HILDA

DON'T STOP BELIEVING

FREYA KENNEDY

Boldwood

First published in Great Britain in 2023 by Boldwood Books Ltd.

Copyright © Freya Kennedy, 2023

Cover Design by Alice Moore Design

Cover Illustration: Shutterstock

The moral right of Freya Kennedy to be identified as the author of this work has been asserted in accordance with the Copyright, Designs and Patents Act 1988.

Every effort has been made to obtain the necessary permissions with reference to copyright material, both illustrative and quoted. We apologise for any omissions in this respect and will be pleased to make the appropriate acknowledgements in any future edition.

A CIP catalogue record for this book is available from the British Library.

Paperback ISBN 978-1-83889-943-1

Large Print ISBN 978-1-83889-942-4

Hardback ISBN 978-1-83533-857-5

Ebook ISBN 978-1-83889-945-5

Kindle ISBN 978-1-83889-944-8

Audio CD ISBN 978-1-83889-937-0

MP3 CD ISBN 978-1-83889-938-7

Digital audio download ISBN 978-1-83889-941-7

Boldwood Books Ltd
23 Bowerdean Street
London SW6 3TN
www.boldwoodbooks.com

For
My sister, Emma,
With love for all the inappropriate humour, support and best
nephews and nieces in the world.

PROLOGUE

The afternoon air is crisp, and the sun hangs low in the sky, as if it would require too much effort to keep shining on this shortest day of the year. It may be a cold December day, but Ivy Lane is just as beautiful as it is on a summer's day – perhaps even more so. It could be the pinch of red on the cheeks of the people outside, standing in their fancy coats as their breath curls in misty clouds towards the sky. It might be the sprays of red berries, of green leaves, of soft eucalyptus and mistletoe bound together – glittering with frost – tied with twine to the iron fencing around The Ivy Inn. It could be the candles flickering in lanterns hung from the trees, or the warm white fairy lights twinkling overhead, glowing brighter and brighter as the sun sinks, turning the sky first pink and orange, then a soft inky blue, before giving way to a blanket of stars.

The chatter among the guests fills the air, along with the clink of champagne flutes and the whooshing sound of the outdoor heaters keeping the worst of the chill at bay. The atmosphere is thick with expectation of what is to come.

There's a certain magic about the wedding that is about to

happen on Ivy Lane. It's the climax of a love story that could only ever have happened on this street, between these people. It's only fitting that the happy couple have decided the courtyard garden of The Ivy Inn is the perfect place to say their vows. With its wide wooden gates open, the assembled guests have a clear view of the bookshop across the street – and the flat above it.

The bride and groom have surprised just about everyone by forgoing tradition and getting ready together in the flat owned by their very dear friends, Libby and Noah – the last couple to get married on the Lane, who also happen to be the owners of Once Upon a Book and The Ivy Inn.

Wanting as little fuss as possible, and clearly not taking into consideration how fondly they are regarded, the bride and groom have decided to simply walk across the street together, hand in hand, to their ceremony.

Noah has arranged for the street to be closed and cleared of traffic for the evening, which has made it possible for it to be decorated so beautifully. He's even gone to the trouble of having a red carpet laid across the cobbles – it wouldn't do to have either the bride or the groom lose their footing should the evening turn icy.

'I hope they aren't too much longer,' says Erin Donohue, the head chef at The Ivy Inn, as she shuffles from foot to foot on impossibly high heels that are very much not her usual footwear. 'These shoes are strictly car to bar and I really want to make sure everything is going okay in the kitchen.'

Her male companion smiles at her reassuringly. 'Everything will be fine in the kitchen. You left very precise instructions. And you checked just ten minutes ago. Before you put those shoes back on.'

'And I can't wait to take them off,' she says. 'They were a bad idea. You should've told me they'd be a bad idea.'

The man raises his hands in mock surrender. 'It takes a braver man than me to tell the ever-powerful Erin Donohue her idea might be a bad one,' he smiles. 'But hang in there. They won't be long now.'

Erin isn't the only guest to be getting a little restless now, waiting for the main event. The happy couple should've arrived ten minutes ago. No matter how pretty the sparkling lights and how fragrant the cinnamon-scented candles, there is only so long anyone is prepared to stand out in the cold for. The patio heaters can't work miracles on a midwinter night.

'Maybe she's getting cold feet?' her companion whispers into her ear.

'She wouldn't be the only one,' Erin says, looking mournfully at her feet. 'I'd give my big toes for a pair of thermal socks right now.'

'You wouldn't look half as fetching though,' he tells her. 'And don't forget, this is their big night. It's important to them both that they have their ceremony under the stars. But hopefully it won't take too long and we'll all be back inside in no time, and you can go and annoy the kitchen staff.'

'And I'm going to change into my Converse and stay in them,' Erin says. 'I'll be throwing some shapes on the dance floor in comfort.'

'You look good to me whether you're in heels or trainers,' he smiles, and she allows him to pull her closer so she can feel the warmth from his body, which adds nicely to the warm and fuzzy feeling she now has inside.

There's more laughter and chatter now before a hush descends over the crowd.

'I see someone coming,' a voice shouts and everyone's gaze turns to the book shop opposite, and the green door to the side from which the husband-and-wife-to-be are set to emerge.

At the creaking of the door to the side of the shop, music starts to play and the sound of the stunning Irish ballad 'She Moved Through the Fair', sung by the angelic-voiced Cara Dillon, fills the air.

But instead of a blushing bride walking through the door with her beau on her arm, there is a very flushed bookseller, her hand clamped to her swollen stomach. Her recently curled hair is already looking a little messy, her make-up streaked with sweat, or tears, or both.

Holding her up is her husband, Noah, whose face is ashen as he supports Libby, and tries to carry both her hospital bag and a baby bag into the street.

'Shit!' he proclaims. 'Bloody, shitting shit.'

The music screeches to a halt before the enchanting tune has even had the chance to really get started.

There's a moment or two of silence as the assembled crowd process the scene in front of them, before the sound of Libby, moaning in pain, jolts everyone into action.

'Why in God's name did we think it was a good idea to close the street and have everyone park somewhere else?' Noah babbles.

'I was supposed to have another week at least,' Libby sobs as Erin rushes over to her and pulls her into a reassuring hug. 'Everyone said first babies never come on time, never mind early. I can't believe I'm going to ruin the wedding.'

'You're not, Libby,' Erin tells her. 'You're just going to make it even more special.' Slipping into organisation mode, she continues, 'Noah, go get the car. Right, you guys,' she says, pointing at the other guests, 'some of you clear the road of these lanterns, flowers and the traffic cones at the top of the street, so Noah can drive down. Libby, let's get you sitting down. This is going to be the best day of your life. You're going to be a mama!'

'But the wedding...' Libby sobs.

'The wedding can still happen,' Erin says. 'If that's what the happy couple want. And it will still be amazing. You've helped them plan the most perfect day, but now you've more important things to be doing.'

Libby sniffs, but she knows Erin is right. Erin is always right. The last six months have proven she's a one-woman tour de force who could run the entirety of Ivy Lane if she put her mind to it. She is, as the Irish saying goes, 'some woman for one woman' – feisty, a little bit bossy (but in a good way) and exceptionally determined. Libby knows she will be wasting her time to even think about arguing with her friend.

As another contraction tightens across her stomach, she realises nothing is going to stop this baby from making an appearance and there's no point in worrying about anything else just now. Apart from, that is, how long it will take Noah to get back with the car and whisk her to Altnagelvin hospital on the other side of Derry so she can get some gas and air!

1

SIX MONTHS EARLIER

All Erin wanted now was a long, cool shower, a bowl of ice cream and prime position on the sofa, with Aaron ready and willing to rub her aching feet. Today had been, in her own words, 'a nightmare of a day'.

An early summer heatwave had brought drinkers out in their droves to The Ivy Inn. Derry people are not accustomed to beautiful weather. The north-west of Ireland is not famed for its sunny weather. So, when the sun shines, the locals waste no time in making the most of it. As a consequence, there hadn't been a spare seat to be had, either inside the pub or in the beer garden, and absolutely everyone seemed to want to be fed. Monday nights were not usually so full on, and if Erin was honest, she'd been hoping for an easy shift with the possibility of closing the kitchen early and maybe – just maybe – getting to enjoy an ice-cold cider in the beer garden before walking the short distance home.

But the fates had other ideas and not only was it the busiest night they'd had since, well, forever – leaving her, as head chef, scrabbling to meet the demand for food – but the air-con and extractor fan in the kitchen had also decided to go on strike. By the time she had closed up the kitchen at nine, her chefs' whites were saturated with her own sweat, she was verging on severely dehydrated, the cupboards were bare and her face was as red as her hair. Almost an hour later, as she had finished cleaning and what little prep she could do for the following day, all Erin wanted to do was get home.

Overheated and overstressed, and having forsaken any notion of a cold cider, she had longed for a distinctly unseasonal snow-storm to hit just as she walked home. She'd happily stand and let the thick snow cover her until she could no longer feel the tips of her fingers or the ends of her toes. She'd welcome the blissful cold, and happily surrender to making snow angels on the ground.

But there was no snow. Or even the hint of a cooling summer shower. There was just a wall of heat and the sun had yet to set. Erin was well aware she was known for her occasional dramatics, but if she hadn't been so dehydrated, the thought of the walk home would've brought her to tears.

At least, she thought wryly, she wasn't going to have to hope Aaron hadn't used up all the hot water before her post-work shower. She lost herself in a glorious fantasy in which she happily stood under icy cool streams of water as she washed the sweat from her body, maybe while she sucked on an ice cube and soaked her swollen feet in an ice bath.

The dream of drying off after, and slipping into her cool cotton shortie PJs, before lying prostrate on her bed with a fan pointed directly at her, kept her going as she walked the few streets home. The smell of barbecues from neighbouring gardens assaulted her nostrils as she passed by. On a different day, the smell may have made her mouth water, but she'd had enough of food and all its aromas for one day.

The only stop she made was at Harry's Shop, the small convenience store a few doors up from the pub, to pick up a tub of Ben & Jerry's ice cream. The arrival of Messrs Ben and Jerry was fairly new to Ivy Lane. The introduction of new stock lines was very much part of the modernisation of the long-established store – which was now under the careful management of Harry's grandson Lorcan. Gone were the sun-faded posters and stickers in the windows dating back at least twenty years, and the battered shelves and fridges. It now gleamed and had lost the faint smell of ham that had seemed ever-present. But it still managed to hold its charm and hadn't morphed into a carbon copy of a small chain store. It had been quite a feat. Erin had to hand it to Lorcan for pulling the store into the twenty-first century while still retaining much of its local, traditional feel.

She'd be lying if she didn't breathe a long sigh of relief to see that Harry was not on his usual perch behind the counter. Much as she had a deep fondness for the old man, his habit of launching into twenty-minute monologues about whatever was on his mind that day was not something she was in the mood to face. No, Harry must've already gone home and Lorcan was alone and, it seemed, just starting to lock up.

'Oh great, I've got here in just in time,' she said.

'I've just cashed up actually,' Lorcan replied with a smile. 'But I know better than to get on your bad side. As long as you're quick, grab whatever you need. I'm meeting Jo at The Ivy for a drink and the only woman who scares me more than you is her!'

Erin laughed, despite her exhaustion. She liked Lorcan – he was kind, smart, caring and, it had to be said, exceptionally handsome. He was the perfect partner for her best friend, Jo. The pair had been together for two years, just a year less than her relationship with Aaron. Who was also kind, smart, caring and... well, maybe not as gorgeous, but handsome all the same. 'I'm scared of Jo a bit myself,' Erin replied. 'Especially with this deadline she's on. She's almost feral at the moment.' A successful author, Jo was working on her third novel and was feeling the pressure of an approaching deadline to submit it to her publisher.

Lorcan smiled, a soft, dopey grin – the kind that only came from being truly in love – and said, 'Yeah, I do love a bit of feral Jo though. As long as I approach with caution and bring Maltesers, it usually ends well.'

Opening the tall freezer at the back of the shop, Erin took a moment to let the cool air wash over her before scanning the shelves for her favourite Phish Food flavour. It appeared the hot weather must have had everyone on the hunt for ice cream and the freezer was close to empty. She could've cried with relief when she spotted one lonely but lovely tub left at the very back of the shelf. As she paid Lorcan, she thought she'd never before been as happy to hand over her hard-earned money.

'If you want, and for no extra charge, I can give you an abridged version of Grandad's speech on how six quid for a tub of ice cream is a "sin before God" and how in his day he'd be lucky to get a scoop of vanilla with some watery jelly on his birthday, and he'd be grateful for it,' Lorcan said.

'I think I'll pass if you don't mind,' Erin replied with a smile. 'It's never the same unless it's Harry himself ranting.'

'It's true.' Lorcan shrugged his shoulders. 'I am no match for his greatness.'

'You've time to grow into the role of Lane curmudgeon yet,' Erin told him. 'But if I don't get home, showered and sitting down soon, I'll be fighting you, and Harry, for the title.'

'You're not even going to let me try and foist some just out-of-date tinned goods on you? Eighty percent likely to be perfectly edible?' Lorcan laughed as Erin waved goodbye, a smile on her face. Harry's habit of gifting out-of-date items to his friends and neighbours was a thing of legend on Ivy Lane.

Minutes later, as she turned her key in own front door all she could think was that she really hoped the ice cream hadn't melted entirely on her walk home.

'Well, that was a tough one,' she announced as she closed the front door behind her. 'I swear those fans better be fixed tomorrow morning or I'll be shutting the kitchen and telling everyone they can get pizza delivered instead.' She kept her voice light, not wanting to start the rest of her night at home with a tirade. 'Noah says he has people coming to look at it first thing, so fingers crossed. I'm going to have to go in early though – we were much busier than expected and I'll need to go and stock up on fresh ingredients to get through another service.'

There was no response. Actually, when she thought about it, there was no noise at all. No TV sounds, or gentle hum of the washing machine. No shower running or the podcast Aaron normally listened to when he was drying off. Just silence. Very unusual silence.

It was possible, of course, that he was in bed already – but it was still early and Aaron was known for being something of a night owl and never settling down until the wee hours. But Erin supposed there was always a first time.

Popping her ice cream in the freezer, she paused to look around the kitchen. It was unusually clean and tidy. There was no trace of Aaron's evening meal preparation, no empty cups or glasses on the worktop by the sink and, in fact, everything was just how she had left it that morning.

She felt a prickle of something run down her spine and this time she was pretty sure it wasn't just another bead of sweat.

Something was amiss.

'Aaron?' she called out, kicking off her trainers and socks and padding through to the living room. She half expected to find him conked out on the sofa, the TV silently running through the save screen of whatever game he had been playing on the Xbox. But he wasn't there, and again the room was suspiciously tidy. There was not a cushion de-plumped, nor a discarded mug to be seen anywhere. And, she realised with a sinking feeling, there was not even an Xbox, or the framed picture he kept on the shelf of him and his best mates on a stag night in Amsterdam.

Erin reached into her pocket and pulled out her phone, not quite sure what she was hoping to see. A message from her boyfriend of three years telling her that he would be back shortly and he'd just decided to take his man-cave belongings out of their living room and put them in some unknown space she wasn't aware of, perhaps?

But there was nothing. Not a message. Nor a missed called. Nor a share of a meme or anything. She realised, in fact, she hadn't received any messages from him at all that day.

After considering her options, she decided to bite the bullet and just call him. It went straight to his answer service. Erin didn't leave a message because she simply didn't know what to say. She was sure she was worrying about nothing – things were okay between her and Aaron... weren't they? This was probably just her overtired mind jumping to all the wrong conclusions.

She walked to the bedroom to find it too was suspiciously tidy. His bottles of aftershave were gone from the dresser. The Tom Clancy novel he had supposedly been reading for the past six months was missing from his nightstand. When she opened his side of the wardrobe, she was greeted, for the most part, with empty hangers. There were a couple of jumpers and shirts – ones he had never really liked – still hanging there, but all else was cleared out.

All she could do was stand, mouth gaping open, as her heart tried to catch up with what her brain was telling her.

'Shower first, think later,' she said aloud, having decided there was absolutely no way she would be able to process anything properly while marinating in her own sweat for a moment longer.

Needless to say, it wasn't the refreshing, relaxing experience she'd hoped for. There was no happy, tuneless singing along to her favourite show tunes while she let the icy water pummel her into blissful submission. Her mind was racing, and her heart wasn't on a go slow either as she tried to make sense of the quiet, empty house and think of a non-catastrophic reason why all Aaron's belongings would have disappeared.

Turning the water temperature up a little, she washed her hair before getting out of the shower, drying off and slipping into her PJs, telling herself with each step that she was just being her usual dramatic self and Aaron would be back by the time she was fully dressed. He'd probably just nipped out to buy her some ice cream. Word would have reached him about the banjaxed extractor fans and how busy the pub had been and he was clearly playing the role of absolute dote of a boyfriend and stocking up on all the ice cream he could get his hands on.

Maybe the clean flat and empty wardrobe had been but mere hallucinations brought on by heatstroke. She was sure that was possible. Hadn't she seen a documentary about it one time?

Except she knew it wasn't an hallucination. This was only confirmed when she opened the wardrobe a second time to find that all his clothes, bar the three ugly jumpers and two hideous shirts, were still gone. It was then she noticed that the designer shirt she'd spent way too much on for his last birthday because she thought he'd look amazing in it was still there too. And it still had the labels attached.

'Fuck,' she swore under her breath as she slumped back onto what had been their shared bed, confusion and hurt clawing at her. To her surprise, tears didn't prick at her eyes, but that, she realised, was probably down to the severe dehydration more than anything else.

This had indeed been the biggest nightmare of a day known to mankind and she was completely baffled as to what the hell had just happened.

2

The ice cream went uneaten. The very thought of it curdled Erin's stomach. Instead, she poured herself a measure of Jameson whiskey and downed it in one – which, in fairness, also made her stomach curdle and she was sick moments later, before lying on the cold bathroom tiles fighting off extreme anxiety.

What was going on? Why on earth had Aaron left? Surely, he owed her an explanation, and an apology. Surely, he owed her the chance to fix whatever she must've done wrong to have him act in this way? Or was he in trouble of some sort? Sick maybe? Nothing about this made any sense. She just simply could not wrap her head around it.

Her feelings of confusion and worry only grew as she tried to sleep later, painfully aware of the empty space on the other side of the bed.

She'd tried to call Aaron again, several times. She'd even managed to leave a quick voicemail asking him to get in touch with her as soon as possible, thankfully managing not to sound as if she was on the brink of tears, even though she was very, very clearly on the brink of tears. She had even phoned a couple of his friends, but not one of them had answered their phones or replied to her WhatsApp messages – leaving her on read.

She considered phoning Jo, but then she remembered what Lorcan had told her about Jo and him meeting for a drink in the pub. Erin was considerate enough that despite her own heartache – which was growing moment by moment – she was not going to ruin her best friend's romantic night. Someone deserved to be happy and in love, and Jo was under so much stress with her book deadline that she needed the chance to relax with her lovely boyfriend.

Besides, Erin was tired. Bone tired. Heartsore and weary. While she desperately wanted someone to hug her and tell her everything would work itself out, she didn't have the energy to try to explain something that she couldn't even make sense of herself.

Aaron was gone. At least that's what it looked like. He hadn't left a note. There hadn't been a big row or even a sense that things were going tits up. Or maybe there had been, and she had just been so busy with work that she hadn't noticed. He'd always told her she needed to delegate more and make more use of the staff she had, especially her sous-chef, Paul, but she'd thought that had been out of his concern for her wellbeing, not out of any feeling he was being neglected or overlooked.

Had she neglected him? She did work exceptionally hard shifting The Ivy Inn's menu from basic pub grub to a menu that had garnered them attention from foodies all through Ireland – North and South. She always thought Aaron understood her need for perfectionism in her work, and her absolute love for what she did. He'd always claimed to be so proud of her when a new review or award nomination came through.

She tried to call him once more, just after midnight, but his phone went straight to voicemail once again. She tried to send him a WhatsApp message – but it wouldn't go through. Was it possible he had actually blocked her?

It was only sheer exhaustion that allowed her to eventually drift off just as the sky was starting to grow lighter.

When her alarm sounded at six, she had to face the realisation that her relationship was most likely over.

This time, the tears started to fall and Erin knew she absolutely, and without a doubt, needed a hug from her best friend. She needed some reassurance that she was not a complete witch who had unwittingly driven the love of her life away due to her supreme unbearable-ness. She needed someone to offer to make a voodoo doll of Aaron and stick pins in it.

Yes, it was early. Yes, Jo had a deadline to meet. But Erin also knew that Jo would absolutely and categorically want to be there for her in her hour of need – even if that hour of need was ridiculously early.

Erin found Jo's number and hit the call button – aware that with every second that passed she was getting closer and closer to losing her composure and the slow trickle of tears on her face turning into a gushing, sobbing torrent. She'd thought she'd reached the stage of her life where she was past heartache. Aaron was supposed to be her forever person, not her three-years-and-on-to-the-next-one person. This was not what she had signed up for.

'Erin?' A croaky, definitely not quite awake yet, voice whispered down the line. 'What's up? Is everything okay?'

What Erin had hoped would come out as 'No, I think Aaron has left me and I need you to come over and help me not have a full emotional breakdown', instead came out as a series of sobs and hiccups punctuated with the occasional recognisable word.

For Jo, it must've been like trying to decipher Lassie's barks and whines when he needed to get a responsible adult to come and rescue an errant child from a well.

'Wait... hang on... Give me a second,' Jo croaked and, between her sobs, Erin could hear her friend tell Lorcan that something was wrong and she'd see him later.

That's what she loved about Jo. There was never a moment's hesitation from her in coming to help her friends when she was needed. That and she lived only two streets away and could be by her side in next to no time when necessary.

As Erin listened to a door close on the other end of the line, she grabbed a tissue and wiped at her eyes – a move she soon realised was completely pointless as she broke down once again.

'Erin, I'm on my way. You'll have to take me as you find me. I'm warning you first because you sound as if you're having a bad enough morning without my appearance traumatising you,' Jo said. 'Whatever this is, we'll sort it out, okay? We'll get through it together. I promise.'

Erin hoped deep in her very soul that Jo was right. She needed that more than anything right now.

Through tears and occasional swear words, Erin managed to dress in a pair of wrinkled linen trousers and a T-shirt that had probably seen better days. She pulled her mass of red curls back into a ponytail and built up the courage to look at herself in the mirror not quite prepared for the blotchy face that stared back at her. Her eyes were red-rimmed but at least had the decency to look the most vibrant shade of blue after all her crying.

There was no denying that she looked a mess though – and right then, in that moment, she felt very much a mess too. Brushing her teeth to maintain at least a hint of proper personal hygiene, she wondered if she could just lock herself away in this house for the full day, not go to work and not have to deal with anyone who wasn't Jo. She could just stay at home today, or maybe forever, and she could adopt a litter of feral kittens and live out her days as the desperate spinster she was clearly meant to be. Stereotypes exist for a reason, she reminded herself – and it's because they had a habit of reflecting reality.

Dabbing a little moisturiser on her face, Erin felt her skin sting, raw from all the tears she had wiped away. She really needed to invest in some better tissues – balsam ones maybe, especially as she would probably be crying her lamps out for the next... well... forever.

She was just descending into a full breakdown when her doorbell rang and she heard the voice of her best friend calling through the letterbox. 'It's only me! I come bearing gifts!'

Amid her tears, Erin gave a half-smile, grateful for Jo and her loveliness. Maybe she should've never moved in with Aaron. Things were so much simpler when she and Jo used to house-share, they were both single and life was all about nights out on the town, or nights in watching *Derry Girls* on repeat.

No sooner had she opened the door than Jo had walked in and enveloped her in a giant hug, whispering soothing words into her ear about how things would be okay and they would get through whatever this was together.

Erin had never been so grateful for a hug in her life.

It was Jo who pulled away first. 'I caught Flora coming out of the bakery to put the shutters up, and the smell of the fresh buns nearly took the breath from me. I managed to talk her into parting with a warm loaf of her finest treacle scone. I picked up some nice soft tissues and some real butter too from Harry's Shop because today is not a day for margarine, no matter how healthy it promises to be. Let me put the kettle on and you can tell me all about it,' Jo said.

Erin nodded, coming to the sudden realisation that she was in fact hungry, and the smell of the fresh treacle scone was whetting her appetite. She followed Jo through to the kitchen.

'So, I gather this is about Aaron,' Jo continued as she took two mugs from the cupboard.

Erin nodded. 'He's gone.' She couldn't help but see Jo's eyes widen in surprise.

'Okaaaay,' her friend said. 'When you say gone...?'

'Left. Left me.'

'Why on earth?' Jo asked, as the kettle bubbled and whistled in the background.

Erin just shrugged. 'I don't know. There's no note. He's not answering his phone. Nor are his friends. He's blocked me on WhatsApp...'

'Holy shit!' Jo said, her eyes wide. 'And you're sure he's actually left you and not just, like, missing, or dead or something?'

For a moment, Erin considered which outcome would be easiest to wrap her head around.

'I mean, should we be phoning round hospitals or calling the police?' Jo asked.

'He took all his things,' Erin sniffed. 'I think that says it all. I don't think we're likely to find some John Doe in the hospital complete with a suitcase of clothes, an Xbox and a mug with World's Best Boyfriend on it.'

The change in expression on Jo's face told her that there was no way the mug would show up anywhere near Aaron, and sure enough, when she stepped aside, there it was on the worktop awaiting a pour of boiling water from the kettle.

'At least he accepts he's not the world's best boyfriend...' Erin said as the tightness in her chest pulled again and she felt more tears coming. 'The thing is, Jo, I don't know what I did wrong. And if I don't know what I did wrong, then how can I process it? I'm used to being able to fix things – you know. If a recipe doesn't work, it will be because it needs more seasoning, or a little longer in the oven, a bit more time to reduce down the stock. So I do that. I do what's needed. But...'

'Men aren't food,' Jo conceded. 'And you do know that sometimes – even though you try your very best to make it all taste amazing, and even though you are supremely talented and wonderful in every way – sometimes, a recipe just goes tits up and needs chucking in the bin. It doesn't make you a bad cook, though. Sometimes the ingredients have gone off, or the recipe you were given was a bit dodgy, or the burners are on the blink or something. Or sometimes, you just don't like the taste.'

'Well, maybe,' Erin sniffed. 'But I'm usually able to work it out, and right now I can't. Because it doesn't make any sense.'

But even as she uttered those words, there was something she couldn't put her finger on niggling at the back of her mind.

She thought they'd been happy. She'd been sure of it, hadn't she? Well, maybe happy wasn't the right word. No one is all big smiles and huge joy all the time. That would be annoying as feck. But they were okay. Content even – and content was a good word, wasn't it? It wasn't a 'meh, doesn't really mean anything word', like nice, or lovely, which were just bywords for vanilla or 'a bit boring but harmless'. It certainly didn't mean they were just settling for something – at least it didn't to her. She'd never been one to settle for anything. That's why she worked so hard and all the hours God sent to make The Ivy Inn an award-winning gastropub.

And Aaron hadn't seemed to have minded too much that she was out working most evenings. He'd been happy staying at home with his Xbox for company, or going out with his mates or, she realised with a jolt, quite possibly building some sort of life that clearly didn't involve her.

She scanned her brain for memories of their recent conversations – for any mentions of new friends, and new female friends in particular, but her head was fuzzy and her heart was sore. Actually, when she thought of it, she couldn't really remember when they had last sat down and had a good old heart-to-heart. When they'd first started dating, they would talk for hours as if they had a desperate need to know every last thing about each other and no detail was too boring. They'd talk into the wee small hours until their eyes were too heavy to stay awake any longer and they'd fall asleep in each other's arms. That didn't happen any more, either – Erin couldn't remember the last time they'd fallen asleep in each other's arms, or even at the same time. She was generally dead to the world by the time Aaron would slope into bed.

'Sometimes, my love, things just don't make sense,' Jo said, pulling her from her thoughts. 'You know, like the success of *Mrs Brown's Boys*, or why anyone in their right mind would apply to go on *Naked Attraction* and shake their bits about for a televised audience. Can you imagine? You'd never be able to show your face on the Lane again if you'd showed your vulva on Channel 4.'

If there was one thing Jo was good at, it was providing just the right level of emotional support and gallows humour when required. Erin couldn't help but snort laugh – and, to her disgust and embarrassment, that resulted in a lovely little snot bubble springing forth from her nose.

Having hastily cleaned it away with one of the super-soft balsam tissues Jo had brought, Erin gratefully accepted the cup of tea and slice of still warm scone from her friend, whose phone pinged with a message at just that very moment.

Erin knew the moment she saw Jo's expression – the way the colour drained from her face – that the message had to be from Aaron and suddenly she realised she wasn't perhaps mentally prepared to find out what she had done wrong and how this relationship she had been so comfortable in had gone so very wrong.

3

'Let me see it,' Erin said, 'What does he say?' Despite her reluctance to read a list of ways in which their relationship had died, she knew she needed answers. She reached her hand out towards Jo.

'Erm, nothing much...' Jo said, pulling the phone out of her friend's reach and showing absolutely no evidence at all that she was anything other than the crappy liar she always had been.

'Jo!' Erin exclaimed, adrenaline now pulsing in her veins. 'Don't fib to me. You know I can always tell when you're lying.'

'I'm not lying,' Jo said, her voice a little overconfident, almost as if she were a child on the stage at a school nativity play delivering her one very important line. It was loud, overpronounced and completely unconvincing. The fact that by that point she was clutching her phone tight to her chest didn't bolster Erin's faith in her either.

There was nothing for Erin to do but fix her expression into her best glare and raise her eyebrow in a way that had terrified many a trainee chef working under her in the past.

'Okay,' Jo said, still holding the phone tight to her chest. 'He wanted me to check in on you and make sure you were okay.'

For one brief moment, Erin's heart soared as she thought of how Aaron clearly cared about her enough to make sure she was coping okay. That surely came from a place of love and respect, and maybe things weren't as bleak as she thought.

'And he said to tell you that he has paid the rent for the next two months, but after that you're on your own because he has to pay for his new place and he can't afford to run two homes,' Jo blurted much too fast, as if she were trying to rapidly pull a plaster off a particularly hairy leg.

So, he had paid up the rent, which could be seen as a good thing and proof that he cared, but he had already rented somewhere new, which was inarguably a bad thing and showed that he had been planning this for some time. Nausea rose from the very pit of Erin's stomach. *How could this be happening?* she wondered. It made no sense.

'Did he say why?' Erin asked. 'Did he give any reason at all?'

Jo's expression was one of pity as she shook her head. 'No,' she said. 'I'm really sorry. He hasn't said anything more than he hopes you're okay and all that guff about the rent. I'll message him and ask him to explain his sad, pathetic self.' Jo's anger was getting ready to take full flight. 'I can't believe he has done this. None of us saw this coming. None of us thought there was anything wrong between the pair of you. You always just seemed to fit together.'

'We did, didn't we?' Erin said, as she clutched her stomach to hold down the wave of bile that was ready to erupt from her gut like lava. Aaron might as well have just punched her square in the stomach or stuck his fingers down her throat to make her retch. 'And he never said anything to Lorcan? Lorcan never mentioned anything to you?' she asked.

Jo shrugged. 'I'm pretty sure Lorcan had no idea. He'd definitely have told me if he had an inkling something was wrong. He cares about you.'

'Can you ask him?' Aaron met with both Lorcan and Noah to play five-a-side football at the local sports centre once a week. They inevitably went for pints after – surely if Aaron had been so unhappy that he was going to pull this stunt, he would have said something or given off an all-is-not-well vibe.

'On it,' Jo said, already tapping a message into her phone while Erin did her very best not to hyperventilate as wave after wave of realisation at what this could mean hit her square in the face. 'Breathe,' Jo told her. 'In for seven, hold for three, and out for seven. And through your nose – both ways. Apparently, that's better than that old in through the mouth and out through the nose line. I saw a documentary. Although, right enough, in that the man liked to jump into icy lakes to find his centre, and surely that means he can't be right in the head. Can you imagine?' Jo shuddered at the thought, as if the temperature had suddenly dipped a good twenty degrees and it wasn't still much too warm for early morning.

Still Erin tried to breathe in, slowly counting in her head. Wondering if she should do a Ross from *Friends* and count Mississippily to make sure she wasn't racing through the numbers. She managed to get to 'Five Mississippi' before she felt as if her lungs might burst, and her exhalation came as a burst rather than a slow, relaxing release of tension, which of course did little to calm the anxiety coursing through her veins.

How could Aaron have done this? How could he not have spoken to her about his feelings? If he'd had a problem with her, why had he simply not sat down and spoken to her about it instead of this? This wasn't something she could rectify. It was a *fait accompli* and that made her both very sad and very angry.

This isn't who she thought Aaron was. He was supposed to be

her person, for the love of God. Hadn't they been ridiculously smug last Christmas and bought each other 'You Are My Person' mugs, and matching Oodies for their joint, cosy sessions of watching *Grey's Anatomy*. (Aaron had made her vow that she would never, under pain of death, reveal his fondness for Grey Sloan Memorial to anyone.) How did you go from being someone's everything to someone's ex-everything in just six short months? And how had she not seen any of it coming? Or had she seen it coming and just buried her head in the sand about it until now?

Had she convinced herself they were just entering the extra-comfortable phase of their relationship, where things slowed down and fell into a routine. She'd read about that. How relationships have peaks and troughs. This had been a trough. She'd told herself that over and over again. But she'd never allowed herself to think it was an 'I've had enough trough' – more just a 'this is a bit meh but it will be grand' trough.

A glass of water appeared in front of her beside her untouched mug of tea, and she heard Jo tell her to take a sip and to try to settle her panic.

'I'm so sorry this is happening to you,' Jo said, 'and I wish I could make some sense of it right now, but I can't. I'll try though and we'll get through it together. But, for now, let's see what we *can* deal with? I'll call Noah and get him to speak to Paul. I'm sure Paul can run the kitchen today so you can take some time to get your head clear, and cry and eat ice cream, and whatever the hell else you need to do. I've the day set aside for writing, but deadlines be damned. The only thing I can't shift around is picking Clara up from school this afternoon. Mum is getting her hair done and I promised Clara some quality sister time. We were going to go to Fiorintini's for a knickerbocker glory – you are of course, welcome to come along.'

Erin wanted so much to hug her friend for being so lovely and thoughtful, and she also really fancied a knickerbocker glory from Fiorintini's – a much-loved family-run ice cream parlour right in the heart of the city. But as she listened to Jo, a steely resolve washed over her, drowning her desire to throw up. She, Erin Donohue, would not spend the day wallowing in her bed, crying into the lovely soft tissues. She also very much did not want to traumatise eight-year-old Clara, Jo's adopted little sister, by weeping all over a delicious, ice-creamy dessert.

She would not leave it to Paul, her very competent sous-chef, to run the kitchen. He was more than capable, of course, but yesterday had put exceptional pressure on them all and it was she who had made of note of their supplies and worked out what was needed to restock after yesterday's rush. And, given the forecast for the coming days, she would also have to take into consideration a possible menu change and an increase in fresh produce. With more people than usual popping in for drinks after work while enjoying the balmy evening sunlight, she'd planned to put together a daily special of a sharing platter of tapas and 'picky bites' for those that liked to nibble while they drank but didn't want a full meal. She wanted to incorporate much more fresh fruit in her desserts over the coming days, too, making the most of in-season ingredients, berries, mango, rhubarb and more. She was excited to feed her passion for preparing delicious desserts and delicate pastries, forged during a placement year as a pâtissière in Paris – and this was the perfect time of year to showcase those skills by creating mouth-watering treats perfect for nibbling while sipping icy cold Prosecco under a setting sun.

Erin may well have felt as if she could crumble onto the floor, but she wasn't going to. She was going to get her bum in gear to get the best and freshest ingredients from her suppliers to draw together the additions to her menu, and she'd need to work out how to present it.

Distraction, she reckoned, was the best way to push down all her feelings about her recently deceased love affair. She'd ask Paul to oversee the main courses, while she would lose herself in sifting and measuring, rubbing cold butter into soft white flour, shaping and rolling, chilling and then baking for the precise and perfect amount of time. She'd make her own compote and coulis, and crème pat. She might even make her own ice cream if she could find the time, and ultimately she would feel better knowing she had spent the day doing something she very much loved. If Aaron was the kind of man who could do this to her, then he was not the kind of man she wanted to spend another minute of her life worrying about.

At least that was what she told herself, as Jo gave her a pitying look and rubbed her hand.

'No,' Erin said as she straightened up and willed her voice to be strong and without even a hint of wobble. 'I will not be playing the role of devastated ex today. I have a kitchen to run and a life to live, and while I'd very much like to join you and the wonderful Miss Clara for ice cream, I will be too busy kicking ass in my wonderful kitchen. But what you can do is ring that brother of yours and check that the air conditioning is going to be fixed.'

'Oh, it is,' Jo said. 'Noah spoke to the engineer last night and he's due at seven. Lorcan is letting him in.' There was a handiness to Jo and Lorcan sharing the flat above the pub, and in Lorcan only working a few doors down in Harry's. Between that and Noah and Libby only living across the street above the bookshop, there was always someone on hand to step in in a crisis.

'Good!' Erin said, and paused. 'And you can also delete that pathetic excuse of a message Aaron sent you and block his number.'

'You don't want to see if he replies to explain himself?' Jo asked.

Erin took a deep breath and thought it through briefly. 'There is no excuse, and no reason on this earth, for him to have done this to me. This is not how you treat someone you have supposedly been in love with for three years.' She felt her voice crack, so stopped, took a deep breath and regained her composure before continuing. 'You are not, under any circumstances, to let him know how I am, or what my plans are. He is no longer a part of my life by his own choice, so he can take a long run and jump if he thinks he gets to peek in at my mourning period from the sidelines.'

At that, she stood up and brushed herself off. She'd get changed into something less 'bag-lady' than her current ensemble. Some Clinique Moisture Surge and Touche Éclat would sort out the zombie look, and her hair could be tamed into some form of submission with the help of some conditioning spray and a good scrunchie.

She would not let this break her, or even slow her stride. She was woman, and she would roar. And continue to build her kitchen empire, with or without a partner waiting for her when she came home from work each night. Calmness descended on her and she couldn't help but think that maybe counting Mississippily had helped after all.

4

It was amazing what keeping busy could do to push all your problems to the back of your mind, Erin thought as she loaded the last of her fresh produce into the boot of her car and prepared to drive on to Ivy Lane to start preparing for the day's service.

Making lists had helped – she had shooed Jo away, telling her she would be fine and that it would suit her better to worry about her forthcoming deadline and not so much about her friend's shattered heart.

Aaron would not break her. She'd make sense of his betrayal in time, but for now she was going to prove that she didn't need him. She could, and would, excel, and she would not lose her stride – not even for one minute.

Normally, she'd order in most of her ingredients from her very reliable and reputable suppliers, but not today. Today, she'd wanted to make sure only the very freshest ingredients made their way into her dishes. She wanted only the ripest beef tomatoes and the most fragrant basil leaves to use in a caprese salad. She'd called her sous-chef Paul and instructed him to make up a dough for fresh crusty rolls and to leave it to prove until she got to the kitchen. She'd opted for Jersey Royals for her potato salad and as a side for lunch – adding an extra buttery richness to her menu. She'd lost herself in the feel, smell and texture of her ingredients, choosing the best organic produce – bottom line be damned. Today was not about scrimping. She made sure to choose only the very best fruits: jewel-coloured berries, ripe and delicious. Her cooking was akin to creating art – knowing exactly how to put the right colours and flavours together – and it was enough to fulfil her in that moment.

Erin got into her car, wound the windows down to let the warm summer sun kiss her skin and took a deep breath. She would be okay. She had been single before and she could be single again. No, none of this made sense. Yes, she felt betrayed in the worst possible way, but she would not show it. Anyone who saw her driving down Ivy Lane, her right elbow poking out of the car window, music blaring, would see her looking effortlessly cool and little else. And, thankfully, the dark sunglasses she wore to shield her from the sun also doubled up as an effective way to hide her red-rimmed eyes.

Channelling her inner Beyoncé and singing 'I'm a Survivor' at the top of her lungs, she approached The Ivy Inn, only to have her attention drawn to a man on a ladder, three doors down, fixing a sign to the wall outside 'Wee Buns', the bakery Flora owned. For sale? Surely not! Flora had been a stalwart on the Lane for as long as Erin could remember and long before. Erin had often thought of Flora as the matriarch of a street where the various shop owners and residents felt more like a family than just neighbours.

Erin parked her car in its usual spot at the back of The Ivy Inn, near the kitchen doors, and decided she was going to go and speak with Flora to try to find out the full story. There had been no hint before now that this might be on the cards, even though Erin spoke to Flora regularly. For as much as Erin had the touch and skill of an expert pastry chef, she was no match for Flora when it came to baking scones so rich with flavour that one slice was never enough, or Guinness soda bread that always went down a treat at corporate functions and weddings. Erin was sure Flora added some secret ingredient that she had never shared, because no matter how many times Erin tried to recreate the magic herself, her attempts never tasted quite as good as Flora's efforts. It was for that reason that she made no apology for making use of Flora's skills on a frequent basis. Almost perfect was not good enough for diners at The Ivy Inn. Only the very best would do.

The bell above the door tinkled as Erin pushed it open. As usual, she was greeted with the smell of freshly baked bread and the sight of trays of jam and icing turnovers, sugar-dusted cream fingers, and an array of different flavours of scones and floury baps.

Flora herself stood behind the counter, her black apron decorated by floury handprints and her pure white hair peeking out from under a hairnet.

'Erin!' she declared. 'Did you have an order placed with me for today? I don't have one. God, maybe I'm losing the plot. I wouldn't be surprised at my age.'

While Flora tried to make her voice light and jokey, Erin knew by the look on her face, there was a touch of genuine fear there. Flora was the elder stateswoman of Ivy Lane. In her seventies, she was of the same generation as Harry and, just like Harry, she too had refused to retire, asserting she loved her job too much. Except now, it looked like she *was* going to retire.

'No, no,' Erin said quickly, to reassure Flora she was very much still in possession of the plot. 'No order for me today. I just saw the sign going up and wanted to check you were okay. Also, I'm really nosey, so I wondered what was going on?'

A flash of relief danced across Flora's face, 'Oh thank goodness. I'd have been mortified if I'd let you down. And yes, darling girl, I'm okay. Well, as okay as a woman of my age can be. I've just had to accept that my knees aren't getting any better and I think it's about time I hung my apron up and enjoyed what's left of my life without standing in a shop all day. My children have been nagging me for years to slow down a bit and there are things I want to do while I'm still able. Do you know, I've always fancied a cruise?'

Her voice was light and breezy, but Erin could still detect a hint of a deeper emotion there. Flora had always insisted she would work until the day they carried her out of the shop in a box, and here she was giving up on her beloved bakery. Erin knew it would be a wrench for her, no matter all her talk of wanting to slow down and enjoy life, and she also knew exactly what a person trying to be brave and think positive looked like because that was exactly what she had been aiming for today herself.

'Oh Flora! Is there no one in your family who could take over the reins so you could keep your hand in a wee bit? You know, like Lorcan and Harry?' Erin thought of how much Harry cherished his ability to keep coming to his shop every day, where he could chat to all his neighbours and customers and feel useful.

Harry had said he never wanted to retire – that he viewed his shop as his home just as much as he viewed the house where he lived – but a number of health scares had made him realise he may have no choice in the matter. Needless to say, he had been more than happy when his grandson, Lorcan, who had initially only come to spend a summer with his grandfather, had offered to take over the reins and carry on the family business.

Just like Harry, Erin couldn't imagine that Flora would cope well with suddenly being cut off from all her daily chats with customers, and the routine that had made up most of her life.

She'd said more than once that she no longer worked because she had to, but because she wanted to.

Flora gave a sad smile and shook her head. 'None of my children were ever interested in the business! They liked eating the buns, but not making them,' the older woman laughed, her soft skin crinkling with a smile that revealed a perfect set of pearly white dentures.

She reminded Erin so much of her own granny that she had to fight the urge to pull Flora into a hug and hope to get a whiff of the same Youth Dew perfume that her granny had worn.

'They have their lives now and I'm for them. Rachel is well settled as a teacher; Marie has a brand new grandchild to mind and Peter... well, his life is in Australia and I don't see that he would give that up to come back and help his poor mother bake baps and cream horns.'

Erin couldn't fight the bubble of emotion that was welling up inside her, no matter how hard she tried to push it down by digging her nails into her own palms. This, it felt, was just one more cosmically bad-timed punch in the stomach by the universe and she wasn't ready for it. There was too much change happening and her world felt as if it might just tilt directly off its axis.

To her shame, she felt a stray tear trickle down her face.

'Oh, love,' Flora said, moving out from behind the counter much quicker than the average seventy-six-year-old and pulling her into a hug. 'All good things must come to an end,' she soothed.

'But not all at once,' Erin sniffed. 'It shouldn't happen all at once. That's not fair.'

Flora crinkled her brow and took in the sorrowful sight in front of her. Blowing her soft white fringe from her forehead, she gave Erin's hand a squeeze. 'Sweetheart, what is it? What's happened? How about I put the kettle on and you can tell me all about it.'

'Oh Flora, I'd love to – but I've so much to do in the kitchen before service and this isn't a two-second story. I think I might still be in shock a little, but long story short, Aaron has moved out.'

Flora's brow furrowed with concern. 'Oh you poor pet. Do you think it might just be some sort of tiff and it can all be worked out?'

Erin considered this for a moment and as much as she would like to cling on to the hope that it could all be worked out, she knew that it couldn't. There was no comeback from moving out and taking all your belongings with you without giving any reason or prior notice. 'I don't think so,' she said, the reality of her situation threatening to fell her. She could not allow herself to think about this now. She had a plan, and that plan was to be positive and make beautiful food until she was so exhausted she wouldn't even have the energy to think about how her life had just imploded. She took in the concerned face in front of her. 'I really can't believe that you'll be moving on,' she said, hoping that would be enough to give Flora the message that she didn't want to discuss Aaron further.

The strategy worked.

'I've done my time here, Erin. Yes, it's a bit scary to let it go – even if it really is getting beyond me – but it's definitely the right time. I want to see the world a little before my knees give out altogether! Go to Australia to see Peter and his family. Maybe take that cruise. Spend more time at the beach. And, besides, the world is changing. It's all baristas and cronuts now – not floury baps and turnovers.'

Looking around her at the almost empty shelves of the bakery, Erin thought the world clearly hadn't moved that far away from its love of traditional baked goods. The morning 'bun-run' was a long-held and treasured tradition in Derry, and even with the passage of years, it was still a staple for many. The day didn't begin properly until you'd had your cup of tea and a tasty bun from the bakery. Yes, there were fewer traditional bakeries now than before, but they were still needed and loved in places like Ivy Lane, where the community felt like a family.

Erin was very much a modern woman, but she loved the old-world feel of the Lane and how everyone still watched out for each other. It was more an extended family than a street of neighbours and shop owners. Places like Harry's Shop and Flora's bakery helped keep that community feeling alive. The conversations that had taken place in each, the gossip, the stories told – they all made up the very fabric of the place. What would come in to replace Wee Buns? A vape shop, maybe – they seemed to pop up everywhere. Or Flora's worst fear of an artsy cronut or doughnut place that charged a clean fortune for something that tasted like mass-produced rubbish. 'Sure what's a doughnut but a gravy ring with notions?' Flora had once said when a pricy new doughnut café had opened in town with every possible flavour on offer. Flora was a purist who had stuck with offering the simple ring doughnut, covered in sugar, or occasionally dribbled with chocolate which was, for some reason, known as a gravy ring throughout Derry. She charged a fraction of the price the fancy café did with its Nutella flavoured this, and blueberry cheesecake flavoured that.

'There's always room for floury baps and turnovers,' Erin said. 'Have you thought of selling it as a going concern? There's bound to be some apprentice baker somewhere who'd be delighted with such a thriving business.'

Flora gave a small smile. 'Sadly, it's nowhere near as thriving as it used to be. As much as I love the place, if I take my rose-tinted glasses off for long enough, it's clear that it needs a little more than I can offer it. I suppose it needs a reinvention of sorts.'

'But then it wouldn't be the same,' Erin said, feeling the sun warm her skin through the shop windows and thinking about just how much this place had been a comfort to her through the years.

'Things don't have to remain the same,' Flora said. 'Life changes and we have to change with it, or risk getting left behind. I don't know where we all get the notion that there's some magical age or life stage where we finally realise this is where we're meant to be. I'm staring at eighty and I don't feel it yet. I'm open to whatever changes come my way.'

As Erin left to start work in the kitchen at The Ivy Inn, she realised she envied Flora in many ways. Not least because the older woman was at peace with how quickly life could change while Erin herself felt cast adrift by the day's events.

5

'I need toast,' Libby bustled into the kitchen at The Ivy Inn and walked straight to the industrial toaster and dropped two slices of white bread into the slots. 'Butter?' she asked. 'The real stuff.'

'In the fridge,' Erin said. 'It's much too warm to bring it out before service.'

'But it won't spread as easily on my toast,' Libby sighed, visibly deflating as she pulled a stool close to her and sat down. 'And it's the only thing that stops this bloody morning sickness.'

'I thought dry toast was the magic cure for morning sickness or ginger n—'

'If you suggest a ginger nut biscuit, so help me, I will cry and maybe throw things,' Libby grimaced. 'They make me feel ill even when I'm not three and a half months pregnant, so they aren't likely to have magical qualities now. And yes, I know dry toast is what normally works, but this is Noah Simpson's baby and just like his or her father, this baby seems to want to do things their own way.'

Despite her pained expression, Erin noticed how tenderly Libby put her hand to her very slightly rounded tummy and held it there. Libby and Noah were #couplegoals – and a pang of jealousy nipped at Erin. She pushed it away and took in the gaunt figure of her friend. If an inspector walked into the kitchen just now and saw this pale woman with dark circles under her bloodshot eyes, hunched over while she clutched her stomach, the place would be shut down within seconds.

'We've run out of butter and Noah said I could come in here and I hope you don't mind,' Libby said, her voice thin and reedy. She was very much not her usual chirpy and assured self. Indeed, she was as clear an advertisement for birth control as Erin had ever seen.

'Of course I don't mind,' Erin replied, overwhelmed with empathy for Libby and her pregnant state. It hadn't been long since Libby and Noah had announced that they were indeed expectant parents, although Erin had suspected it for some time. Though not a mother herself, she had seen the same slightly green around the gills look that Libby seemed to sport on a daily basis on her cousin's face during each of her three pregnancies. That, and Libby's sudden aversion to after-work drinks kind of gave the game away long before the official announcement. Erin had mined her cousin for hints and tips on how to tackle morning sickness, but unfortunately for Libby, none of them seemed to be particularly effective. Apart from, that is, the toast – but only if it came with real Irish butter. So Erin made sure to keep a loaf of white bread by the toaster at all times – day and night – should the boss's wife need to urgently fight off the urge to be sick.

'I'm told the sickness will pass soon,' Libby said, in much the same manner she had said it every day for the last three weeks. As if she believed saying it so often, as an affirmation, would will it into reality. Initially, Erin had soothed and smiled and said she was sure she was right, but now she just nodded and set about taking some butter out of the fridge and giving it a few seconds in the microwave to soften it.

'You are an angel put on this earth by God himself,' Libby sighed as she took her first bite of toast and for a moment Erin wasn't sure it was she, or the toast itself, Libby was directing her praise at.

'Hardly,' she snorted. 'Sure I only warmed some butter. I think it takes more than that for your big wings and halo these days.' She ignored the part of her that felt warm and fuzzy at the compliment. If there was ever a day when she needed a kind word, today was it.

It was then she noticed the expression change on Libby's face. 'Erin, are you okay?' she asked, before dropping her voice to a whisper. 'Have you been crying?'

Clearly the Touche Éclat was not doing the sterling job Erin hoped it would to hide the signs of her emotional turmoil.

'Onions!' she said, much too loudly. 'I've been chopping onions.'

'I thought I was supposed to be preparing the onions?' a male voice from across the kitchen called.

Both Erin and Libby turned their heads towards the voice. Paul, Erin's sous-chef, was standing with a knife raised as he chopped fresh basil leaves to make a pesto.

Shit, Erin thought, having forgotten that Paul was in earshot and well able to contradict the only excuse she could think of that was unlikely to draw further questions.

'Erm... you are. You did. I just needed some extra for this sauce and I figured it would be quicker if I just did it myself,' Erin mumbled.

'What sauce is that?' Paul called and Erin could gleefully have throttled him.

'Never you mind,' she said with fake jollity, before turning away from Paul's confused gaze and back to Libby, who looked equally as confused. Erin was not ready to have this conversation. Not now and not here, and definitely not in front of her staff. 'Onions,' she muttered again. 'They were really strong,' she added and she set about continuing to season some chicken she was intending to roast while trying to push down all the little bubbles of anxiety that keeping popping up. Had she done something wrong she wasn't aware of? Had Aaron done something really bad? Was there someone else? The thought made her want to vomit, as she tried to examine his behaviour over the last few weeks and months. Had there been new aftershave? She didn't think so. Was he sneaky with his phone? She had trusted him so implicitly, she never really paid attention. Because they were a couple and that's how it was. She knew him – except she didn't. Not at all.

Oh God, she suddenly remembered they'd booked an all-inclusive holiday for August that they'd have to cancel. Would they get their money back? It had cost a clean fortune and they'd only made the final payment a week ago. Why did he do that if he was planning on leaving, and all evidence pointed to the fact he had very much planned his flit?

Her spiral into the depths of depression was interrupted by the door to the kitchen swinging open and Jo marching in, her face like thunder. Erin surmised it must not be a good writing day.

Whenever Jo hit a bout of writer's block, she would inevitably show up in the kitchen, cross and frustrated, and start sniffing around the desserts for something she'd describe as 'medicinal'. She'd label these little visits to The Ivy Inn as one of the perks of being a part-owner of the establishment, and also as a much-needed change in scenery to get the wheels of creativity turning again.

As soon as Jo set eyes on Libby, she paused, just for a moment, before blurting, 'Don't judge me, Libby Quinn. Just because you know I've already had two chocolate brownies from the coffee bar this morning. These are serious times. This deadline is growing ever closer and my characters are refusing to behave.'

Libby raised her hands in mock surrender. 'I am judging no one,' she said. 'I'm mainlining buttery toast to stop myself from puking my guts up. Eat what you want. Enjoy it. For the sake of us who can only eat toast at the moment. Oh, and as you well know, it's Libby Simpson now.'

'You were Libby Quinn when I met you and you'll be Libby Quinn always, no matter if you're married to my brother,' Jo said with a smile.

Erin had already reached into the fridge and retrieved a passionfruit creme tart – one of Jo's favourites – from the selection she had made that morning before she'd had to switch her attention to lunch prep. 'Sit down, eat this – tell us what those horrible characters are up to and then get back to work,' Erin said, delighted to have the distraction of Jo's visit steer the conversation away from her red-rimmed eyes and puffy face.

'But you're preparing for service,' Jo said, her voice less certain than before.

Erin simply handed her a pastry fork. 'It has been rumoured that I can do two things at the same time, such as listen and prep. Besides, I've this place nearly in order now and there's little more to do before the orders start coming in.' And she was right – she had worked her socks off and managed her team of two beautifully so that they were ready for the lunchtime rush and had a start on preparing the tapas for the evening's sharing platters. She had been able, as she had hoped, to lose herself in her work.

'And... and well you've enough else on your mind without me whinging on,' Jo said, now two forkfuls down on the tart and feeling the soothing power of pastry and cream.

'I. Am. Fine,' Erin enunciated as she raised her eyebrows and gave a small nod that screamed, 'Not now!'

'Are you really though?' Jo said, having clearly not picked up on Erin's facial hints – no doubt due to the fact she was too busy ogling the pastry in front of her. 'I mean, how can you be?'

'What's this about?' Libby asked and Erin felt her heart sink.

She wondered if it was an appropriate time to fake her own death just to avoid answering the question. Instead, she decided simply to direct the conversation somewhere else. 'Did you see Flora is selling Wee Buns?' she blurted. 'I saw the sign go up this morning when I was coming to work. She says it's time for her to hang up her apron and that she might go travelling, maybe even go to Australia to see her son. I just can't believe in a matter of weeks or months the bakery won't be here any more.'

'Oh,' Libby said, and Erin couldn't help but notice her crestfallen expression. 'But she's a big part of the Lane. I don't want things to change.'

'Change isn't always a bad thing,' Jo soothed. 'I'll really miss Flora, and her buns if I'm being honest. But it'll be good for her to see some of the world, especially at her age.'

'I know,' Libby sniffed. 'It's just, nothing ever stays as it is for long, does it?'

It was at this point Erin felt herself start to choke up. Directing the conversation towards Flora's news was meant to be a distraction, not a roundabout way of reminding her about the transient nature of life.

'Being pregnant is making me extra soft,' Libby snuffled. 'Hormones are dangerous things. I don't feel in control of myself any more, so any change is knocking me sideways. I want this baby to grow up on the Lane knowing this community and feeling the same warmth we all feel. What if someone awful moves in to Flora's shop and wrecks the tone of the place? Those vape shops are opening up everywhere. I don't want to be enveloped in someone's bubblegum flavoured vape smoke every time I walk up and down the street. Or, what if it's one of those big chain coffee shops? They might steal all the business from my coffee bar in the shop. This street isn't big enough for two coffee shops.'

'Don't worry,' Jo said, with what Erin recognised as a wicked smile creeping onto her face. 'It will probably be an adult shop.'

The look of horror on Libby's face was almost enough to make Erin laugh. 'Jo, stop winding her up! For goodness sake!' she grinned before turning to Libby. 'I'm sure everyone had the same worries when you bought your shop. We didn't know who was moving in and what they were going to do, but it all worked out for the best. So try not to worry.'

'I suppose,' Libby said, as she stood up and shook the toast crumbs from her skirt. 'We'll just have to hope it's someone nice. Maybe another bakery, or a craft shop, or something that just fits, you know?'

There was a pause while all three women contemplated the situation. Erin couldn't help but wonder herself about what would happen next on the lane.

'I'll tell you something,' Jo piped up, as she waved her pastry fork in the air, 'if you opened a shop that sold these and only these, I'd say you'd be onto a winner. I mean, seriously, this is one of your finest efforts, Erin – and even better I've just had an idea about how to make my characters behave. The power of pastry wins again!' she declared with a grin as she polished off the last bite of the tart and got up to leave. 'You are a magician,' she enthused, as she kissed Erin on the cheek. 'And I love you.'

Erin felt her friend give her hand an extra squeeze – one which told her she had the best people in her life and everything would be okay.

She couldn't help but smile as Jo practically danced from the room, her spirits clearly high. And while she knew that her friend had been joking about her opening a pastry shop, something in what she had just said made Erin feel the smallest little fizz of excitement start to bubble up in the pit of her stomach.

She couldn't, could she? Yes, she loved the kitchens here. Loved the restaurant. Noah and Jo had given her carte blanche to make it her own, but the thought of opening her very own business – being able to concentrate on pastries and cakes – that would almost be a chance worth taking. And the start-up costs wouldn't be too insane? The place was already fitted out as a bakery.

Then again, she had just been dumped by the man she thought she would spend the rest of her life with and there was a good chance she wasn't thinking rationally. Wasn't there an old adage that you should never get a drastic haircut after a break-up? Surely the same logic applied to considering opening a business of your very own?

But still, if Libby could chase her dream and open the bookshop, and Jo could chase her dream and become a successful published author, and even if Flora could chase her dream and plan a trip to Australia, or to cruise the high seas, then why was Erin holding herself back?

'Libby,' she said, 'how did you go about buying the bookshop?'

6

The more Erin thought about it, the more excited she got at the prospect of finally having a business to call her own. A place that would help her rise from the ashes of whatever the hell had just happened with Aaron. It was something she could think about to push down all the sadness, and all the questions that were bubbling through her mind about what exactly was going on with the man she had thought she would spend the rest of her life with.

Yes, part of her wanted to storm over to the insurance brokerage he worked in and demand answers right there in front of all his colleagues, but a bigger part of her wanted to make sure she showed she could be strong and she did not need him. Whatever motive lay behind his actions, what Aaron had done was cruel. Just the morning before, they had been debating what colour to paint the living room – although now that Erin thought about it, Aaron wasn't debating so much as listening, but still, he didn't stop her. He didn't say 'Well, actually, paint it whatever colour you want because I won't be here. I'm moving to a lovely new gaff – without you.'

But she was determined not to show him how much he had hurt her. If it had been his plan all along to blindside her and leave her high and dry, then he had done it. He had won. She wasn't going to invite him to the after-party.

And every time she felt a bubble of emotion rise in her, she battered it back down by thinking of just how her new business could shape up. She adored working in The Ivy Inn. It had taken her a long time to build up her reputation here. When she had first started, it had been standard pub grub fare, and while it had been perfectly lovely and popular with the customers, it didn't showcase her true skills. The menu offered nothing out of the ordinary – but she had changed that, one brioche toasted sandwich and beer-battered asparagus spear at a time. She was incredibly proud of her achievements and she could not have asked for better bosses than Noah and Jo. In fact, if there was anything that would hold her back now, it would be giving up the kitchen that she had made her own and the fear of letting Noah and Jo down.

But both her bosses knew where Erin's true passions lay and how she had long dreamt of being her own boss one day– owning a place where she could utilise the very best of her skills to make her favourite dishes time and time again.

And for Erin, that meant a place where she could create the finest pastries and desserts. A shiver of pleasure ran through her when she imagined creating trays of pastel-coloured macarons, cream-layered Mille-feuille, shortbread that was light and crumbly with just enough snap to send Mary Berry into orgasmic delight. Of course, she'd add an Irish touch to some of her products – just the right amount of Guinness or whiskey added to a sauce, batter or creme could give it a rich flavour. She'd certainly enjoy experimenting with different recipes.

She thought of the pâtisseries of Paris and how she would stop in the street just to look in their windows at the sheer variety of treats and treasures on offer. She thought of how she was taught that the secret to the perfect *pâte feuilletée*, or puff pastry, was butter that was cool, but not cold, and lots of patience, or that the secret to making the perfect Beignet lay in making sure not to crowd the pan when deep frying. How she would stand at those windows and dream that, one day, she might be able to bring the delicate touch needed to be a master *pâtissière* back home to her beloved Derry.

Until now – until she had to deal with the shock that Aaron had planned and executed his move out of their home and out her life without giving her a chance to even ask why – she'd always thought that particular dream would forever be just that. Filed in the same part of her brain as her dream that she would one day meet Chris Hemsworth and he would instantly fall madly in love with her. Or the dream that she would one day be asked to perform as a backing dancer for Beyoncé. It was stored in the folder of dreams that would probably never, ever come true – but that day something inside of her snapped. There was nothing to stop her now. No planning for a life with Aaron. No continued saving towards a deposit to buy a house of their own, paying for a wedding or having children she had never been sure she actually wanted. No making decisions in which she put his feelings above her own. Perhaps Wee Buns going on the market this day of all days was a sign that life doesn't always work out the way you think it will, but it can still lead you to where you are meant to be. This could be her time to shine and it would be all of her own making.

Erin let that thought keep her going while she dealt with the lunchtime rush and the evening stampede. She fought off the painful feelings of Aaron's betrayal by instead thinking about ordering branded boxes tied with ribbon to sell her delicate creations in and maybe even a queue at the door for her treats.

More than once, Paul asked her why she was smiling as she

slaved over the hot burners, and she simply smiled back at him. 'Oh nothing,' she said, or, 'Wouldn't you like to know?' While the truth was that she couldn't wait to finish up for the day and go to pick Libby's brains about her experiences of opening her own business on Ivy Lane and making a roaring success of it.

And Aaron could watch from the sidelines, gutted that he had let her go.

* * *

Adrenaline could only take you so far, Erin realised as she wiped down the countertops one last time and looked around her kitchen. The day had been as busy as she had ever known it. The tapas platters had gone down a bomb, as had the dessert selection she had prepared offering bite-size tasters of some of her favourites. Paul had added a watermelon sorbet to the menu that absolutely blew her mind and was a firm hit with their customers.

Still, she had been relieved when she could call end of service and set about righting her kitchen. As she listened to the chatter continue from the beer garden, it seemed she was one of the only people on the premises who had intentions of getting home at a decent hour – and sober. But being around people comforted her. The sound of laughter – raucous and joy-filled – soothed her. Okay, it also made her a little teary as she remembered all the summer nights she had left the kitchen and found Aaron at a table waiting for her with a grin and an ice-cold cider. It hurt that he wouldn't be there tonight, even though she couldn't quite remember the last time he had actually come along to wait for her. The habit had died off somewhere along the way without her really noticing. Maybe, she thought, that had been part of the problem. But just as soon as that thought entered her head, she pushed it away. She was not going to wallow or allow herself to sink into the same sorry state she had been in when Jo had come to her aid that morning.

'Hey,' Paul said, as she stood at the door letting what little cool breeze there was wash over her. She turned her head to see him standing with a pint of icy water, complete with a slice of lemon. 'Take a drink and rehydrate,' he said, as he handed it to her.

'Thanks,' she replied and she revelled in the feeling of the cool condensation on the glass in her hands. She held the glass to her forehead to cool herself down a little before taking a long drink. 'That was a busy one,' she said. 'Thanks for your hard work. We pulled that off.'

'We did,' Paul said with a smile as he leaned with his back against the counter. 'The tapas went down so well. Maybe we should look at a variation on it at different times of the year.'

Erin nodded. As much as she normally loved talking about food and menus, she was worn out from the adrenaline fuelled rollercoaster of emotions that had been running through her all day.

'That's a good idea,' she said, aware that her response lacked her usual enthusiasm.

Of course, Paul noticed. 'I'm not trying to pry or anything,' he said. 'But are you okay? You've not seemed quite yourself, and that business earlier about chopping onions? You weren't, were you?'

Erin coloured, and found herself embarrassed at just how transparent her emotions were.

'Tell me to feck off if you want.' Paul said. 'But you know I'm always here as a listening ear if you need one. We're a team, after all.'

She looked up and saw the genuine concern written across his face. The crinkle in his brow, and the way his eyes were fixed on hers. As her second in command in the kitchen, she trusted Paul implicitly as a work colleague. He had also proven to be a useful sounding board over other matters in recent years too, but she wasn't sure she was ready to tell him about the break up. Just as she hadn't been ready to tell Libby, or Noah, she wanted to have had some time to try and process what had happened before she told Paul,

'I'm not going to tell you to feck off,' she said. 'And you're right, I'm not quite myself but I'm not ready to talk about it yet.'

He nodded. 'Okay. But you know I'm always willing to listen if you need to sound off about anything?'

'I do and I appreciate it,' Erin replied, and offered him a small but warm smile. 'Thanks for noticing and for asking,' she added. 'This too shall pass, and all that!'

'It will,' Paul said. There was a pause where the two colleagues just existed in the same space for a while before Paul said his goodbyes and said he would see Erin the next day.

After she watched him leave, Erin breathed in deeply, took her apron off and walked on aching feet through the bar, to where the crowd had thinned out. Sitting on the sofa close to the window was Libby, with Paddy, The Ivy Inn's resident rescue dog lying beside her, his head resting on her lap. Even as Erin approached her, she could see Libby's eyes drooping. Maybe this wasn't the time to discuss business strategy after all.

Slipping into the seat opposite, Erin was almost afraid to speak in case she frightened Libby back into full consciousness. Or Paddy for that matter.

As it happened, Paddy just lifted his head slightly and gave a sleepy wag of his tail to indicate his pleasure at her arrival before dropping his head and closing his eyes again. This, of course, startled Libby, who widened her eyes and straightened herself, trying desperately to look as if she had been fully conscious the entire time.

'Erin, sorry. I... I'm... I was just resting my eyes...' Libby stuttered.

Erin couldn't help but smile. 'I imagine it's hard-going – keeping the shop running and growing an entire new human being.'

Libby's hand went instinctively to her tummy. 'I didn't expect to be so tired all the time,' Libby sighed, 'or so nauseous, but I have to trust that it's all going to be worth it.'

Paddy lifted his head again, nuzzling it now against Libby's tummy as if he was aware of the precious cargo therein.

'If you're too tired to talk business, I understand,' Erin said, aware that while she would understand, she would be a little disappointed too.

Libby stretched. 'I don't think you're getting me at my best right now, but look, when is your next night off? Come round to ours, or I'll come to yours, and we can talk through your business plan and finances, et cetera.'

Erin didn't dare say she didn't have a business plan as such, or at all for that matter. In fact, all she really had was a broken heart, a kernel of an idea and the hope she could make it all work. And that would have to be enough.

'I'm off Thursday and Friday night – would Thursday work?' she asked, trying to work out just how much of a business plan she could pull together before then while also running the kitchen.

'Yep,' Libby said. 'Although Noah will be working here, so you won't have his business acumen. We could ask Jo along too though? She knows just about all there is to know about making this place work.'

'That's a good idea,' Erin said. 'Any and all help appreciated. I mean, it might be a non-starter but—'

'Everyone thinks their idea is a non-starter to begin with,'

Libby said. 'I definitely did with Once Upon a Book, but look at it now. It takes a lot of work, but you're not scared of hard work. I do have one concern though.'

Erin raised an eyebrow but didn't dare speak; she was too afraid of what the concern might be.

'What will we do without you? I can't imagine this place without you running the kitchen, and I know Noah would be really sorry to see you go. We'd support you, of course, and be delighted for you. I'll be your best customer,' she smiled, 'but you've really made this place your own.'

Erin didn't like to think about it, but she supposed she was going to have to at some stage. 'I have to work it all out – and God knows if it's even doable. This might be the shortest-lived dream in history. I may get cold feet and decide to stay here forever,' she smiled.

Libby reached across the table and gave her hand a gentle squeeze. 'It's a big decision, but exciting too. Let's look at your figures and see what we can make happen. Thursday night. At mine? And, of course, Aaron is more than welcome to come round with you too – assuming it's a joint venture?'

Erin's stomach sank at the mention of his name, and at Libby's well-intentioned assumption. But she still wasn't ready to have that conversation. She was not ready to say the words out loud again. So she nodded her thanks, stood up and gave Paddy a little stroke just as she saw Noah approach.

'I see my beautiful wife is tired,' he said, and Erin watched as he smiled warmly at Libby. 'Will we get you home, darlin'?' he asked.

'That would be very lovely indeed,' Libby replied, and she shifted in her seat, prompting Paddy to grumble with discontent.

'You can come too, fella,' Noah said, reaching down to scratch

Paddy right behind his right ear, which was his very favourite spot. 'It's our week to have you with us.'

'So the custody arrangement between you and Jo is still going well?' Erin asked, although she already knew that it was. Paddy certainly wasn't complaining about getting spoiled each week either with Jo and Lorcan, or with Libby and Noah.

'The very best,' Noah said. 'And Paddy is very excited about becoming a big brother. Little Paddy will be so lucky to have the best dog in the whole of Derry looking out for him.'

'Little Paddy?' Erin asked confused, while Libby rolled her eyes.

'That's what this eejit keeps calling the baby. As if, one; it's a forgone conclusion it's a boy, and two; we would name our baby after the dog,' Libby said.

'You'll grow to love it,' Noah said, as he slipped Paddy's lead on and winked at Erin. 'Won't she, Erin? It's a lovely name. A good solid name. For a boy, or a girl.'

'Eejit!' Libby laughed and swiped at him playfully.

This, Erin thought, this was what love was, and it wasn't what she'd had with Aaron.

That thought stayed with her as she walked home with a lump in her throat the size of a small island.

7

At least she had slept, Erin thought the following morning. Exhaustion had won through and she had drifted off almost as soon as her head hit the pillow. She had slept so well in fact that she didn't even wake at two in the morning desperate for a wee as usual. To her shock, when she had first opened her eyes that morning, it was already light and she could hear the sound of traffic on the street outside. Instinctively, she had reached across the bed expecting to find Aaron there, but, of course, she was only met with cool sheets and the realisation once again that everything had changed utterly in the last forty-eight hours.

Their flat felt different without his presence. He hadn't managed to strip away all traces of himself, but his essence was gone. There was no shaving gel for her to use on her legs when she had her morning shower. No manly scented shower gel sat beside her own, and no shortage of freshly laundered towels. The laundry basket was empty, apart from the clothes she had stripped off the night before, and when she was dressed and went to make herself a coffee, it seemed strange that there was exactly the same amount of milk left in the carton as there had been the previous day.

Every part of their home was changed and, to her shock, she even found herself feeling strangely bereft at the sight of a still clean and tidy living room, with no gaming controls lying around or empty crisp bags discarded on the sofa. She had no one to moan at for living like a teenager.

The place even smelled different without him in it. She'd never, in all her days, thought she could ever find herself missing that slightly sour tang of Aaron's body odour or the pungent aroma of his discarded football boots.

She even missed the noise of him. Just the everyday sounds of someone walking around the flat, putting on the kettle, opening and closing cupboards, or singing tunelessly along with the radio.

Erin looked at her phone wondering if he might have at least tried to get in touch with her. She wondered if she would find twenty late-night 'I'm sorry, I made a terrible mistake' messages. But there was nothing. Surely he wouldn't just leave it at speaking to her via Jo on WhatsApp? Did that sum up the depth of their relationship after three years spent together? She deserved an explanation. At the very least. Surely he didn't hate her enough to just cut her out? She wasn't a monster – or was she? Was she so deeply unlovable that he felt he'd no choice but to ghost her?

As she sipped the coffee, which now tasted much too bitter, she logged in to her Facebook and saw that, predictably, she was blocked from his profile. He couldn't have made any big announcement about the split, though, or she would've been inundated with 'You okay, hun?' messages from people she only barely considered friends who would be dying to hear all the gossip.

A surge of anger tightened in the very pit of her stomach. How dare he, she thought, how dare he decide he was the one to call all the shots in how this relationship ended. She accepted that if he wasn't happy he had every right to leave, but surely he could've spoken to her about how he was feeling first? He could've given her the chance to change, or for them to work together, or at least to tackle all this messy stuff amicably. Instead he had taken the coward's way out and sneaked away while she was at work before cutting off all contact with her and leaving her high and dry.

Well, two could play at that game. She went through her phone and blocked his number right back. Then she changed her passwords to Netflix, Prime and Apple TV. He'd have to fork out for his own subscription now and that would leave him cut off from the latest drama on *Below Deck*. Take that, Aaron, she thought, knowing in her heart that Captain Sandy would back her one hundred per cent. Just as she would her cancelling his phone contract, which had been taken out under her name as part of a friends and family deal. If he could cut her so callously out of his life, she sure as hell could do the same right back at him.

It gave Erin a moment or two of satisfaction until she wondered whether or not it would've been better if she had adopted a position of appearing to be completely unbothered by his actions.

'Gaaaahh,' she shouted, her voice echoing around her too quiet home. 'I am not this person! I am a strong, confident, independent woman who is about to start her own business and reclaim her fabulousness!' Of course, as she said this, she turned and caught the reflection of a woman as pale as a corpse in winter, with hair as frizzy as candyfloss, staring back at her. Despite her epic night's sleep, dark circles framed her eyes and, if she wasn't mistaken, the mother of all spots was brewing on her chin. 'My appearance doesn't matter,' she said, with slightly less vigour. 'It's who I am and what I am going to achieve that counts.'

And what she was going to do, first of all, was get through another blistering day in the kitchen at The Ivy Inn while calling the estate agent and inquiring about the sale price of Flora's bakery. She had savings, but did she have enough, or was this dream a non-starter from the off?

* * *

Erin was very much lost in her own thoughts as she walked to work. She'd popped her AirPods in and was listening to an audiobook, but she knew she wasn't really listening. It was just noise as her mind raced through everything that had happened with Aaron, and everything related to this mad notion she had had to buy the bakery. She'd have to go back a fair bit and listen again if she wanted the rest of the story to make sense.

The morning sun was warm, with just the gentlest of breezes offering a little reprieve from the heat. If she closed her eyes, Erin could almost imagine she was on holiday, the faint scent of her jasmine bodywash evoking memories of long summer nights in a Spanish taverna.

It was only the sound of a very familiar voice, in a very strong Derry accent, that pulled her away from her thoughts, her audiobook and her memories.

'Isn't it a great morning?' the low, just a little bit gruff, voice said.

Erin looked up to see Harry standing outside his shop, his face turned towards the sun. For a man in his late seventies, he was looking well. Better, Erin thought, than he had done for a while and certainly better than he had looked just a couple of years ago when he'd scared everyone on the street by collapsing behind the counter and ending up being rushed to hospital. Having Lorcan take over the lion's share of the business was clearly agreeing with him.

'It is a great morning,' Erin replied with a smile. There was something about Harry that meant even on his grumpiest days, people couldn't help but be incredibly fond of him.

'I'd say it will be another busy one for you down the street. I couldn't get over how busy it was yesterday. All that chatter going up and down the place and people coming in to buy ice cream and ice pops. We just about kept up with demand. We've had to double our orders this last week – and they say they don't know when the weather will break. Reminds me of the summer of 1976. Of course, that was way before your time – when was it you were born? The eighties maybe? Of course, 1976 feels like twenty years ago, but I suppose it wasn't. I was a young man then – well, young enough. And my boys were still at home...'

Erin nodded and smiled in all the right places and didn't attempt to answer any of Harry's questions. That wasn't how Harry operated. He just liked to talk and share his stories and was happiest when he had someone listening – whether they wanted to or not. It was just his way, and the Lane was richer for it. Just as it was with Flora, although perhaps not for much longer.

'So, Harry, what do you think about Flora's news?' Erin asked, breaking him off amid tales of the tar melting on the roads and the warm, sticky smell in the air back in 1976.

Harry blinked, looked up the street towards the bakery and looked back at Erin. If she wasn't mistaken, she could see a certain sadness in his eyes. 'Well, I know the bakery has become a bit too much to manage for her,' he said. 'And I know she wants to enjoy life away from work, and I understand that. But I think I'll miss her all the same. She's been here almost as long as I have and we've been through the best of times and the worst of times together. When this whole place was going to ruin during the

Troubles, we were able to keep our shops open, and there were times no one had any money, and everything was done on tick. I don't know how we kept going, but we did.'

There was a wistfulness, and a sense of pride, in his voice that made Erin feel more than a little emotional herself, even though she knew that she was already fragile and didn't require much help slipping into a maudlin state.

'You two are the heart of the Lane,' she said with sincerity.

'Ah now,' Harry said as he reached out and gave her arm a friendly squeeze. 'The Lane is about more than just one or two people. Sure, it's you young ones who have brought life back to the place and kept it going. The time was always going to come for a changing of the guard.'

Erin nodded, although a big part of her wished it didn't have to happen.

'And it's exciting too,' Harry continued. 'For Flora, you know. She hasn't always had it easy, but she's going to enjoy what is still to come. That takes a lot of guts, especially at our age. Sometimes I wish I had her nerve. I've not seen much of the world – always been much more of a homebird – but it's too late now, I suppose. All the same, I wish her well – there's no one that deserves happiness more.'

Still, Erin couldn't help but notice his gaze was fixed on the bakery. She couldn't say for certain, but there seemed to be something to his expression that cut a little deeper than just friendship and wishes that he may have travelled more and seen a little more of the world. It even seemed more than just an emotional realisation that things were changing on the Lane and there was no way to pause time and stay in the moment.

A bubble of emotion rose up in Erin, which she swallowed for fear Harry would ask her what was wrong and she would either start blurting out the whole sorry truth about Aaron doing a bunk, or worse still, would try to cover it up by saying something completely inappropriate that would traumatise the very life out of this lovely old man. Something like 'time of the month' that would turn Harry's face the colour of tomatoes and perhaps cause his already weak heart to give up altogether.

So, instead, she took a deep breath and told Harry she would chat to him later and she hoped he had a lovely day.

Still even as the busyness of the kitchen took over, Erin couldn't help but think of the older man and the sad look in his eyes and felt that a little of the ache in her heart was for him too.

8

The following day began with a surprise Erin absolutely had not been suspecting. Sadly, it was not a good surprise. Despite having come home from work late and exhausted the night before (making sure the kitchen was good to survive a day with someone else in charge was not a task she took lightly), Erin had struggled to get to sleep. It may have been because of the heat – her bedroom was too hot, but she hated sleeping with the bedroom windows open in case some masked intruder broke in and killed her in her sleep. The fact that her flat was on the second floor and there was a definite dearth of climbable surfaces on the exterior walls of her property did little to assuage this fear. Usually, she settled herself with the knowledge that Aaron would protect her. He had slept on the side of the bed closest to the window for this very reason, and while he could've found it hilarious that his adult girlfriend was afraid of imaginary intruders with Spider-man-style climbing skills, he had never once made her feel like her fears were ridiculous. Now she had no one to reassure her that her mind was not twisted and wonky, and she still had that fear to contend with. So, the windows had stayed closed and she had tossed and turned under her summer duvet for hours – because, despite the heat, she could not countenance sleeping on top of the covers in case monsters stole her toes in the middle of the night. That part, at least, she was willing to accept was an irrational fear, and yet she could not rid herself of it.

It could also have been because of the three glasses of wine she had downed when she got home, while watching *The Notebook* and crying herself into a state of hyperventilation at the notion of all love being fleeting and, sure, what was the point anyway – because the love of your life could just leave one day and never look back, or get some shitty illness and forget all about you in the first place.

The wine may have made her sleepy, but she had entered that stage of her thirties where alcohol had evolved in its war against her and woke her in the middle of the night with palpitations and anxiety about every little thing she had ever done wrong in her life, ever.

So by 9 a.m., when Erin had planned to be up, dressed and ready to work on her business plan for Libby, she was instead climbing back into bed desperate for even an hour of restful sleep. And that, of course, was when Aaron had decided to get in touch with her.

Of course, she had blocked his number on her phone, so instead he had used his best mate Connor's phone to send her a short and to-the-point text.

It's Aaron using Connor's phone,

As soon as she opened the message to see those first words, she felt her entire body tense up so tightly, she was genuinely worried she might be about to twist herself inside out.

I've left some stuff in the flat and I want to call round to get it, but wanted to check you were okay with that first? It's not much - some bedding and towels, some stuff from the kitchen.

Erin ran through what was actually in their kitchen to try to work out what he was talking about it. Bedding and towels, she could kind of understand. She knew there were some duvet sets and threadbare towels in the airing cupboard which he had brought with him when they had moved in together. She'd arrived with a couple of shopping bags from Dunnes Stores, filled with brand new Carolyn Donnelly collection towels – as well as matching bed linen. She couldn't remember the last time, if ever, they had used any of the towels she suspected Aaron had lifted from the back of his mammy's airing cupboard – maybe ones she was saving to use as cleaning cloths. They were so old and battered, she figured they were even beyond the use of a charity shop, but if Aaron wanted them back, he was welcome to them.

But the kitchen? As a chef, she prepared most of their food at home and she prided herself on her home kitchen being as efficient and well stocked as her work kitchen. Only the best-quality utensils, copper-bottomed pots and sharpest knives were allowed in her space. And she had bought all of those.

She typed back – her protectiveness over her beloved safe space superseding any feelings she may or may not have about Aaron super-ghosting her.

Stuff from the kitchen?

She just managed to hold herself back from typing 'Stuff from *my* kitchen?'

It was a painful ten minutes until he replied with a sad face emoji, which made her want to call him up and scream at him. A sad-faced emoji? In what part of what world was that an appropriate response to the former life partner you'd just walked out on with no warning?

As Erin tried her best to compose a response in which she did not belie her true feelings about what an absolute arse-face he was, a second message popped in.

Look, things are a bit tight at the moment. What with setting up in the new gaff and all. So, I was just going to come and pick up a few things from home? Not being cheeky, but I did do the last big food shop and—

Erin didn't know whether to laugh or cry, or possibly whether it would be appropriate to do both. He was actually getting in touch with her now, just three days after he had turned her life on its head, because he was a bit skint and wanted to claim some of the food shopping he had done the week before? Was this eejit for real?

Well, Erin thought, rising to her feet, he was welcome to it. She grabbed a reusable bag from the cupboard and started to fill it with a selection of the food her former partner had purchased. Then she stopped, her anger rising now, and emptied the bag again. If he wanted to treat her home like a one-stop shop or a glorified food bank, he could go to hell. Yes, he could have some of the tins and packets from the back of the cupboards, but she was certainly not going to make it easy for him.

It was, perhaps, a little vindictive, but wasn't she entitled to be a little vindictive given what he had put her through? She considered opening the air-sealed jars and punching holes in the tins to make sure the food spoiled, but she could not, in good conscience, countenance food waste. So, instead, she thought she would go for some low-key passive aggression instead. She gave him only tins that did not have a pull-ring opener, and she made sure she only chose food close to its expiry date. She packed a bag of spaghetti knowing that he preferred fusilli, and opened the multi-pack of cereals he had bought, giving him the boxes he didn't like. Oh yes, she kept the Frosties and the Crunchy Nut Cornflakes. He could have the ordinary Cornflakes and Rice Krispies. He could snap, crackle and pop off as far as she was concerned. She added all the Ready Salted crisps from the multipack and the shop-branded versions of Jaffa Cakes which tasted like pure evil, and left the bag outside the door of their flat in the hallway, along with a black bin bag containing the threadbare towels and bed linen. She hoped that was message enough to him that he was not to enter the flat – that he had lost all access rights to the home they had shared.

Once that was done, she sent him a text saying his belongings were in the hall as she didn't want him in her space, and if they weren't lifted by lunchtime, she would be disposing of them at her earliest convenience. She also asked him to slip his key under the door.

He didn't even have the manners to reply and so, not knowing when he was planning to land on her doorstep, she decided to take her paperwork out of the flat and away from the possibility of coming face to face with Aaron.

It wasn't that she didn't want to shake him hard and demand he explain his sorry self to her, but more that she'd had enough of this break-up being entirely on his terms and being forced to just swim against the current of his tsunami of bullshit.

He couldn't just land over with some probably made-up excuse about needing scruffy towels and tins of beans and think she would fall at his feet and invite him in. Right at that moment, Erin told herself she couldn't care less if she ever caught sight or sound of him again, but that when she did – and there would have to be some sort of reckoning at some stage – she was abso-lutely certain she wanted it to be on her say-so and when she felt suitably armed and prepared to show him what he had thrown away.

So, she packed the file containing the printouts from her current and savings accounts and the rough calculations she had been working on. She also packed up the notebook, filled with her own take on classic recipes which she had taken the time to beautifully illustrate, one day imagining she would be able to bake and sell these confectionaries in a glass-fronted shop. Between the pages, she had stuffed photos she had taken in Paris, images torn from magazines or printed out of design ideas she wanted to recreate in her dream world. Pictures of pastry boxes tied with ribbon or string. White and gold china cake stands, handwritten labels – everything with an air of elegance and warmth. It wasn't much in terms of a business plan, but she was confident it was a start, and that had to count for something.

Leaving her flat behind her, she didn't stop to glance back-wards at the bags outside her front door. In fact, she didn't want to look back at all – Erin's focus was now squarely on her future.

9

'So, I suppose, the most important thing to look at in all this is your budget,' Libby said, from her position of lying prone on the sofa with the window open and a fan pointed directly at her. She sipped gingerly from a glass of iced water through a straw before resting her hands once again on her stomach. It wasn't in a protective way, more of a 'please God make this sickness stop' way and Erin couldn't help but feel incredibly sorry for her. Libby was not experiencing any sort of pregnancy glow. She had lost weight, and was paler than usual.

When Erin had arrived, Libby had pointed out the little red dots around her eyes which she explained were burst capillaries.

'That happened because I had the audacity to drink pineapple juice,' Libby had explained. 'Half a glass and I was running to the bathroom and throwing up so violently, I broke my own face!'

'That can't be right,' Erin had said, horrified at her friend's experience. 'Have you spoken to your doctor or your midwife about this? There must be something they can do to help?'

Libby had sighed. 'That's what Noah says. I mean, I did mention it at my booking-in appointment, but, you know, millions of women get morning sickness and just get on with it. Besides, everyone keeps telling me it will pass any day now. Please God, it will.'

Erin hoped for Libby's sake she was right. And a little for her own sake too. Erin was not a brave little soldier when it came to illness and there was little she hated more than feeling nauseous or throwing up. In fact, apart from the man she thought she would be spending the rest of her days with running off and starting a new life without her, it really was at the top of her list of least favourite things.

She also happened to have a very suggestible mind and an incredibly empathetic stomach. So, while she knew that pregnancy was not contagious and morning sickness was not airborne, looking at Libby switching between a shade of fresh corpse to an even less appealing pale green around the gills and back again was enough to give her a queasy tummy.

Or maybe it was thinking about her budget that made her feel like her stomach was caught in a spin cycle. Erin wasn't clueless by any means – she did balance the budget in the kitchens of The Ivy Inn quite admirably, taking into consideration the cost of ingredients, and designing a menu that offered top-quality food with a decent profit margin. It was she who decided the price of each dish, weighing up the overheads but also what was a comfortable price point for their customers. But working with numbers was not something that came naturally to her, and it never had. In her school days, she'd even been known to bunk off the occasional – or perhaps not so occasional – maths lesson to avoid coming face to face with Mr Thompson – her teacher and arch-nemesis.

Erin drew in a long breath, and wished it was she who was sat in front of the fan instead of Libby. It was too warm and she was beginning to feel a little overwhelmed. Or sick with nerves maybe. Because the truth was, she knew that this was going to be a tall order – even with the savings she had squirrelled away over the years.

The shop itself was on the market at a fair price – Flora had definitely priced for a quick sale – and Erin had worked out that she could just about pull off a twenty per cent deposit. But that didn't leave her a lot left to play with – especially now that she would no longer have Aaron to split bills with.

Yes, the shop came with space upstairs – space which the estate agent specs described as 'multifunctional' and 'could be renovated into living space'. It was possible that Erin could maybe live there – but that depended on the amount of work that would need doing to make it habitable.

It could be the case she'd have to juggle her new venture with continuing to rent her current flat, and that was going to be pricey. She could, of course, always rent out the second bedroom.

And yet the thought of sharing a place with someone new made her nausea grow even more.

It was different when it had been Jo. They'd been best friends since the dawn of time. They'd had the occasional disagreement, of course. There was a particularly weird but very-intense-at-the-time stand-off over who bought more toilet paper. Rolls were carried in and out of the bathroom by the toilet user as and when needed for a total of eighteen days until it just didn't seem to matter all that much any more and life had returned to normal.

But even in the midst of Loo-Roll-gate, Erin knew that Jo had her back and always would have. They were compatible as house-mates and friends and, most importantly, Jo was not some crazed weirdo who was likely to have a nosey through her underwear drawer while she was at work or leave toenail clippings on the coffee table.

Aaron had taken a little more time to break in as a housemate.

Mostly because he had never lived with a woman before who was not his mother, and like most Derry men, that mother had spoiled him rotten. He'd barely known how to switch on the washing machine and Jo was fairly sure he genuinely thought bathrooms were self-cleaning, but she had soon corrected him on both matters.

Where she and Aaron had clashed at times, there was always room for forgiveness and understanding because, ultimately, they loved each other very much and it's relatively easy to forgive almost everything from a person you adore. It would not be so easy with someone new; some stranger to adapt to.

Erin was thirty-two. All her long-term friends were beyond the age of looking to rent a room in someone's home. That felt very much like something you did in your twenties when you were first starting out. Erin didn't *want* to still be living like someone in her twenties. She wanted her own space. She loved being able to come home from work, strip off item by item as she made her way to the kitchen to pour a glass of wine or open a bottle of beer without fear of being spotted in her comfy knickers and bra. And she loved being able to sing, badly, at the top of her lungs while she did the housework without fear of judgement. Most of all, she just loved that she didn't have to spend hours of her life making small talk and building a new friendship with somebody. She needed her house to feel like her home.

Yes, the prospect of another flat-share – especially with someone who would be a complete stranger – was something that brought her out in a cold sweat. But she might just have to suck it up to make this work.

'Erin, have you looked at the figures in much detail?' Libby's voice pulled her back into the here and now. She wondered how long she had been lost in her own thoughts and how long Libby had been waiting for a reply.

'God, yes, sorry. Well sort of. This wasn't exactly in my plan three days ago and then Wee Buns went up for sale and Aaron...' She trailed off, having realised that she hadn't actually told Libby – or anyone apart from Jo and Flora, for that matter – about the break-up, and even though she knew in the pit of her stomach that it was final and done and there was no going back, she didn't quite know if she had the emotional capability to say it out loud just yet. 'Well... it doesn't matter about Aaron,' she mumbled. 'Really it was Flora's shop going up for sale. It had made me feel all sorts of emotions – about this place, and what it means to me and what matters. And I'm not getting any younger either.'

Libby nodded. She understood more than most. Hadn't she sunk the redundancy money from her copy-writing job and the healthy inheritance her grandad had left for her into opening Once Upon A Book? Hadn't she felt compelled to chase that dream?

'Well, you're not staggering towards your pension years yet either, but yeah, this is probably a good time to do it,' she said. 'You know, before you and Aaron tie the knot, or settle down with babies. That changes things, you know. It gets a lot more serious then.'

There was a pause. A beat in which Erin wondered if Libby was expressing some of her own feelings about her impending motherhood and how it would change her relationship with Noah. Was Libby actually worried? Surely not. Noah and Libby adored each other. They were each other's ride or die; which Erin conceded could have a different and funnier meaning in Ireland than anywhere else. They were simply made for each other.

Then again, Erin would have said she and Aaron were solid three days ago. Her mind flitted to the value-branded tinned sardines she had left out for him, and the tinned Irish stew that was an affront to Ireland and all who lived there. She secretly hoped one or both of them had gone off and would give him an awful dose of the runs when he ate them.

It was only when she realised that Libby was, once again, staring at her that Erin realised she hadn't actually replied.

'It must be scary,' she said. 'The unknown and all that. But you guys, you love each other so much. It's clear to everyone when they see you together how you just work. A baby won't change that. It will just make it better.'

Libby lay back down again and groaned. 'You must think I'm awful moaning about being pregnant and how it's going to change things. I know it's the miracle of life, perfectly natural and the fulfilment of some sort of womanly destiny, but pregnancy doesn't seem to agree with me. I'm tired. My boobs are ginormous already and hurt like absolute bastards. I mean, you only have to look at them from across the room and they ache. And the only pregnancy glow I'm in danger of getting is positively radioactive. Worst of all, I did it to myself!' Libby cried.

'Well, great and all as you are,' Erin said, 'I do think there was someone else involved in the process. Tall, owns a pub, likes to tell really corny jokes...?'

Libby had the good grace to laugh a little. 'I don't think there's a prouder daddy to be in all of Ireland,' she said, 'but what I mean is... well... it's a bit like going out on the lash and having the mother and father of all hangovers the next day but knowing you made the decision to drink like a gulpin and brought it on yourself. I got knocked up by choice and it's hard going, Erin.' Another groan from Libby made Erin wince in sympathy.

'You poor thing,' she soothed, holding the glass of water up close to Libby so she could sip from it without moving her head. 'But just remember, at the end of it all, you get to have a little mini you or a little mini Noah to love and cherish.'

A smile broke out on Libby's face. 'I know. That keeps me

going – the thought of meeting this little one and getting to know them and watch them grow. And I get to do it all with Noah. I know he'll be a brilliant dad. He's already so excited. I've had to hold him back from decorating the nursery just yet, but that doesn't stop him arriving home a couple of times a week with a new onesie, or teddy bear, or pack of nappies.'

Erin was warmed by the obvious love in Libby's voice. There was no doubt in her mind that she and Noah would make for the best parents. She'd seen how Libby interacted with the kids who came into Once Upon A Book to choose a book in the beautiful Children's Book Nook towards the rear of the store. Her Saturday morning Storytime sessions were always jammed and, to her credit, Libby took it all in her stride – even if one of the babies took a crying fit that had a domino effect on all the other children in the store.

And as for Noah – he had been born to be a daddy. Erin saw that every time he interacted with his little sister, Clara. Between Jo, Noah and everyone who knew little Miss Clara, that child knew nothing but love and fun. Noah seemed to work extra hard at making sure Clara's childhood was as happy as it could possibly be.

Erin felt a pang of sadness for him, knowing how his own tragedy had led him into foster care when he was a teenager. He was lucky to have been placed with the Campbells and to have gained Jo as a sister, and this little baby who was making his or her mamma so very unwell was going to be loved so much by so many.

'You're very lucky,' Erin told Libby. 'I know this sickness is tough, though. Are you sure you are up to talking figures with me just now? I understand if you can't face it. Maybe you should just get a nice long sleep?'

'No! No, I'm grand. Honest. Talking about something exciting like a new business might just distract me from the nausea. And as long as you don't so much as glance in the direction of my boobs, they'll be grand too. So how about you run me through your outline and the ballpark figures.'

'Okay,' Erin said, sitting down on the floor with her legs crossed and looking at her little notebook of dreams.

'Please understand these are very, very, very much ballpark figures. And it's a really big ballpark. I'm hopeful that not every-thing will cost as much as I've allocated, but I know some things will probably cost more. This is my position, though. I have some money in savings. Some in my current account and some in an ISA. I figure it would cover about a twenty per cent deposit on the shop and leave enough for a basic refit. I'd need to do a lot of the work myself to save on labour costs and I think I may have to be very canny in my purchases. It's important to make sure I have ample capital for equipment and ingredients. Those are two areas I don't want to skimp on. The equipment isn't cheap.'

'I don't imagine it is. I know what it cost me to kit out the small coffee area downstairs, and that was nothing in comparison to what you'll need. Does Flora have any equipment you can buy and continue to use? It's worth asking her – she might throw it all in as a job lot. Ovens, mixers... I don't know... Those thingies for doing the wee footery bits?'

'Thingies for doing the wee footery bits?' Erin asked, smiling and with one eyebrow raised. She knew baby brain was a thing, but she'd need more clues than 'thingies' and 'footery'.

'Aye, you know, all the cutting and decorating tools and... I don't know, plates and stands and that kind of thing? But, look, you know what you need, it's just worth looking at different ways to source it all. Downstairs, we used a lot of reclaimed items, vintage finds and auction pieces,' Libby said. 'How much of a refit do you think the shop needs? Obviously, you'll want to do it justice, but is there shelving, for example, that could be given a facelift and fit with your vision?'

'I was hoping that might be the case,' Erin said. 'I didn't want to speak to Flora until I knew if it was viable at all – but you're right. Speaking to her might help me know just how viable it is.'

'But your business will be different, won't it? It won't be turnovers and snowballs and cream fingers?'

'No, it won't be. It will be a pâtisserie – lots of pastries, fresh cream desserts, biscotti and macarons, wedding cakes and the like. So not much of a bun with a cup of a tea at eleven in the morning kind of a place,' Erin said and she could envisage it all as she spoke. How it would look. How it would smell. How she would revel in the feel of flour tickling her nose, and dough in her hands. The beauty and the science of taking raw ingredients and mixing them in exactly the right way to create delicate and delicious works of culinary art. It's what made her heart sing.

'And you think you have twenty per cent of the deposit?' Libby asked, and Erin was once again jolted back into the reality of numbers and money and scary business decisions.

'Yes. Ideally, it would've been better if I could've put ten per cent down and invested the rest into the refit and into making sure I have a decent contingency fund, but I read that you need a bigger deposit for a commercial mortgage so...'

Libby blew out of a breath and pulled herself to sitting up again. 'You do. Is there any way you can stretch to more than twenty per cent?'

'I can't. As it stands, I will be cutting things pretty tight,' Erin said as she watched Libby's face for her reaction. She was getting serious 'I'm about to pee on your parade' vibes from her friend.

'Twenty per cent is still decent,' Libby said, in a voice that Erin noted was extra soft and soothing. The kind of voice someone uses when they are just about to drop a mega bombshell on someone but wants to do it gently. 'I hate to say it, but you should be warned that it's tough getting a mortgage at the moment. We've just remortgaged a new deal for the bookshop and we found that lenders are less likely to take a risk these days. Every penny extra you can put down goes in your favour. An extra few thousand can make all the difference. I mean, I know it's not easy. People don't have thousands of pounds hidden under the mattress or down the back of the sofa these days. Or any days for that matter. But is there a family member who might be able to help you out?'

Even though it was still incredibly warm in Libby's living room, and even though she could feel the strength of the sun shining in through the window, Erin couldn't help but feel a shiver of disappointment, which very quickly turned into a big, cold, dirty deluge of depression. There was no way she could get her hands on any more money. Her parents, who certainly had money squirrelled away, had essentially cut her off financially when she had shunned a law degree in favour of the culinary arts. Disappointment in her life choices radiated off them in waves whenever she saw them, so asking for a loan or an investment would only add to their disdain. It didn't matter to them that she had won a scholarship to study for Le Grand Diplôme – a professional chef diploma – with extra study in pâtisserie at Le Cordon Bleu, a prestigious culinary school in London. Or that she had spent a year honing her pâtisserie craft in Paris. All they could see was that she was now working in a pub kitchen – and they didn't bother to learn that her reputation as a chef with talent and potential was growing day by day. She wouldn't give them a chance to reject her again, nor would she waste her breath trying to explain herself once more.

'Is Aaron going to co-sign, and invest into the business too? Does he have savings he can tap into? I'm sure you've already asked him?' Libby said, her face full of concern for Erin.

She absolutely did not trust herself to speak, so instead she shook her head and tried to focus on her breathing.

'You could be lucky and find the right lender,' Libby said with a lack of conviction as she reached out to rub Erin's shoulder to comfort her. 'Let's stay positive!'

But Erin knew without a doubt that if Libby were to touch her, or show her any kindness in that moment, she would lose control of her emotions. So instead, she shuffled backwards.

'I was stupid to even think it was possible,' she stammered, as she climbed to her feet. 'And sure, even if I did get a lender, then no doubt the equipment would be too much or something else would go wrong – like they'd find rising damp, or I'd forget to buy all the wee footery things.' She tried to laugh at her parroting of the word 'footery', but it came out more as a strangled sob instead. She couldn't help but feel she'd just made an eejit of herself – taking the notion of a shop and thinking she had the knowledge, and the money, to make it her own. Just a few days ago, this was nothing more than a recipe book she'd hand drawn and memories of her time in Paris. It was a pipe dream and she'd hurtled full speed ahead at it. Because she was grieving her relationship. Because she wanted to show Aaron she didn't need him. She'd thought she could do it and had run at it not realising just how hard any setback, or even whisper of a setback, would hit her. She was a stupid, stupid woman.

'Erin!' Libby called out as Erin, her heart thumping and a flush of humiliation or stress or something rising from deep within her, tried her best to scoop her belongings back into her bag. 'You don't give up at the first hurdle. Not without trying. God knows if I had given up every time we hit a bump with this place, my life would look very, very different right now. I'd probably be working in some horrible unfulfilling job, and I'd be single and, admittedly, I wouldn't want to throw my guts up, but I wouldn't be happy. You have to take a chance if you want to make a change.'

Erin heard everything her friend said – of course she did. But all the time, her own negative monologue continued to run at full speed in her head, drowning out Libby's motivational speech about taking chances. This particular hurdle was at least six feet high and even an Olympic gymnast would struggle to get over it. And what if there were another one waiting for her down the road? She either had enough money or she didn't. And at this stage – before she'd even had the chance to do the full costings – it looked like a distinct possibility she didn't. Maybe she should just scrap the whole idea now instead of allowing herself to dream it for a while longer before it all blew up in her face.

'I think I'd better just go and I'm sorry for wasting your time. You must think me completely stupid,' she blurted, her face now as red as her hair and annoyed at herself for losing her cool.

'Erin!' Libby said, exasperation heavy in her voice. 'For good ness' sake. Let me take a look at the figures and see if I can spot any slippage?'

'You're not going to find a slippage that amounts to thousands of pounds,' Erin said. 'I was being stupid at rushing at something just because I'd seen a for sale sign. Life doesn't work like that, does it? There's no closing of one door and opening of another. Not for real people. Not for people like me.'

She watched as Libby blinked at her, clearly unsure of what level of breakdown she had just witnessed.

'Well, we absolutely won't know if any doors will open if I don't look at the figures,' Libby replied, her voice quiet but firm. The kind of firm that reminded Erin of Mr Thompson, the maths teacher, and she knew better than to say no to him. Or Libby.

And so, with a degree of reluctance, Erin handed over her figures and her notebook of dreams and excused herself to go to the bathroom, where she looked herself straight in the mirror and acknowledged her emotions were all over the place at that moment and her reactions could possibly be construed as a little overdramatic.

Erin took a deep breath. She could do this.

10

The bags were gone from outside the flat when Erin got home. A small of part of her had held on to the hope that when she opened the door and made her way inside, she would find the bags, and Aaron, waiting for her. That he would fall to his knees and tell her he had made a huge mistake and he'd realised almost as soon as he had tried to exist outside their little love nest that he was nothing without her and even the bad times they had together were better than most people's good times. That home did not exist for him outside of these four walls.

It had felt like home from the day they came to view it. It was very different to the flat she had shared with Jo. While it had been modern and sleek, this flat oozed character and charm. It had sash windows, and real wood floors and an original fireplace which Erin loved in the winter. They'd known immediately it was the place for them, when they couldn't stop grinning as they had walked around it, hand in hand. Erin had been able to imagine exactly what her life was going to look like – how her infrequent nights off would be spent cuddled up on the sofa with Aaron watching box sets, or drinking wine and talking about their future. She could imagine how those conversations would morph into sessions of lovemaking that were extra-long and extra orgasmic because they'd know there was no chance of anyone walking in and catching them at it, or listening in from a neighbouring bedroom. She'd squeezed Aaron's hand, and he had squeezed hers back as they had looked around the kitchen – her mind already filled with ideas of meals she could cook for them and how she could make the bijou space a decent working kitchen. How it would feel and smell like home. How she could use the second bedroom as a dressing room/office/guest room. It was up to them because this would be their home. It wasn't a palace, or even particularly fancy, but they'd known straight away that it was perfect for them.

And even after two years, she'd still loved it and had thought of it as their love nest. She'd still thought they were as solid together as the walls surrounding them. Even if they didn't cuddle on the sofa as much as she'd hoped, and there were more and more times when she was too exhausted on her nights off to stand and cook a gourmet meal, so they'd simply order in a takeaway, or, increasingly, eat separately. Maybe they'd grab something when they were out with friends. Or just make up a quick sandwich. Erin had even been known, to her secret shame, to just take a packet of chocolate digestives to bed with her and munch through them while she read her novel or binge-watched *Married at First Sight* on her own.

Maybe she should've spotted that something was wrong, but was that what wrong even looked like? All couples went through slumps over time, didn't they? No one stayed forever and ever madly in love all the time. The butterflies and heart-thumping, dizzy-making yearning of being madly in love wasn't sustainable – or even that comfortable. The honeymoon stage was known as the honeymoon stage for a reason – it didn't last. It couldn't last. It was fuelled by adrenaline and dopamine and the need to get to know everything about each other – every thought in their head, every inch of their body – intimately. It was exhilarating but you couldn't live your entire life as if you were at the very top of the rollercoaster, just about to hurtle downhill before looping the loop. It would be exhausting.

Erin had always believed when love was done right it was the process of falling in love over and over again with the right person, which, by definition, also meant falling a little out of love with them from time to time. That there would inevitably be times when it became about the practicalities of getting the rent paid, or making sure the bins were put out. Or times when it was perfectly normal to fantasise about putting a pillow over your snoring partner's face or realise the odd way they ate pasta gave you the really bad ick. An ick so bad you were sure you'd never be able to remotely find that person sexually appealing ever again (with Aaron, it was the slurping and insisting on eating every kind of pasta with a spoon). But those were the times when you worked at it and fixed it. That's when your brain got to hit a reset button and there was something in how that person makes you toast in bed when you're hungover or how they remember your favourite chocolate bar, or just how they make you laugh like no one else has ever made you laugh, and you got that swooping, rushing, falling feeling again – perhaps less intensely, but it was there all same. More comfortable now, because the fear that it was not going to last should be gone. That whatever came their way they would work at it and through it and find their way back to the top of the rollercoaster. Because that was how real love actually worked. That's how real problems were dealt with.

You didn't just ghost the person you'd already chosen baby names with. You didn't just move out without warning. Who does that? She certainly never thought Aaron would be the type to do it, but he had. There was no escaping that particularly ugly reality.

But still, she had hoped she was wrong. That this had all been some sort of epic misunderstanding that she just couldn't think of a suitable explanation for.

And within that hope was the idea that Aaron might just have been inside the apartment waiting for her. That his tins of on-the-turn food would be back in the cupboard, and his clothes would be hanging in the wardrobe.

Okay, so she didn't know how she would react to that – whether she would want to give him another chance or whether she would, as Jo's little sister, Clara, would say 'yeet him into space'. But she'd have liked to have had the choice.

Especially that night of all nights.

Because after two hours of brainstorming and number crunching, not even Libby Quinn's brilliant business mind had been able to find a way to help Erin achieve her dream.

They'd discussed first of all buying the bakery as a going concern and continuing to run it just as it was until she could give the pâtisserie the glittering start in life she dreamt of. There was no doubt that an 'if it's not broke, don't fix it' approach would require a significantly lower investment in the first place. But running an ordinary, if well loved, bakery had never been Erin's dream. When she had allowed her mind to imagine just what her perfect life would look like, she'd think of croquembouche and tarte tatin instead of floury baps and sugar-coated gravy rings – and if she was going to sink in every penny she had in savings, and probably sell some of her own belongings to make it happen, then there could be no half-measures.

As hard as she had tried, she could not help feeling incredibly disappointed, even if this had only been a pipe dream until a couple of days ago and she'd never really considered how to do it properly. It all left her with a feeling that she was failing at life – unable to maintain a relationship, or start a business and realise her dream. While her friends, Libby and Jo, were absolutely smashing it and finding their happy ever afters too. Childish as it might have been, she had to fight the urge to stomp her feet in protest and scream that it wasn't fair.

Libby had tried to be reassuring. She had said all the right things. All the platitudes were wheeled out. 'What's for you won't pass you,' was said more than once. Along with the reassurance that the universe would provide when Erin was ready to receive.

It was only the fact that Libby was pregnant that stopped Erin carrying out an act of violence on her after that particular comment. Erin knew she was ready. She'd wanted to scream that she was more than ready. That the bakery going up for a sale was a sign she couldn't afford to ignore. This *was* the universe telling her that this was for her, and it would be a crying shame to let it pass by.

She needed something that would distract her from the ache in her heart and from the desire to have someone hold her in his arms, kiss the top of her head and tell her how incredible it was to love, and be loved by, her.

But when she opened the door into an empty flat, there was no one waiting to hug her. The cupboards and wardrobe were as bare as when she had left them. The whole place was quiet, without the rumble of Aaron's gentle snores reverberating out of the bedroom, or the quiet hum of the TV to greet her. There were no crumbs on the worktop or discarded trainers in the hall ready to trip her up. She was on her own. Completely.

Tired and emotional, Erin walked through to the bedroom, and pulled the curtains across to block out the last flickers of the day's light. Not even the soft streaks of pink, orange and red across the sky could lift her feeling of melancholy.

So she took time only to slip out of her sneakers, shorts and T-shirt before she climbed into bed in her underwear, and pulled the duvet up over her face.

To her immense relief, she fell straight to sleep and didn't wake until there was an unholy hammering at her front door.

11

It took a moment or two for Erin to process that it was morning and the noise that had woken her was real and indicated there was someone banging on her front door as if there was some sort of emergency.

The jolt from peaceful dreaming mode to full-on fight or flight mode was as jarring as it was confusing.

Of course, the first thing she did was reach her hand across to the other side of the bed to give Aaron a shake so he could get up and tackle whatever threat had just descended upon them. That in itself prompted an immediate spike in anxiety as she found his side of the bed to be empty, and her brain had yet to reset to her new single reality.

The persistent hammering did not give her time to grieve his loss however, and she jumped out of bed in a state of panic, and practically ran to the door sure that there must be some momentous and probably bad news afoot to have someone knock so violently and not give up.

And that was how she found herself standing in her knickers

and bra at her open front door staring at Libby, Jo and – most embarrassingly of all – Noah.

Noah at least had the decency to avert his gaze. Libby's eyes widened and Jo, who was not known for her subtlety, said: 'Not even a matching set, Erin! This is simply not good enough if you're trying to seduce us!'

Of course Erin hadn't remembered until that point that she *was* standing dressed only in her slightly greying but exceptionally comfy white M&S T-shirt bra and her favourite pair of Wonder Woman-themed pants. As the realisation dawned on her, her hand flew immediately to her crotch to hide any visible bikini line strays that may be popping out to say hello. She had been planning on booking a wax this week, but her impetus to have hair ripped from her most sensitive area had lessened somewhat after she had been dumped. Her other hand flew to her chest and she turned away, horrified that, of all people, Noah had seen her in her scanties. Jo had seen this not so glorious sight before and Libby was perhaps the least judgemental person she knew and unlikely to be horrified at the sight of sagging knickers, but her boss? Her particularly cool and sexy boss? No – the thought was mortifyingly embarrassing.

She cursed her laziness at just peeling off her outer clothes and jumping into bed the previous night, but then again, she was in the middle of a very traumatic break-up and should be allowed to cut herself some slack.

'Oh arse!' she muttered under her breath as she left her three friends standing at the door while she made a beeline back to the bedroom to grab jeans and the crinkled T-shirt from the day before. She pulled her unruly red curls into a high ponytail, grabbed a flannel to give her face a quick wipe and brushed her teeth.

All the while, she wondered just why on earth her three

friends were at her front door first thing in the morning and what was so important that they'd had to virtually break it down to get in. Perhaps she had missed calls from them? But when she looked to her bedside table, where she would normally leave her phone to charge, it wasn't there. Come to think of it, she couldn't actually remember plugging it in the night before, having been too intent on just hiding from the world under her duvet. Sure enough, it was still in her bag and the battery was dead.

Had Jo been trying to call her and maybe panicked when she couldn't get an answer? Or had something happened with Aaron? More than just sardine poisoning? Maybe a small bout of psychosis that could be easily fixed but which would explain why he had just walked out like she meant nothing to him? She could absolutely live with that.

But no, it couldn't be that something was wrong. Jo wouldn't have made a joke about her mismatched underwear if something truly life-altering had occurred. No one ever softened someone up for bad news by laughing at their Wonder Woman pants.

To steady herself, Erin took a deep breath. The uncertainty of not knowing exactly what she was going to face made her feel a little uneasy. As did the thought that Libby and Noah would likely want to know where Aaron was. Was she going to have to explain to them that Aaron was now her ex? Right now?

They probably had already noticed the lack of an Aaron-shaped figure in the room, or the absence of his musky man-scent, or discarded games console controls strewn across the floor.

A thought crossed her mind that maybe, just maybe, Aaron had consulted all three of them on how to win her back and this was step one in that process. She didn't quite know how she would respond to that.

A quick glance in the mirror told her she was passable as a functioning, clothed adult with no underwear on show, and she walked back to the hall, where her three friends remained standing at the front door seemingly not sure whether or not it was safe to come in.

Was it the horrified expression on her face that had put the fear of God in them? Or simply the sight of her knickers?

'You can come through, you know,' she said, faintly amused now by how awkward they looked. 'But you better hurry up and tell me why exactly you were all on my doorstep at this time of the morning on a very rare Friday off.'

'That's my fault,' Jo said. 'I did try to call you late last night and then this morning, but your phone kept going directly to voice-mail and you never let the battery run out on your phone, so I got a little worried. And also, you know what I'm like when I get an idea in my head and last night we came up with an idea and I said you'd want to know about it as soon as possible...' She was the first to walk into Erin's living room, followed by Noah, who mouthed 'sorry' at her as he walked past, and Libby, who smiled and held up a bulging bag from Wee Buns and a bunch of slighted wilted carnations.

'Harry said you didn't seem quite yourself the last time he saw you, so he asked me to bring you these,' Libby explained and Erin couldn't help but feel a swell of emotion rise up in her. It was a mixture of a fondness for Harry and his quirky ways and a feeling of gratitude that she had these people in her life at a time when everything felt as if it were falling apart.

'Now that I know you're still alive, I'll put the kettle on,' Jo shouted from the kitchen. 'We can get a cup of tea or coffee and then get down to business.'

'What business is that?' Erin called back to her. 'And I'm sorry about my phone. I was exhausted last night and just needed to sleep.'

She knew that Jo would be able to read her like a book and

know that meant she had not only been exhausted the night before but also that she was heartbroken and not functioning at an optimal level.

'We may just have a solution to your problem!' Libby blurted with a grin, and a flicker of something that Erin couldn't quite put a name on ignited somewhere low in the pit of her stomach. Fear or excitement? At that stage, it could have gone either way.

Her shoulders relaxed a little as Jo handed her a cup of tea. Libby and Noah both had smiles on their face and Jo wore an expression that screamed 'I'm so excited, I might vomit' – which Erin knew only too well from all the times she was in her friend's company and her friend had, indeed, vomited with excitement. Or too many WKDs.

'First of all,' Libby said, 'we should just let you know that Jo told us about Aaron and we're really sorry.'

'Don't be mad at me!' Jo blurted before Erin could answer. 'I just thought they needed to know the full picture and I know it's very raw and you don't know where it might ultimately end...'

Tears pricked at Erin's eyes. 'It already has ultimately ended,' she replied. 'I still don't know why, but it's fair to say there is no coming back from this.' There was a slight shake in her hand, which she forced herself to still. She would not let a single tear fall or show any weakness now. 'I'm sorry I didn't tell you both about the break-up,' she said to Libby and Noah.

'You have nothing to apologise for,' Noah said. 'You're not obliged to fill us in on all the comings and goings in your life. But we are sorry we couldn't support you from the start.'

The tightness that had squeezed her chest squeezed even tighter until she wasn't sure if she would be able to expand her chest enough to inhale another breath, or if there was one stuck in her chest waiting for her to let it go. All she could do was shake her head.

'We probably don't say it enough because we are always, always on the go, but you are not just a very vital part of our business, Erin, you know you're part of our family and we love you. We need you to know if we can be there for you in any way, then we will be there for you,' Noah said. 'No questions asked.'

Erin couldn't hold it in any longer. She raised her hand and, as calmly as she could, told Noah to 'Shut up!'

It was unlikely he could've looked any less shocked than if she had just slapped him square across the face.

'No. I didn't mean it like that... I don't... It's just, please, I'm asking you, all of you,' she said, her voice cracking. 'Please don't be nice to me, or kind to me, because I'm just about keeping my shit together and I know I won't be able to if people are kind to me.'

'But you do know you deserve people being kind to you, don't you?' Jo said, as she crossed the room and sat on the arm of the chair beside her friend, wrapping one arm around her shoulders. 'And you know, not to sound all cheesy and stuff, but we are a safe space where you can always lose your shit without judgement. We're here for all the shit searching, always.'

Erin snorted, and smiled, even as her eyes betrayed her and started to leak. 'I love you all – but I am not ready to be in my feelings just yet. I know Aaron and I are over, but I am not ready to grieve it yet, so I just want to keep those feelings bottled up for a bit. If that's okay?'

But even as she spoke, Erin knew that the grief she had been holding deep inside her was bubbling perilously close to the surface. There would only be so many times she would be able to push it back down.

'Well, in that case, I'm not sure we'll be able to tell you what our solution to your problem is, because it will make you cry. We hope. But in a good way,' Jo said.

Erin glanced at the sofa, where both Libby and Noah sat, hand in hand. Noah was smiling and Libby was openly crying.

'Hormones,' she sniffed, having sensed Erin was looking at her.

'Oh dear, sweet baby Jesus, my tea is going cold and I haven't even had a bun yet. Can you get on with telling me what this intervention is all about?' Erin said.

'This is the exciting part,' Libby replied.

'We think you should buy Wee Buns and transform it into the loveliest pâtisserie in the country,' Jo added.

'Well, so do I, but you do realise it's not quite as simple as that,' Erin said. 'I mean, last night, Libby and I went over the figures. And we couldn't make them work – as hard as we tried. There's no way I can put more finance together and, probably, even if I could just about swing it, it would mean risking absolutely everything I own in this world and getting into a really scary amount of debt to do so. But that's really just a moot point anyway, because, believe me, I'm nowhere near to being able to swing it. I'm not saying never, but short of a lottery win, it's not going to happen just now. So I have to be okay with that. And maybe actually buy a lottery ticket!'

When she stopped talking, Erin realised her voice had taken on a distinctly high-pitched quality and that all three sets of eyes were directly on her and all of them belonged to fairly bemused-looking faces.

'Maybe we could just calm things down for a moment,' Jo said. 'And hear us out.'

'I don't see how anything you say could make a difference,' Erin said, that little fluttery feeling back in her stomach. 'The fact is, I'm too financially challenged.'

'Let us show you what we were thinking before you go and

sign yourself into the poorhouse,' Noah said, before he nodded to Libby.

'Okay, so when you went home last night, Noah and Jo called round after the bar had closed and I'm sorry, but I talked to them about your idea because it is a brilliant idea. It's exactly the kind of business we need on the Lane. And you're someone who knows this place, and cares for this place. Who feels invested in the Lane continuing to do well and grow,' Libby said.

'It's in all our interests to have someone who shares our vision for the Lane coming on board here,' Noah added.

'But the problem is,' Jo said, 'we really don't want to lose you entirely from The Ivy Inn. You're too important for us to lose you so that you can put every ounce of your energy towards starting a new business.' Jo beamed as she said this and Erin couldn't help but feel confused.

'You want me to open my own business, but you don't want me to leave The Ivy Inn?' she said. 'I think I might need a couple of paracetamol to get through this.' She made to stand up to go and grab some painkillers to fight the headache now starting to build behind her eyes, only to feel Jo reach for her hand and pull her back down.

'Sit down and listen just a minute. I'll get the paracetamol. You concentrate on what Noah and Libby are telling you!' Jo instructed. 'We have a plan.'

'You have a plan?' Erin asked, and three heads moved in unison, nodding in front of her.

'We want to go into business *with* you,' Noah said. 'The pâtisserie as an offshoot of The Ivy Inn kitchens. The business would absolutely be yours, but we'd be your investors. What we'd want in return is for you to be able to keep your influence in our kitchens, and maybe we could look at some shared branding to reinforce the link between us all. You get your dream business.

We don't lose you as, say, executive chef. We all make an invest-ment which will reward us all. There's nothing to lose!'

It was at that point, as tears flowed freely down her pale white cheeks, that Erin realised she had lost the battle to keep her feel-ings in check. It sounded like the answer to all her prayers – even the ones she didn't realise she had said.

12

It was gone ten and Libby had left to go and open the bookshop. Erin had left Noah and Jo to drink their tea while she cried a little in the shower, then dressed in her red ditzy-print midi dress which should have clashed with her hair, but didn't. It was a dress she wore when she was feeling particularly positive about life, and while she still had one hundred and one questions, she actually *was* feeling very positive. If nothing else, she had learned that these people – her friends – saw her as someone who really mattered. As family.

That was a new feeling to Erin, who didn't really know what it was like to have family who believed in her wholeheartedly. A family who, it seemed, actually loved her unconditionally. Her parents seemed to have missed out on those genes. They had been very focused on their careers and not so much on raising the one and only child they had brought into this world. Sometimes she had wondered if her arrival on this earth had simply been a tick on a to-do list for Gerry and Helen Donohue. Every move in their carefully planned life was designed as part of a checklist of things expected of a successful, well-to-do couple. 'Have at least one child' was on it, between 'buy a detached house on the Culmore Road' – the poshest part of the city of Derry – and 'get a dog'. More than sometimes, Erin had wondered if her parents loved the different dogs that had been family pets through the years more than they loved her. Certainly, they showed the dogs more affection. Her mother would at times make it feel like a failing in her that she did not respond to every command with as much ease as a pooch hoping for a sliver of chicken from the fridge. The decision to turn down an offer to study Law at Queen's University in Belfast had been the last straw for them. They still invited her over occasionally. They weren't monsters. But they also weren't her cheerleaders.

Their approach to parenting was a big factor in Erin's reluctance to have her own children. But Aaron had managed to talk her round to the idea that someday they would be parents. So Erin had vowed things would be different for her children. She and Aaron would only ever get a rescue dog, and preferably one as gentle and loving as Paddy at the Ivy Inn. There would be no pure breeds or show dogs in their future. Just gorgeous, extra-fluffy, kind-of-stupid-in-a-cute-way rescue dogs who had more love to give than the Donohues ever had.

Erin had often wished that someone could rescue her. That they'd choose her and show her unconditional love for the rest of her days. She'd imagined there would be a great romantic lead in her life. She'd thought that Aaron had filled that role in her happy ever after, even if he didn't quite fit the image of the rugged love interests on the covers of the romance books in Libby's shop. But now she knew it wasn't him.

But her rescue might just have come in the most unexpected of ways – when her friends had showed up at her door ready to look after her and give her the tools to rescue herself.

Jo, Noah and Libby were all very genuine with their offer.

They desperately wanted to invest in her business, and in her. They believed in her – probably more than she had ever believed in herself. The butterflies in her stomach had morphed to the size of giant colourful birds who were swooping and soaring and making her feel like she was going to throw up. But in a good way. If such a thing existed.

Erin quickly fixed her curls up into a messy bun on the top of her head and walked back into the living room, where she had left Noah and Jo poring over her very rough business plan.

'Thanks for sharing this,' Noah smiled as Erin sat down opposite him. 'Libby had said there was a good framework here, and I have to agree. There's a lot to be done, but this is a good starting point. So let's work out how to go about this. First things first, let's call the estate agents and arrange a formal viewing of the bakery.'

'I'm sure Flora would just show us around,' Erin said. 'Surely she'd be happy to?'

Noah shifted a little in his chair. 'She might be, but it's always better to go and see a place with an unbiased eye. If we arrange it through the agent, we don't have to worry about offending Flora if we spot things that need work or find any unexpected problems.'

Erin clearly had a horrified look on her face because Jo immediately jumped in. 'We're not saying there *will* be problems, but it's always potentially tricky when you're buying from someone you know.'

'Oh, okay,' Erin said, her heart racing. This was all starting to feel like it could actually happen. For real.

'Now, the multipurpose space upstairs – are you considering refurbing that and making it your home?' Noah asked.

Erin shrugged. 'I'm open to it, but I suppose it depends on what needs doing and how much that would cost, and you know how hard it is to get tradesmen on board.'

'Well, we're lucky there. I'm sure Libby's dad, Jim, would be more than happy to come on board and he has sway with a lot of tradesmen.'

Erin had forgotten that Libby's dad was a builder who had helped her transform the flat above the bookshop into a really lovely home. And Noah was right, he did know a lot of good tradesmen – many of whom had done various jobs in and around The Ivy Inn over the last couple of years. Terry the Spark – who was always given that full title for reasons Erin didn't know – had done some work in the kitchen just a month before.

'That's a good idea, if he's free, of course. And if the place isn't in too bad a state.'

'As long as it has decent plumbing, it should be doable. We could certainly factor in some of the costs to our investment too,' Noah said.

'I can't ask you to do that!' Erin insisted. 'The shop is one thing, but not my living quarters.'

'Taking care of you increases the chances of the business being a roaring success,' he countered. 'And, of course, we love you. You could maybe consider some of it a bonus for taking on the position of executive chef?'

This was all incredible – and a lot to take in, especially in such a short space of time. Life really can change in a heartbeat, Erin thought.

'Well, let's get a viewing booked in and have a good look and take it from there. Once we know what we're looking at, we'll be able to see if there's a way we can make this work,' Noah said.

Jo clapped her hands together excitedly and grinned. 'I have a really good feeling about this. I'm so excited! I can't wait to tell Lorcan all about it. Can I go to the viewing too? I'd love to cast my eye over it all.'

'Erm, Jo, should you not be working on your book?' Noah asked. 'Your deadline approaches.'

'Deadline, schmeadline,' Jo said with a roll of her eyes. 'What does that matter when it comes to issues of such importance as my best friend and her fancy pâtisserie and the next step towards making Ivy Lane the best place to live and work in all of Derry.'

There were times when the brother/sister dynamic of Jo and Noah came sharply into focus and this was one of them. 'Jo, it matters a lot. You have made me promise that I am to kick your arse every time I see you slacking and, and I quote, "tie that arse to the chair if necessary" if I see you procrastinating and not writing,' Noah said.

Jo simply rolled her eyes a second time, while shaking her head. 'Well obviously, I didn't really mean that.'

'Yes, you did. In fact you said, "Even if I tell you I didn't really mean it, I want you to force me. And if I refuse, you can bring out the big guns and call Mum,' Noah said while Erin allowed herself to revel in the gentle back and forth of their banter.

'You wouldn't dare!' Jo admonished. 'Don't forget, I'm a crime writer. I have many ideas about how to dispose of bodies.'

Erin knew, just as she knew Jo would, that Noah would absolutely dare and no threat of being offed by a nosy crime writer would stop him. He was incredibly proud of what Jo had achieved and he was going to make sure she kept on achieving more and more. Even if it meant him playing the role of the bossy big brother from time to time.

'Noah's right and you don't need your mum to tell you that,' Erin said. 'You really should be writing.'

'If I write a chapter, can I come?' Jo asked, her expression so pleading it reminded Erin of Clara when she wanted a sneaky scoop of ice cream each time she visited The Ivy Inn kitchens.

As Erin nodded to agree, Noah added: 'But I want to see proof! I'll be asking Lorcan to check your work, young lady.'

As Jo stuck her tongue out playfully at her older brother, Erin smiled. She didn't need Aaron. She didn't even need this place. She just needed these people, and their support, and the increasing possibility that her business dreams were about to come true.

13

The estate agent had been only too happy to arrange to show Erin and Noah – and Jo if she had her work done in time – around Wee Buns. Even better, he could arrange the viewing that very day, which Erin tried to see as a positive sign from the universe. The viewing was scheduled for two o'clock, which would be just after the lunchtime rush and around the time the shelves would be looking bare and Flora would be starting the clean-up and prep for the next morning.

The bakery always closed its doors at four in the afternoon to compensate for the ridiculously early starts to the day, with Flora often in her kitchen from shortly after five in the morning. Erin tried not to think too much about how early she would have to start work at the pâtisserie. She wasn't afraid of long hours or hard work, but she had never really had cause to be an early riser before. She'd manage though, if it was for her dream. Maybe, she'd even start to enjoy it. After all, there would be the added benefit of having her evenings free again.

But first, she had to cast a very discerning and non-emotional eye over her potential investment and Noah was by her side to make sure she did a good job of it.

The estate agent was a small round man, with greying hair and wide-rimmed glasses. When he gave them a smile and introduced himself as Adrian Quigley, Erin realised he reminded her of a mole, which was a perfect match for his first name. She internally prayed she would never make the mistake of calling him Mr Mole, as she doubted he would appreciate the reference to either a small, blind mammal or the acne-ridden teenage anti-hero from the famous books by Sue Townsend.

He seemed to be nice and Erin had noted with pleasant surprise that when he spoke, he addressed her first and didn't treat her like she was the little wife or clueless assistant. To her relief, this meant she was able to immediately discount him from her 'Slay the Patriarchy' kill list.

'Well, you're the second viewer for this quaint bakery, which can be sold as a going concern if that interests you,' he said, as he delivered what was clearly his well-prepared spiel. 'The owner is retiring and has no plans to pass the business on to family, so you don't have to worry about sitting tenants. That always makes these things much easier to deal with, don't you think?' he remarked, in a voice that was so quiet, both Erin and Noah had to lean in to hear what he was saying.

'And are there more viewings booked?' Noah asked.

'I believe so, yes,' Mr Mole replied. 'But I don't have those details with me at this time. We are confident that this property will sell quickly, however. I'm sure you'll agree it is very realistically priced for this area – which seems to be enjoying a little renaissance all of its own. Do you know this area well?'

Erin was about to reveal just how well they knew the area, when she felt Noah take her hand and give it a squeeze. A squeeze she rightly interpreted as 'play your cards close to your chest, for now'.

'Ish,' she replied. 'It seems lovely.'

'Oh, it very much is. There has been significant investment in this Lane in recent years, with the expansion of the bar, refurbishment of the convenience store and the opening of Once Upon A Book. That draws a big crowd. Footfall is generally good, and we have seen the price of domestic properties rise above the average rate. It's attracting more professionals and a surprising number of families looking for starter homes or to downsize later in life. So, all in all, this would be a good investment for anyone who wants to get in early in the regeneration of the wider area.'

'That's interesting,' Noah said. 'We'll keep all that in mind.'

'It would be pertinent to do so. This place won't hang around for long. Now, would you like the tour? The shop is still open and the owner is here today, but she has assured me that she will be dealing with the demands of her business and not interfering in our viewing. I know some people find it awkward to have a good poke around while the owners stand and watch.' Mr Mole laughed, silently, his round face crinkling so much his eyes all but disappeared.

Erin was not exactly sure what he was laughing at. The use of the word 'poke' perhaps? Or maybe he had said something truly hilarious and she just didn't catch it because he spoke at a volume only the bionic man would be able to hear. She forced herself to smile and nod before he turned to open the door that led into the shop.

A wave of emotion washed over Erin as she walked through the door. She wondered what Flora would think when she saw her, and Noah, coming to view the bakery. Would she be pleasantly surprised? Hopeful that it could mean her business wasn't going to retire with her? The excitement that had been fizzing in Erin's stomach suddenly switched to nausea-inducing nerves, and she felt a cool sweat start to break out on her forehead. This was big. Even being there looking at this property was a move that just a few days ago she didn't think she'd be making any time soon, if ever. Once Flora set her eyes on her, it would be out there that Erin Donohue had a dream to be her own boss and own her own place. There'd be no putting it back in the box after that.

'Are you coming?' She heard Noah ask, as she blinked back into the moment. 'You're blocking the doorway, if nothing else. And it's important to look in all the nooks and crannies.'

To her immense relief, Flora was not behind the counter or front of shop. That gave Erin at least a moment or two to try to steady her racing heart.

She could hear Mr Mole speaking (just), but even if she could hear him clearly, she doubted she would be able to pay him too much attention. It was as if she was seeing Wee Buns through new eyes. As if she was experiencing the sounds, the smells and the feel of the place for the first time.

Flora had always been extremely proud of her bakery and kept it beautifully maintained. The paintwork and trimmings were pristine. The window frames were solid, and the flooring was covered in slate tiles which all appeared to be in perfect condition. It was a good foundation to start with. Erin tried to imagine how much, if any, of the current shelving she would be able to make use of. She'd need chiller cabinets, but something that didn't look too industrial. She'd love to create a little consultation area where clients could come in for tastings or to discuss larger orders or cake designs. She wondered as she looked up at the high ceilings, would it be too much to hang a crystal chandelier from the ceiling that could act almost as a sun catcher, reflecting rainbows of light around the room? It could be truly breathtaking in the early-morning light, with the scent of freshly baked pastry in the air and the tinkle of a bell above the door. She'd have to get one of those old-fashioned brass bells on a coiled spring. Or maybe it would get very annoying very quickly? These were questions she was going to have ask and decisions she was going to have to make if this went ahead.

'I don't think I realised how beautiful she has it before,' Erin said to Noah, who had a notebook and was scribbling furiously.

'And there are plenty of power points here,' he said, pointing to a bank of sockets behind the counter and focusing on the more practical details.

'All inspected and up to code,' Mr Mole said. 'You're lucky with this one. The current owner is a very conscientious lady. This place has been a real labour of love for her.'

'It has that,' Flora said, shuffling out from the kitchens. She stopped when she spotted Erin and Noah and looked between the pair.

As hard she tried, Erin couldn't read exactly what the expression on Flora's face was saying. Was it 'Oh, it's you!' in a nice way, or 'Oh, it's you!' in a 'what is going on here?' way.

To her shame, Erin felt a hot flush of embarrassment rise in her. As if she had been caught doing something she absolutely should not be doing and had landed herself in a whole heap of trouble.

'Well, this is a surprise,' Flora said. 'I didn't think I'd see the pair of you here.'

'It's... it's... all been a bit sudden really,' Erin stuttered. 'And, really, we're just looking at this stage, and I'm sorry, I don't want you to think we're happy to see you leave or are trying to push you out.'

Mr Mole looked absolutely baffled. Noah looked at Erin as if she had lost the run of herself and Flora broke into the widest smile imaginable, the bright white of her dentures fully on show. 'Oh, love, I'd never think that you were happy to see me leave, even if *I'm* happy to see me leave. Actually, it makes me really happy to see you looking at the place. I'd like to say this is purely a business to me, but we all know it is much more than that. This place and this street, and you people.'

'So, I'm guessing you're all acquainted?' Mr Mole said and Erin felt bad for not coming clean to him right away.

'We're neighbours,' Flora said. 'Noah here owns The Ivy Inn, and Erin is their award-winning chef, and a master baker in her own right!'

Erin's blush only grew darker. 'I'm not sure that topping a poll in the *Derry Journal* for nicest pub lunch really counts as award-winning, but I'll take it!'

'And you should. Don't hide your light under a bushel!'

'I'm always telling her that,' Noah said. 'Not every chef spent a summer in Paris working in an exclusive pâtisserie, or had a couple of years working in some of London's best restaurants. How we ever managed to get her back here to work in the Inn is beyond me – but I'm glad we did. She's elevated us to new heights.'

Erin knew how Noah and Jo had managed to get her working in the Inn and it wasn't a glamorous story by any means. She'd come home from London out of a sense of duty and guilt when her mother had been unwell, and had enjoyed the calmer lifestyle out of the big city. When her long-time friend Jo approached her, and told her she could have free rein of The Ivy Inn kitchens – within certain limits, of course – it was to retain its gastropub vibe – she had decided to at least try it out. And she had loved it. It was even better when she and Jo decided to house share together. Those early days seemed like forever ago now, but she still adored the life she had built on the Lane.

'Ah, well, very good,' Mr Mole said, cutting through her reverie. 'I imagine having a knowledge of the area and businesses here puts a whole new slant on things.'

If Erin wasn't mistaken, she thought she could practically see the pound signs flashing in his eyes. No doubt he thought he was onto an easy sale.

'Don't be pressuring these good people!' Flora scolded. 'If it's right for them, they'll take it. If it isn't, well, sure, then no harm done,' she said with a smile, and reached across for Erin's hand.

The touch of the older woman's soft skin on hers infused in Erin an understanding of just what this place meant. Each wrinkled line and age spot on Flora's hands told a story of years of early rises, of measuring and kneading, of dusting cakes with sugar. Of struggling to keep the power going during the strikes of the seventies. Of hauling down the shutters to try to protect the shop from damage during the riots that so often accompanied the worst of the Troubles. Of shaking the hands of generations of customers, baking their children's christening cakes and then putting together a parcel of pastries and buns to be sent out to their wakes when the time came. She never charged for the parcels she sent to wakes. It was her way of thanking those families for their years of custom. It was her way of showing solidarity in their loss. Erin thought of all the times those hands had lifted a cloth to wipe down the counters at the end of a long day. How often they had restocked the shelves. How Wee Buns had first opened when Flora was just a teenager – and her uncle had held the reins until he had left it and all it meant to her in his will. She who had left school at fifteen and worked almost every day of her life since in this shop.

Erin had to stop herself from saying she'd find a way, even if it meant selling a kidney, to make the shop her own. She had to force herself to be sensible and keep her mouth shut, but she did give Flora's hand a gentle squeeze, one she hoped would convey her hopes, dreams, desires and, most of all, her admiration for the older woman.

14

Erin's excitement had only grown with every step she took around the bakery. Having never seen its inner workings before, she had been unsure of what to expect. Flora had confirmed the equipment she had was not included in the sale price, but that she was open to reasonable offers. She'd winked when she'd said that and squeezed Erin's hand with reassurance.

Flora had run a tight ship and the kitchen was pristine, with the equipment relatively modern and in good working order. There was a deck oven, which was perfect for the breads Flora made so beautifully, and a smaller rack oven, more suitable for the delicious pastries Erin wanted to prepare. She'd have to upsize the latter and it wouldn't come cheap, but given the quality of the rest of the kitchen, hopefully with the investment from her friends she would be able to make it all work.

There was a walk-in fridge and a decent-sized freezer. The mixers were perfect and Flora obviously shared Erin's belief that in a kitchen there should be a place for everything and everything should be in its place. Erin could already picture herself bustling around and preparing her orders. She'd need staff, of course. That was a given. The work was too labour-intensive to be able to combine the baking with the selling, and if Noah still wanted her to keep a foot in at the Inn, it would be a lot to juggle. But she'd make it work. If Flora could make it work and keep it open for fifty odd years on her own, then surely Erin would be able to do so, with the help of Noah, Libby and Jo.

At the back of the bakery, Mr Mole led them out through a set of fire doors to a large enclosed yard which had space for much more than a set of bins. An image of a small, seated area, perfect for the warmer months, popped into Erin's head. She could maybe put up a canopy and sell hot chocolate and freshly baked cookies or flaky pastries in the colder months and in the run-up to Christmas. She almost squeaked out loud with excitement at that thought.

Upstairs required more work – aside from a room used as an office and a functional but old and basic toilet and sink, it remained very much a blank canvas. Erin couldn't help but wonder why Flora had never made more use of the space. Beyond the office and small WC, there were three other rooms, varying in size, that were just used as storage. Erin could envisage transforming them into a living room, a kitchen and a bedroom with an en suite. She could retain the office and the small WC to be used by staff. All in, it would make for a lovely one-bed apartment. With a door and wrought-iron steps leading down into the yard, she would have the choice between creating her lovely little outdoor tea-room, or a beautiful city garden where she could relax, on the off chance she would get any time off at all.

She had never had such an experience before – one where she had walked into a place and envisaged it exactly how it would be or felt immediately at home. It was enough to distract her from thinking about the flat she had loved for the past few years, and even from thinking about the *man* she had loved for the last few years. If someone had mentioned Aaron's name to her in that moment, she'd have asked 'who?' and it wouldn't have come from a sarcastic or bitter place.

As Erin followed Noah and Mr Mole back downstairs and into the kitchen once again, she tried to ground herself. Just because she wanted it, and just because it was perfect for her in every way bar the start-up cost, it didn't mean it would be hers. There were so many variables at play – what Noah and co. could invest being the biggest one, but also who else had an interest in buying the property and what they were willing to pay. She understood that Flora was retiring and wanted not only to spend whatever years she had left living her best life, but that she also wanted to make sure she left a nice nest egg to her family after her passing. She'd want that nest egg to be as healthy as possible.

'What's for me won't pass me,' Erin told herself as she crossed her fingers and dared to hope it might actually happen.

When Noah turned back to look at her, and raised his eyebrows in a silent 'well, what do you think?' she had to stop herself going full Veruca Salt and screaming 'Give it to me now!' Dignity, she reminded herself, was important at all times.

She smiled instead, and hoped it didn't have a slightly manic appearance to it. Mr Mole was talking about making offers and the marked interest in the property (which seemed to have increased in direct proportion to the enthusiasm Erin had shown for it), but Erin could only think about the centre island work-space where she could delicately put her creations together amid the sound of the mixer and ovens whirring and the delicious smells that baking created – hints of vanilla and cinnamon, of chocolate and sugar.

She still had a smile on her face when she walked through to the shop floor. She immediately saw that Flora was doing her very best not to pounce on her and ask her what her plans would be.

They both knew that, as odd as it felt to them as people who had known each other for several years, this was where Mr Mole had to step in and do his work. It was a game played out between buyers and sellers and enthusiastic estate agents the world over.

Erin tried very much to focus on what he was saying, but it was little use. She'd get Noah to go over it all, in great detail, later, when she could properly absorb it all.

They were just finishing up when the door to the shop opened and in bustled Harry, with one of his trademark bunches of slightly wilted flowers and a smile as broad as she had ever seen across his face. Did Erin sense gossip in the making?

Harry had a naturally ruddy complexion anyway, but it darkened further when he saw Erin and Noah. He immediately tried to hide the flowers behind his back, but quickly realised that they had already been seen and held them in front of himself. 'I... well... I'm just on my way home and these flowers, well, they don't have much life left in them – bit like myself, really – but I thought maybe you might get some enjoyment out of them?' He reached out towards Flora, who had developed a delicate pink blush herself.

Erin looked between the two and took in their reactions. Was this just a neighbour handing over some of his overstock, or was it a declaration of something more? Did he hope that Flora might be able to get some enjoyment out of him as well as the multi-coloured tulips and baby's breath? Was there a budding romance under all their noses all this time and they'd missed it?

'That's very kind of you, Harry,' Flora said with a smile. 'But now, tell the truth and shame the devil, you realised there was a viewing down here and you just wanted to get a gander at who was looking about the place?'

Erin's eyes flew to Harry's face to see his response. He blinked a few times, and she saw his jaw tense as he tried to think of the right thing to say and find the ability the to say it without stuttering. It was quite the experience – to see Harry Gallagher look flustered. There was nothing that usually put that man off his stride and less still that left him at a loss for words.

'There's nothing wrong in wanting to see who I might be working alongside in the future,' Harry said, in a manner Erin recognised as remarkably similar to Clara's truculent pre-teen sass. He was embarrassed. He'd been caught out.

She looked back to Flora for her response, having come to the conclusion that this was better than an episode of *EastEnders* for dramatic tension.

'I suppose not,' Flora said. 'And you wouldn't be you if you missed out on some juicy bars.'

'Are you saying I'm a gossip?' Harry replied, fully indignant in his response.

'No, I'm saying you like to know the bars. You like to be fully aware at all times of what is going on around you.'

'I never liked that expression,' Harry said, as he moved the focus of the conversation away from himself. 'It makes no sense. Why do we call the news or the gossip "the bars" anyway? Is it because the bar is a place where gossip is shared? Or does that expression have its etymology somewhere else? Is it just a Derry phrase, do you think?'

Just as Erin couldn't help but smile, she noticed that a similar expression had crept onto Noah's face.

'Harry Gallagher, I know your style. Change the subject so no one knows you're just a nosy old goat,' Flora said, but Erin would have had to be blind and deaf not to pick up on the real affection and warmth in her voice.

'You know yourself, Flora, I always had to know everything that was going on. Mary would've had me hung, drawn and quartered if I'd not gone home every day with some scandal or craic for her. And sure, there was no harm in it,' he said.

'That's the truth. Those were the days,' Flora replied.

'Never a truer word spoken,' Harry agreed, with a wistful air. 'God, do you remember when our children were wee and knocking about playing on the street while we were stood behind the counters in the shops.'

'Happy times,' Flora said. 'The world's a changed place since then.'

'It is,' Harry concurred. 'But these young ones aren't doing a bad job of keeping this place as nice as it always was. I think we've been lucky with them.'

Erin smiled as she felt her heart swell at the thought of being considered a part of the family here on Ivy Lane. She also couldn't miss the way Harry and Flora were looking at each other. She very much hoped that when she reached her seventies, she too would have friendships that meant the world to her and more.

15

The heat had not abated and Erin sat in the beer garden with a glass of iced cider in front of her, which she swore was probably the nicest drink she had ever had in her entire life. She felt as if she had walked for forty days and forty nights through the wilderness before reaching this little oasis of calm. She savoured the cool, crisp taste as it slid down her throat, where it both quenched her thirst and cooled her down. She didn't say it out loud, but it felt like a celebratory drink. She felt it in the very pit of her stomach that she was going to realise her dream – a dream she had discounted because of Aaron and the life she thought they would build together.

After the tour of the bakery, and after listening to Flora and Harry talk, Erin had realised something. When she thought of opening her own pâtisserie, she felt excited – giddy even. Damn it, she felt alive for the first time in a long time.

It was a marked contrast to how she had felt when she was with Aaron and when she thought about a wedding, and buying a house, and having children. It wasn't that she didn't want any of those things, but when she thought of them, it was more in a 'that would be nice' way rather than a 'I'm so excited by this, I might throw up' way – and surely your dreams – the really big ones that you really have to push yourself to achieve – they should make you feel like you might throw up a little. Hadn't David Bowie once said to also step a little outside of your comfort zone? To go a little deeper than where you feel safe, to where your feet don't quite touch the bottom – because that's where the magic happens? Or something like that.

The notion of getting married to Aaron had been lovely at the time. Even her parents liked him enough to approve of their relationship, which, although it shouldn't matter to her, had helped. Her mother had been hinting for a while now that after three years, it really was time to think about taking things to the next level. She had seen genuine excitement in her eyes at the very thought of her daughter getting married. Erin had wondered if it might have become the way in which they put their differences aside, and while that would be a positive thing, it didn't change the fact that her life with Aaron had been the safe option. It certainly didn't involve her moving outside of her comfort zone. But this new adventure? It did and she loved the very notion.

'It's going to be good, isn't it?' she said to a sleeping Paddy, who was sitting on the bench beside her, his dark fur warmed by the sun. These were Paddy's favourite days – when the garden was full and the sun was warm and there was always someone on hand to stroke him, or feed him morsels of their food.

Erin had tried desperately to look nonchalant as they had left Wee Buns earlier, even though every cell in her body was vibrating with a feeling of belonging. She was not known for her patience or her poker face. If she wanted something, she went for it, and she wore her heart not so much on her sleeve, but in every single facial expression she made. If she could've signed the paperwork to buy there and then, she would have, but she had known she had to sit down and have a very serious discussion with Noah, Libby and Jo about their proposed investment. And it was entirely possible that Noah would shake his head and declare it was a bad deal.

But he hadn't done that. Not at all. As they had walked back up the Lane towards The Ivy Inn, he had been quiet. Erin had recognised this as thoughtful Noah working through the figures in his head; either that or he was trying to work out how to tell her it was a non-starter and she knew, absolutely, that the worst thing she could have done was to interrupt him. So she had walked beside him in silence – her own mind racing with ideas and recipes and hope.

It was only when they had reached the cobbles outside The Ivy Inn that Noah spoke. 'I think it's a sound investment. At least, it has the potential to be a sound investment. I've asked Mr Quigley to talk to Flora about the possibility of also buying the equipment you might need and what cost that would involve.'

'Mr Quigley?' Erin had asked, completely confused as to who Mr Quigley was.

Noah had looked at her as if she had lost the plot. 'Mr Quigley who we just spoke to and who showed us around the bakery? Mr Quigley – Adrian.'

'Ah, Mr Mole!' Erin had gushed. 'Because he looks like a mole!'

'Please don't ever call him that to his face,' Noah had said, as he rolled his eyes. There was a hint of amusement in his expression though, so Erin was sure she hadn't just blown the chance of getting him to invest by showing herself to be an airhead. 'Anyway, Mr QUIGLEY,' he had continued, with emphasis on his surname, 'has said he will come back to me as soon as possible. Then we'll know if this is doable or not. I don't want to low-ball Flora and it probably wouldn't go in our favour – not if there are other viewers lined up. It is priced competitively, so I think the asking price will be the lowest we could dare to go. Let's get the full picture first though. Yes?'

Erin had nodded and offered a silent prayer up to any higher being who happened to be listening that it would indeed be doable.

'Let's grab a drink and sit outside,' he'd added. 'We can talk some more and I'll see if Libby and Jo are able to join us. Drinks are on me,' he'd said with a smile and that was an offer that Erin was not going to refuse. And if a part of her had thought she'd love to call Aaron to tell him about it all, she'd pushed it down. He had opted out of their life together and she was going to focus on the future and not the past.

Erin was jolted from her thoughts by the arrival of Jo, pale, drawn and make-up-less, wearing what she was pretty sure was one of Lorcan's T-shirts, a pair of jersey shorts, Ugg boots and with her mass of curls tied up in a sequin-embossed scrunchie – which just had to have been borrowed from Clara.

Her friend reached across the table and lifted Erin's glass of cider with her left hand, raised her right hand in a 'do not even talk to me' gesture and took a long drink before sitting it back on the table.

'Do not ask me how the writing is going and everyone will get out of here alive,' Jo said.

'That good?' Erin replied.

'I just need a couple of drinks and some distractions.'

'And if I can be so bold,' Noah said as he arrived at their table with more drinks and sat down beside Jo. 'You could do with a shower too.'

Erin's eyes widened as she waited for Jo to lose what little shit she had left, but to her surprise, that didn't happen. Jo simply lifted the drink Noah had brought for her and took another long swig before she spoke.

'Your face could do with a shower,' she teased back in a childish mocking voice.

Thankfully, Noah laughed, and then Jo did, and Erin couldn't help but join in. It felt like the first proper laugh she'd had in days and that in itself made her feel good.

At that moment, a pale-faced and tired Libby appeared, and Erin immediately shuffled across the bench, waking Paddy from his blissful sleep, to make room for her.

'Still feeling rough?' Erin asked, concerned by the dark circles under Libby's eyes .

'I've been better,' Libby said as she gingerly sipped at her glass of iced water. 'But Jess advised me to ask my doctor for some anti-sickness medication and I've to pick up the prescription later. Hopefully it will help.'

'Fingers crossed,' Erin said, remembering that Libby's long-time best friend Jess was a GP and would have an idea how to offer help more practical than just a glass of iced water.

'Noah, you are going to have to move heaven and earth to make this one up to Libby,' Jo said, taking in the pitiful sight of her sister-in-law. 'This is going to have to be the mother and father of all push presents.'

'Push presents?' Noah asked, one eyebrow raised.

Erin was just as confused, so she simply shrugged at him. 'Never heard that expression before,' she said.

'The present a partner buys the mother of his newly-pushed-into-this-world child as a token of appreciation for the mammoth task she has just performed on his behalf,' Jo explained. 'Do none of you heathens watch reality TV? Diamonds, cars, designer handbags... it's all to play for!'

It was, Erin noted, Noah's turn to pale.

'Don't look at me like that,' Jo cut in. 'A bunch of carnations from Harry's Shop won't cut it. In fact, I've warned Lorcan to beat you over the head with them if you even try.'

'I don't care about push presents,' Libby said. 'I'd settle for being able to eat something without feeling as if I'm going to meet it again in the near future. That's the only present that matters to me. That and a healthy baby, of course.'

'Hopefully this medication will work,' Jo soothed. 'Or you'll reach the stage of pregnancy where it all calms down a little.'

Libby nodded. 'Please God let it be soon, but that is not what we are here to talk about right now. We're here to talk about the bakery and making it a huge success!'

Erin watched as Libby took another sip of her water. It was time to decide whether or not they were going to go for it.

'Noah tells me the building is in perfect shape, or as near as,' Libby said.

'Oh!' Noah said, as he looked up from his phone. 'I can happily confirm that Flora is willing to sell on whatever equipment you may need at a fair price. Unfortunately, I don't have that price yet as she needs to know exactly what you might want to keep.' He turned the screen towards her so she could read the message Mr Mole had just sent.

Erin felt a flutter in her chest again. Her head was already full of everything she wanted to keep. And everything she would need to get. She felt as if she was staring at some internal computer screen and had twenty different tabs open in front of her – all of them filled with ideas and plans for her pâtisserie. Well, almost all of them. One contained all the unanswered questions about Aaron, but she very quickly minimised that and went back to thoughts of recipes and colour schemes.

'Obviously, we'll need to have this all drawn up by our solicitors, but having talked to Libby and Jo, and having run the figures – allowing for investment in equipment and refurbishment to the shop and the upstairs accommodation – we think it can work. It will be tight, but it's doable,' Noah said.

Erin would have liked to look back on that moment and recall how she whooped and cheered but then immediately got down to the business. But while there very much was internal whooping and cheering, her external reaction was to burst into tears, just as Lorcan rounded the corner and approached the table, pint in hand.

'Was it something I said?' he asked. 'Should I just leave?'

'It... it's... not y-you,' Erin stuttered through sobs as Lorcan sat down beside Jo. 'I think... we might be b-buying a bakery.'

'Well, that's the best news I've heard all day!' Lorcan beamed.

'I think it would be wise to make an offer as soon as we can. More viewers are due to call just after five. It won't stay on the market long,' Noah addressed Erin, while Jo handed her a napkin to dry her tears.

'So how will it work with the restaurant here?' Lorcan asked. 'Will you be leaving?'

Erin wanted to tell him how it would work, but apart from the title of executive chef, she didn't have any more details to go on. A moment of doubt flashed through her mind. What if she was taking on more than she could chew?

'Here's what we were thinking, although we're open to ideas,' Noah began and Erin sat up straight. 'Erin, you will still design the menu, train the kitchen staff to cook to your standards and, if possible, be on site for any high-profile events. Beyond that, you concentrate on the pâtisserie side of things, which we'd like you to use our branding with. I mean name it what you like, but it would be good for us all if it had a small "At The Ivy Inn" or "With The

Ivy Inn" in the logo somewhere, don't you think? It allows you to carry over the success of the Inn to your business, and hopefully drives some business back our way too. It's a win-win as far as I can see.'

Erin nodded. 'Yes, yes, of course.' This sounded doable. In fact, it sounded brilliant.

'And, to top it all off, your first order will be to provide desserts for The Ivy Inn. We're even thinking of launching an afternoon tea in the function room.'

Erin was too overwhelmed to speak, so she just nodded.

'I've printed out this breakdown of our projected investment and expectations therein,' Noah continued. 'There are a few options. We can profit share, or we can view the investment as a loan of sorts. To be honest, the first option appeals to us more. It's riskier for us in the short term, but offers much more potential for growth in the long run. We can invest roughly forty-five per cent of the start-up costs, which would leave you as the majority share-holder. To be clear, we will be silent partners. This is your baby.'

Erin gasped at the investment offer. They really must believe in this idea, and in her. She vowed that she would not cry again and started to scan over the figures. Numbers blurred in front of her eyes. This was where she needed someone with a business head to look them over and tell her whether or not they were sound. The only problem was, her usual business advisors were sitting opposite her and were behind the proposal in the first place.

She lifted her glass to her lips and took a long, cooling drink in the hope that alcohol would steady the shake in her hands. It did. A little. 'This is scary as hell,' she said.

Her four friends chimed in with a chorus of 'Yes. We know,' – each of them going on to list the times they had to push away that self-same fear Erin was almost suffocated with at that moment, and let it be replaced with excitement and positive nervous energy.

Noah had been just as terrified when he had taken on owner-ship of The Ivy Inn – and he had battled the same nerves every time he grew the business. Under his management, and with the help of Jo, it had grown from an occasionally busy pub serving traditional pub grub to a destination gastropub which prided itself on using local and seasonal ingredients.

Libby had taken a run-down, almost derelict, former drapery and turned it into a bookshop that was not only a beautiful place to visit and buy books, but which had become a place where creatives could meet for a coffee, or work on their next book.

And Jo? Well, Erin thought her best friend was perhaps the bravest woman she knew – putting her work out there for everyone to read, and everyone to review. That took guts and it hadn't always been easy. But, she thought, none of them had ever regretted it.

'But it's exciting as hell too?' she added.

'YES!' her friends chorused, voices so loud that Paddy, usually quite docile, sat up, gave them the most cutting doggy side-eye any of them had ever seen in their lives and let off a short but sharp warning bark, before resuming his resting position on the bench.

'So...' Noah said. 'Do you want to make the official offer or will I?'

It would've been so easy to leave that task to Noah, but Erin was going to girl boss this like a queen. This was her dream. It was her wish. She would make the offer and she would make this dream happen.

'I will,' she said with confidence. 'I want to sleep on it first, but I think it should be me.'

As the five of them, and Paddy, talked into the evening, discussing what would be their best strategy, Erin realised that the feeling that was washing over her was one she had not felt in a long time. It was contentment. It was happiness. It was, she realised, hope.

16

Perhaps it was because her head was so full, but when Erin got home that evening, the flat felt less empty. Nothing had changed about her home since she had left that afternoon to go and view Wee Buns, but, at the same time, it felt as if *everything* had changed.

She tried to remind herself that nothing was for certain yet. There was a long way to go to make the pâtisserie happen – mortgages, machinery, refurbishment, marketing, recipes that stood out... but she felt it in the very pit of her soul that this was her thing and it would happen. This was the life she was supposed to live.

What that said about the last few years with Aaron was anyone's guess, but she didn't want to think about Aaron just then. She didn't want to miss telling him about her plans or asking him for ideas. She didn't want to miss how he loved making lists and would've pulled out a notebook and started scribbling things down (in bullet points, obviously) as she spoke, his face becoming more and more animated. No, Erin absolutely did not want to think about him in that way, or any way if it could be helped. She wanted to stay in the joyful bubble that she had left the bar in – just tipsy enough to feel as if she could and should sing a happy song at the top of her lungs, but not tipsy enough that she would have a hangover when morning came.

As she ran herself a bath, she thought about the flat above the bakery. It was just a shell of a thing – bare walls and bare floors, but enough space for an en suite bathroom with a large shower to wash the day off. There wouldn't be room for a bath, but she could live with that. The room she had earmarked as the bedroom caught the light in the evenings, which meant the courtyard to the rear of the building would be a little suntrap in the right weather. She'd need to put new windows in to dampen the noise from the street, but that was doable. In fact, her friends had made her believe it was all doable.

When she slipped into the water and under the suds, Erin closed her eyes and imagined what life would be like a year from now. She poked and prodded at every possible variable of what might it might look like. And none of her outcomes made her feel the kind of sad she used to feel when she and Aaron were both at home together but not communicating.

God, she realised, maybe Aaron had been right to leave. Maybe whatever they had shared together had drifted away long before now and him pulling the plug and leaving had been a kindness in its own way. It had needed an act of supreme courage to stop them both sleepwalking into a future that would fulfil neither of them. Is that what Aaron had done? A mercy killing of sorts. It was brutal, yes. But was it just brutal in the way pulling a plaster off a cut was brutal? Kinder to get it over and done with quickly so the healing could be more effective.

But no, she thought, it was not an act of courage. Courage

would've involved him talking to her first. Courage would have involved allowing them both to come to the same joint conclusion that what they had had run its course. It would've involved them both having the chance to say what had needed to be said.

Courage did not leave an innocent party feeling humiliated and confused. Courage shouldn't leave one person feeling solely responsible for the failings in a joint relationship.

As these darker thoughts started to swoop in, Erin slid under the water to a place where all she had to do was concentrate on the air in her lungs and the way her heart now pounded sending her blood whooshing around her body. Aaron was not a courageous man. He was a coward. And the only way to truly move on from whatever damage the last few days had done to her would be to talk to him. Face to face. If she didn't, that would make her as much of a coward as he was.

Once she was dried off and dressed in a pair of her comfiest M&S cotton knickers and an oversized T-shirt that had once been Aaron's but had long since been claimed as her own, Erin poured her a glass of water and carried it through to her bedroom. It was dark by then and the street below was growing quiet. Thankfully, she found the drone of cars as they approached then drove away soothing, just as she was soothed by the way the curtains billowed with the gentle evening breeze.

She reached across to close the window as usual, then stopped. It was time to put her big girl pants on. She was on the second floor. There was no easy access to her window, unless you were Spiderman, and if truth be told she wouldn't be adverse to Tom Holland climbing in through her window. The air was thick and hot and the breeze would be blissful while she slept. Which, she decided, she would do on top of the bedsheets. Take that, scary monster who didn't even exist and certainly didn't hide under her bed. This was her time to be brave, and to slay all her personal demons – real or not. And she knew exactly where she had to start.

She had to get a message to Aaron that she wanted to talk to him, but, of course, he had blocked her on social media and from his phone. Jo had described Aaron's blocking as 'a complete dick move' and Erin hadn't been able to argue – or admit she'd then done a bit of blocking herself. Even if it was him who had started it.

Sitting cross-legged on her bed, she resolved to message the man she had loved for three years – a man who had once told her that she had made him believe in love, which now made her want to vomit. And she would have to do it through his best friend, Connor, whose phone Aaron had decided was the only acceptable channel through which messages could be sent. As if it wasn't bad enough that all this had happened in the first place, she had to undergo the further humiliation of Connor reading all of her messages first.

It wasn't easy to think of the perfect way to say 'you better get your ass over to this flat and talk this out' without coming across as desperate and needy, or mildly threatening. After she had typed, deleted and retyped a message at least twenty times, she settled for:

Connor, can you please ask Aaron to get in touch so we can talk through the end of this relationship like proper grown-ups. Then we can both move on with our lives.

Her finger hovered over the send button for five minutes before she simply closed her eyes and stabbed at the phone, sending her words flying through the cybersphere to Connor's phone. It was out of her hands then, and she was going to try to keep it out of her mind until either Connor or Aaron replied.

With that done, she switched off her bedside lamp, plugged her phone into charge and lay back on her pillows. How was it possible to be both so tired and yet so wired at the same time?

Erin woke from what was, at best, a half a sleep every half-hour, unable to resist the urge to look at her phone to see if Connor or Aaron had replied. Even when it had gone 3 a.m., also known as the witching hour, in which no good text messages are ever sent.

Finally, at around half past four, she switched her phone off altogether in the hope this would be the key to her finally being able to drift off. Dawn had already broken and the world would soon be awake – while she had succeeded in nothing more than a light snooze. If she didn't get more sleep, she'd be facing a long, hard day – one that would test her emotionally and mentally, as well as physically.

'Just an hour,' she pleaded with her overactive brain. 'Just enough to feel a little rested before I commit myself to the biggest financial commitment of my entire life.'

Her brain, thankfully, listened and sleep washed over her. In fact, it washed over her a bit too well and she was woken once again by the sound of someone pounding on her door.

Her head was still thick with sleep and her eyelids heavy when she reached for her phone to see what time it was. Of course, the screen was dark and the banging at the door was too loud and too insistent for her to wait to power up her phone and check the time.

In a half daze- she hauled herself out of bed and down the hall to open the door and tell whoever was trying to batter their way in to chill the feck out.

Without so much as saying hello or giving Erin the chance to speak, Jo bustled her way into the flat and walked straight through to the kitchen, where she began to root around in the cupboards.

'This is becoming a bit of a habit,' Jo said, as she lifted two cups down and glanced inside them to make sure they were clean, which, Erin thought, was ridiculous, given her obsessive kitchen hygiene practices. 'I've brought buns from Flora. I'll make some tea. You get dressed. Something which covers your pants, preferably. You can't look back on this moment and remember that you were wearing your comfiest knickers, a Today FM T-shirt, and little else.'

'I... I didn't sleep well. What time is it?' Erin stuttered. Her mouth was bone dry and her mind was still fuzzy around the edges.

'It's almost ten,' Jo said.

'What the fu—'

'I know!' Jo interrupted. 'I've been trying to call you, but it just kept going straight to voicemail, so once again I'm coming over here to make sure you are okay and still on this planet.'

'I need to get to work. And to the farmers' market. I'll not have the best pick of produce at this stage though. Damn it, I switched my phone off a few hours ago because I was tired and couldn't sleep and I...' Erin paused, aware that if she told her friend about the message she had sent to Connor, said friend would very likely flip out.

'You what?' Jo said.

'I... erm... I'm going to get dressed. You make the tea. There are travel cups in the cupboard beside the cooker. We can drink our tea on the way to work,' Erin muttered and with that she turned to go to her bedroom.

'There's no big rush about work,' Jo said. 'Paul has taken care of it. He sensed you've a lot going on right now, so he took care of the orders, and he went to the farmers' market first thing this morning. He had Jackie come in to start on prep.'

'Good... that's good,' Erin said, relieved that particular worry was off her shoulders. She was lucky to have a sous-chef as reliable and thoughtful as Paul. He'd definitely make a good head chef when – or if, she reminded herself – the pâtisserie opened. 'But I still need to get ready.'

In her bedroom, her phone lay on the bed, and its unilluminated face taunted her. She knew she needed to switch it back on – it would be impossible to call Mr Mole at the estate agents without it – but suddenly the bravery that had made her want to talk everything out with Aaron had disappeared. Getting the closure she so clearly wanted would probably involve him saying hurtful things as he outlined their joint, and her individual, failings. Closure would be messy before it was final, but she supposed – feeling brave or not – she knew it had to be done. There was no escaping it.

She switched the phone on, her heart thumping while it powered up. To distract herself, she pulled on her comfiest maxi-T-shirt dress and slipped her feet into her favourite red Converse. Then she looked at her phone. There were three new message notifications.

The first, which was the most recent, was from Paul, telling her he had everything under control and prep was well underway for another busy Saturday.

The second was the one she was waiting for from Aaron, via Connor. Was it a suggestion of when to meet, or how to put this whole sorry episode to rest? No, it was not. It was a:

I'd like to take a little time before we talk.

This was followed by a request that she reinstate him on her

Netflix, Prime and Disney+ accounts as he was, after all, paying her rent for the next two months. The sheer audacity of the man at least made her laugh to counterbalance the rage she felt at his 'needing a little time'.

The third message – and this was the real punch to the gut – was from her mother.

Erin, is it true that you and Aaron have parted ways? I thought wedding bells had been ringing! What has happened?

Erin swore, loudly, at her phone. There was no 'how are you?' or 'I'm so sorry to hear that' – just an expression of disappoint-ment that there would be no engagement and no wedding. Well, it was her turn to 'need a little time' before she answered that particular message because she was sure if she did, there and then, she would say something that her parents would never let her forget.

So, with adrenaline – or maybe it was rage – coursing through her veins, she pulled her hair back into a messy bun of copper curls, slid her sunglasses on top of her head and walked back into the living room, where Jo had two cups of tea waiting along with two sugar-coated cream fingers.

'Can we go?' she asked. 'Bring the buns with us and grab a coffee at the Inn? I want to speak to Noah to confirm our offer and whether or not we're bidding for the equipment too, and I want to take the pressure off Paul as well. He's been busy these last few days.'

'If you want,' Jo said, a look of confusion on her face. 'But the tea is ready?'

'Coffee will be better. I'll make you a caramel latte,' Erin said, as she felt her skin itch with desire to get moving to release some of the nervous tension that was tightening every muscle in her body.

'You're the boss. Or you will be,' Jo said.

'That's the plan,' Erin replied, but as she pulled the door to her apartment closed behind them, she couldn't help but notice the shake in her hand.

17

There were certain key events in Erin's life that she expected would make her feel like a proper grown-up. Moving out of her family home for the first time. Her first day in charge of the kitchen in The Ivy Inn. When she and Aaron had made mutual declarations of love and had their first discussion about what they would call their hypothetical children in the future. There was her first parking ticket. Her first smear test – which was yuck, but very important – and the time she had received a letter telling her she was on the register for jury service.

But none of these actually *did* make her feel like a legitimate grown-up. It all felt a little bit like playing at being a grown-up and she had waited for the day to dawn when she fully accepted her place in the world as a proper adult with proper adulting responsibilities. Surely, she'd thought, the day was bound to come when she wouldn't automatically look for a more grown up grown-up to take charge in a crisis, or when she didn't wish she didn't have to do adult things, like phone to make a doctor's appointment or arrange for her boiler to be serviced.

But it wasn't until she was sat in Noah's office at The Ivy Inn, a spreadsheet of figures in front of her, that she started to feel the weight of the real grown-up world on her shoulders.

'It's time to seize the day,' Noah said, as he pushed the office phone in her direction.

'I will,' she replied, her mind a blur of numbers and ideas and responsibilities that would soon be fifty-five per cent hers. That was scary enough, but it didn't scare her as much as thinking about the forty-five per cent investment from her best friends that she would absolutely have to make work. 'Well, I might not seize the day, but I'll do my best to carefully hold it and hope I don't break it,' she said, with a voice that was as far from her usual confident self as was possible.

'You won't break it,' Noah reassured her. 'We have faith in you. Look, it's been amazing to have you here in the kitchen. You've helped grow this place so much and I don't think you even realise what a talented chef you are. But I know Jo and I have always felt a little guilty that we were keeping you to ourselves when your specialism is in baking the most amazing pastries and cakes. We know you love it. We've seen it with every new recipe you've tried, with every cake you've baked for our birthdays and for my wedding. You worked in Paris – it would be a crying shame not to share that talent more widely. So it's about time you did that, and had faith in yourself. This is your moment and if you don't pick up the phone and call the estate agent and make that offer, then I will be forced to continue with this inspiring and motivational speech until you change your mind. And, to be honest, I'm rubbish at it. That's where Libby and Jo come into their own. I'll only mutter some more nonsense at you, and maybe sing or something.' He smiled and she smiled too, her heart warmed by his kind words and also a little terrified at his threat to sing. Everyone at The Ivy Inn was well aware just how tone-deaf Noah was, thanks to his insistence on performing the 'Fairytale of New York' at Christmas karaoke every year.

'Okay,' she said. 'I'll do it. If you promise not to sing.'

'I will not sing even one note if you pick that phone up right now and put in your formal offer. Whispers on the street are that another two viewers are due today, so there is no time to waste!'

So Erin did what he said, even though her heart thudded in her chest and her palms sweated so much she was borderline afraid the phone would slip from them – and even though having such a grown-up, proper conversation felt completely alien to her.

To her surprise, it was all a bit anticlimactic. Mr Mole didn't whoop with joy. He simply thanked her for her interest and said he would run the offer past the vendor. She asked him when she would be likely to hear a response and he replied with a very flat, 'When the vendor has had time to consider your offer.'

'So, you've done it then,' Noah said as she put the phone down and tried not to feel too deflated.

'I have,' she said. 'And now I have to wait.'

'Good thing you've a busy lunchtime service to distract you,' Noah said. 'That will keep you from obsessing about it too much.'

She gave him a half-smile that she knew looked as fake as it felt. 'You know so little about women,' she replied. 'We can multi-task like queens. I can plan and prepare the best lunchtime service this Inn has ever known and have a full-on menty b at the same time stressing about this offer.'

'Menty b?' he asked, a look of genuine confusion on his face.

'Mental breakdown,' Erin told him. 'Menty b is what the cool kids call it. The TikTok generation. You're going to have to get up to speed with all the lingo if you're going to be a dad.'

'I'm hoping that our baby won't be having a menty b any time soon or come out demanding their own TikTok account, but I suppose you never know these days,' he said.

'Still, pays to keep up with the trends now, so you're not the sad dad in the corner with zero cool points,' she said.

'Are you actually trying to give me a menty b right now?' Noah said, as he glanced at himself in the mirror. Erin imagined he was checking out whether or not he had already started to morph into a dad-bodded version of himself.

'Not at all,' she told him. 'But there is comfort in having a mental breakdown with others.'

'That's true,' he said. 'It's out of your hands now for a bit.' There was a pause before he spoke again, his tone more earnest this time. 'I know this is stressful on top of all the other stress in your life at the moment but hang in there. Look, I know you have the girls to talk to about what has happened with Aaron, but I'm here for you too. He's an absolute asshole for treating you that way, and when I next see him, I'll tell him as much. But, for now, let's put all our energy into manifesting this dream for you. Isn't that what the cool kids would say?' he ended with a wink.

That was when she realised, fully, for the first time that she really, really wanted, and needed, this to work out for her – and for all of them – all of her friends who had become family. The realisation hit her like a tidal wave and she felt a rush of blood to her cheeks as her eyes welled up once more. It was supposed to be Libby who was the hormonal, sobbing mess, not her, but it seemed that was all she could do these days.

Erin wiped the tears from her eyes and tried desperately not to give in to them. 'I'm such an eejit standing here crying over him,' she managed to stutter.

'Hardly!' Noah protested. 'You loved him, Erin. There's no shame in loving someone and there's certainly no shame in showing your emotions when that goes wrong. Give yourself a break and allow yourself to have a cry. You've absolutely no need to be embarrassed in front of me.'

To which she ugly cried, letting out the knot of pain that seemed to have taken up permanent residence in the pit of her stomach. Yes, she could pretend she was totally kicking ass and claiming her life back, but *this* did hurt. What Aaron did had wounded her.

She felt Noah wrap his arms around her and pull her into a brotherly hug, soothing her until her sobs turned to little shudders of spent emotion.

'Better out than in,' Noah said when she had stopped crying and had pulled away from him. 'I'm not a big supporter of this "just move on" and "everything is a positive lesson" nonsense. We all need to process the negative feelings too. It's okay to be sad about Aaron and excited about your business at the same time.'

'Thanks,' she said. 'You're right.'

'I'm always right,' Noah replied. 'Just like I'm right that, for now, this is not in your control and you just have to be patient.'

She nodded, and said, 'What I can control is today's lunch special, so I'll do that.' Given that the warm spell had yet to break, she had a feeling it was going to be extra busy once again and she was grateful for it. It would be a very welcome distraction from all that was running through her head.

'Exactly,' Noah said. 'And I promise I will patch the call through to the kitchen if he phones back – even if you are really busy.'

'Thanks, Noah,' she said. 'You're a decent person, you know. And don't let anyone tell you otherwise.'

'Away!' he scolded, with a smile. 'Get to work!'

'Yes, boss!' she said as she left for the kitchen, doing her level best not to be distracted by the desire to hear the phone ring.

* * *

Thankfully, lunch service was as busy as predicted – if not more so – and Erin found she didn't have the time to lift her head, and because it was a Saturday, there was no marked break between lunch and dinner service – just a slightly quieter spell before the madness of the evening would begin.

Erin took advantage of the lull to walk to Harry's Shop so she could fulfil her craving to indulge in a Polly Pineapple ice lolly. There was nothing like it, apart from its sister ice pop, the Pear Picking Porky, to quench a person's thirst on a hot day. If there was something Ireland did right, it was ice lollies. Erin fully intended to sit on the small stone wall outside the Inn, but away from the bustle of the beer garden, to enjoy ten minutes of peace and quiet and to give her feet a much-needed rest before things got busy again.

Both Harry and Lorcan were in the shop when she got there. Harry was perched on his stool behind the counter surveying his kingdom, while his grandson was busy restocking the shelves.

'Erin, how are you?' Lorcan asked in his posh English accent. 'Another busy day?'

She nodded. 'We're flat out, but I'm on a break and I'm going to make the most of it before the evening crowd starts to arrive.'

'Yeah,' he said. 'The nice weather has brought everyone out in their droves. Jo has taken to spending even more time writing at her mum's to escape the chatter floating up from the garden.'

Erin knew her friend loved her flat above the pub, but she also knew that Jo was easily distracted and didn't like to miss out on anything that sounded like fun. There's no doubt it would've been hard for her to stay focused on working on her next book while summer was in full bloom below.

'I didn't want to ask her,' Erin said. 'But how's the book going?'

Lorcan grimaced a little, then smiled. 'We always say it's hard going, but the truth is, she's loving it. Even the tough days. It's hard work – much harder than I ever thought writing a book would be – but it means so much to her to be able to spend her days doing something she loves so much.'

'Love your job and you'll never work a day in your life,' Harry chimed in. 'That's what I've always believed. And sure, here I am, happy as Larry in this shop when the whole world would have me retired.'

'Chance would be a fine thing, Grandad!' Lorcan said with a wry smile. 'Sure, we tried to get rid of you and have you off enjoying the rest of your life, but you follow me here every day anyway!'

'That's the difference between me and you, sunshine,' Harry said. 'You think enjoying your life means not being here in a place of work, surrounded by the people and things you love. What would an old duffer like me be doing in any retirement? Sitting in the house on my own reading the paper and talking to the birds in the garden? I'd go off my head with boredom within a week.'

'Sure, you could take a leaf out of Flora's book and make plans to travel the world!' Erin said.

There was a momentary pause before Harry started to speak again, one which Erin realised could mean a hundred different things. But it was the sadness that swept across his face which intrigued her most. Was he sad that he'd never taken the bull by the horns and travelled the world himself? Or was it, as she suspected, about something much deeper than that?

'What would the likes of me go to Australia for?' Harry said. 'All those hours on a plane. My back would be killing me before we flew over England! And I'm not Flora. I don't have family on the other side of the world. I'd be travelling on my own to a place I'd never been. At my age? I don't think so. And remember, I've a dodgy heart – can you imagine what would happen if I took unwell.'

'Sure, you could always go with Flora and she would mind you? She seems to be quite fond of you, and you her too, if you don't mind me saying,' Lorcan said, with a cheeky wink.

Erin couldn't help but be intrigued. 'What's this? Is there gossip afoot here, Harry? Is there romance blossoming between you and Flora?' she said, as she took her ice lolly from the freezer and followed Lorcan to the counter so she could pay for it. To her surprise, she saw Harry blush, just as he had blushed the day before when he had arrived at the bakery with the flowers for Flora which he claimed meant nothing.

'Don't be so ridiculous!' Harry replied. 'A man of my age isn't about to be gadding around looking for a new lady friend! Besides, what would your granny think?'

'Granny would want you to be happy. She's gone a long time, Grandad,' Lorcan said – his tone soft. 'All I'm saying is... if you've feelings for Flora, well, life is too short...'

'It doesn't matter how I feel or don't feel for my friend Flora,' Harry said. 'As you have already pointed out, she's off to travel the world soon and I doubt we'll see her again on the Lane, so it's better I continue as I am. I'm happy with my lot here, and let's just leave it at that!'

'But, Grandad—' Lorcan began as he scanned the ice pop at the till.

'But Grandad nothing!' Harry said, his voice stern. It was the first time Erin had ever seen him look properly cross and flustered in all the time she had known him. 'Let's just help Erin get her ice pop here, and then get on with our day and never worry about talking any more nonsense about Flora and trips around the world or anything else. Those shelves aren't going to stack themselves, Lorcan. The last thing we want to do is leave those boxes lying there and someone coming in and tripping over them! It's a health and safety nightmare!'

Erin couldn't bring herself to look up at Lorcan for his reaction. It was clear he had hit a nerve when it came to his grandad's feelings for Flora, and Erin got the distinct feeling this was not the first time the subject had come up in conversation.

Regardless of his words, there was something in Harry's expression which told her the old man cared for his longest-standing neighbour – probably more than he realised. She felt sad that Harry didn't feel he could allow himself the chance at happiness that could come with injecting a little romance into his later years. She may well be sworn off relationships for the time being, but that didn't mean she didn't believe in happy ever afters.

18

'Oh God, yes. We're totally convinced that Harry has a notion for Flora,' Jo said that evening as they nursed a couple of cold drinks on her sofa after work.

'Has he ever actually admitted it?' Erin asked, before she raised her glass to her lips and took a long refreshing drink of perhaps the nicest glass of white wine she had ever enjoyed in her life. This was a drink she needed – not just because it was still much too warm and she had worked much too hard – but because it was night-time and no call had come from Mr Mole, or Flora, or anyone in response to her offer and her nerves were in ribbons.

Lorcan was sat opposite her on the brown leather sofa, with Jo resting her legs across his lap. Erin felt a tingle of jealousy when she watched how he gently rubbed Jo's aching calves. She would give anything for a leg and foot rub just then, but she knew it would be more than a little creepy to ask her best friend's fella for one.

'He has never admitted it. The man isn't one for doing feelings. You know Harry – he'll kill you with kindness and spoil you with presents from the shop, but he doesn't say how he feels. Not unless he's talking about Granny.'

'I never knew her,' Erin said. 'She was way before my time.'

'She died much too young,' Lorcan said, and Erin watched as a sadness washed over him. 'She was a remarkable woman. I suppose you'd have to be to put up with that grumpy arse, day in and day out. But she was brimming with kindness, you know. When we came home in the summer holidays, she made sure we had the best time. It was like our proper childhood.'

'You didn't want to spend your holidays somewhere more exotic than Derry? As lovely as it is here, it wasn't exactly jumping with things to do back then,' Erin remarked.

'Said with the innocence of someone who didn't grow up in a land-locked big city,' Lorcan replied. 'It had everything to do. The beach on one side and the mountains on the other. Fields to run about and play in. Craic to be had. And Granny always ready to slip a few pounds into my hand on the way out the door.'

'I suppose,' Erin said. 'I never thought of it that way.'

'Most people don't when it comes to the place they grew up. But this was magical to us and a big part of that was Granny and Grandad. I think they were the kind of couple that made me realise what love should look like.'

Erin felt her heart flip and she glanced to Jo, who was staring at her boyfriend with a look of pure adoration. The two of them were the kind of couple who helped her realise what love should look like – and, more importantly, what it shouldn't.

'But I don't think Granny would be too bothered by Grandad finding a new love. He's mourned her a long time and no one could ever question how he felt, or feels, about her. But I've seen the way he lights up when Flora comes into the shop. I've listened to the way they banter together. They're like an old married couple anyway most days. He's been in fierce form since the shop went up for sale. I'd hate to see her leave and him not let her know he has feelings for her. '

'Lorcan Gallagher, look at you being all romantic,' Jo said.

'As if you don't know that I'm a romantic old fart,' he replied and leaned across to kiss her softly on the lips.

Erin felt a complicated mix of emotions. She was, of course, happy that her best friend had found one of the few good men still in existence. And her heart was very much warmed by the story of how much Harry and his wife had loved each other. She even felt a little hopeful that love could still properly blossom between Harry and Flora, but she also felt just a little lonely too. She knew that if she drank any more wine that loneliness might well turn into a fairly unattractive maudlin state and her emotions were already wrung out.

'I think I'd better make a move,' she said, swigging back the last of her wine before she stood up.

'Why don't you stay?' Jo said. 'For a little bit, at least?'

'No, I'll leave you two lovebirds to your evening and go home and get a decent rest before the traditional Sunday madness kicks in.'

'Let me walk you home, at least,' Lorcan offered.

'No need. Sure, it's only five minutes away,' Erin replied, lifting her bag and swinging it over her shoulder.

'Doesn't matter,' Lorcan said. 'We wouldn't want you walking home alone. It's starting to get dark.'

Erin couldn't help but feel warmed by Lorcan's offer and she remembered the evenings when Aaron used to insist on walking to the bar to meet her at the end of her shift and walk home with her. She wasn't sure exactly when that had stopped, but it had been months since they had walked down the Lane, hand in hand, each of them tripping over their words to try fill the other in on their day – as if it had been weeks and not just hours since they had last been together. It had made Erin feel so special and more than a little smug at the time. She'd been sure it wasn't just because they were in the honeymoon phase of their relationship – this was how it was always going to be. They were different from other couples. What a naive eejit she had been.

'Thank you,' she said graciously to Lorcan. 'Jo, you've got a good one there, you know.'

'I know,' Jo grinned as she moved her legs to allow her boyfriend to stand up. 'He's a keeper.'

They smiled at each other and Erin watched the interaction and the way their eyes met. They'd been together almost as long as she and Aaron had and yet there was still a very obvious spark between them.

'Right, you guys, let's stop the kissy faces before I have to shout at you to go get a room!' Erin said.

'How about I grab my jacket and walk with you both?' Jo suggested. 'Then you don't have to walk back on your own, Lorcan.'

'I'll be fine walking on my own,' Lorcan said. 'You stay here and relax. It's been a tough week for you with this book. So feet up and I won't be long. Use the time to unpick that latest plot hole!'

'If you insist!' Jo said, reaching for the wine bottle and pouring herself another glass. 'It has been a tough week and wine always helps me overcome my writer's block.'

As much as she loved her friend, Erin couldn't help but feel relieved that Jo wasn't joining them. She didn't want to feel like a third wheel as they all walked together, her on her own behind the happy couple as they strolled hand in hand, laughing and joking, before dropping her off at her sad little flat and leaving with their arms still wrapped around each other on their way back to their flat, where they would no doubt have noisy, passionate sex with multiple orgasms and declarations of undying passion and love for each other.

Erin shook the thoughts away and reached over and kissed her friend on the cheek. 'Now, enjoy your downtime. See you tomorrow.'

Jo raised her glass in salute to her friend. 'Love you, Erin. Hang in there, kid. It's all going to come good.'

Erin nodded in response. She had to believe her friend was right.

Night had almost completely fallen as Erin and Lorcan left the flat and started walking the short distance home. The sky was a mix of darkest ink with just the smallest swirls of pale blue belying the warm day that was still desperately trying to hang on to its existence for dear life.

Lorcan seemed quieter than normal as he walked beside her, with his hands deep in his pockets and his shoulders hunched. After the long day in the kitchen, Erin didn't have the emotional energy left for small talk and she tried to reassure herself that they could probably get away with some companionable silence at this stage of their friendship anyway.

Once they had turned the corner at the top of the Lane, she heard Lorcan clear his throat. 'Erm, Erin... I've something to ask you and I know the timing might be really shitty for you, so if it's inappropriate, then just let me know and I'll stop talking and we can pretend this conversation never happened.'

She stopped walking and turned her head to look at him. Even in the half-light, she could tell his face was flushed – in much the same manner his grandad's had been earlier when they had spoken about Flora in the shop.

'What is it?' she asked.

Lorcan, who was usually chatty and brimming with confidence, couldn't meet her gaze. 'This is a bit awkward,' he said.

Erin started to run through all the possible reasons Lorcan would need to talk to her and which of them might make for a difficult conversation. The glass of wine she'd drunk just a short time before started to sour in her stomach as her nerves took over. Was this about Aaron? Did he know something she didn't? Another woman, perhaps? No – he'd have told Jo that before now. He'd have no reason to keep it from her. Shit, she thought, maybe it was about the bakery. Was he one of the other interested parties? Maybe it wasn't a crush on Flora that had Harry looking so flustered whenever her name was mentioned. Maybe it was a crush on her business. Lorcan had a good head for business – there was every chance he may well want to expand his grandad's empire to take over the running of a popular local bakery too.

'It will be more awkward if you don't speak soon,' she said, 'because my mind is running through every possible scenario and none of them are particularly good, so I'm about two seconds away from having a stroke with the stress of it all.'

He paled, the flush disappearing from his cheeks. 'Jesus! Don't have a stroke. It's not stressful. Honest. Look...' He shuffled from foot to foot like a shy teenager trying to find the courage to ask the girl he liked for a snog at the back of the disco. Thankfully, of all the possible scenarios running through her head at that moment, the prospect of him asking her for a snog was perhaps the least likely. At least she bloody hoped he wasn't. That would be the very definition of awkward. He was a handsome man, but A) she viewed him as a sort of brother figure, and B) he was in a long-term love affair with her best friend. Even thinking about snogging him gave her a mad case of the ick.

She tried to read his face for a reaction and watched him take a deep breath.

'The thing is,' he said, 'you might have realised that I love Jo. Like, I am crazy in love with that woman. I love her in a way I've never loved anyone else and I can't imagine ever wanting to spend my life with anyone but her. I don't want to be insensitive to what you're going through, and you are her very best friend in the world, but... well... I had been planning to ask her to marry me.'

Erin felt her heart skip a beat. Oh, this was perfect. Lorcan was the perfect man for her beautiful friend and she totally believed they would live a long and happy life together. She was so sure of it that she didn't feel so much as a pang of heartache at her newly single status. This was Jo and Lorcan. It was meant to be. 'I think that's a wonderful idea,' she said. 'Assuming you are still planning on asking her because I can't think of a single reason why you wouldn't go ahead with that.'

'Well, it might be a bit shit for you with the break-up and everything,' he said.

'It's not shit for me to see my best friend get her happy ever after,' Erin replied, and she meant it. There was nothing about this, even the timing, that was shit. This was all good.

'And you think she'll say yes?' Lorcan asked, with a sincerity that took Erin by surprise.

'Why on earth would she not? She loves you, Lorcan, and you two are so good together. Her mum and dad love you. Clara adores you. And even I think you're pretty sound, for a wee English fella,' she laughed.

'Cheers, Michelle from *Derry Girls*,' Lorcan smiled back.

She grinned at him. 'I'm just keeping it real,' she said. 'You have my seal of approval anyway. I think it's a brilliant idea and the timing is perfect in its own way. There's no way it's going to upset me just because my relationship has crashed and burned. I appreciate you asking, of course. It speaks volumes as to the kind of person you are,' she said as they walked.

'I've been wanting to ask her for the longest time,' he said. 'But there was always something or someone else to consider. I didn't want to take away from Noah and Libby's wedding last year. They deserved their big moment. And then Jo had a deadline... and another deadline. Then she was promoting her book and travelling all around the place and what I didn't want to do was make her achievements somehow about me by proposing in the middle of them. The focus very rightly had to stay on her. But then I came to realise there's always going to be something, isn't there? There will always be an obstacle in the way if I let there be, and I was making it into a huge thing that it didn't need to be. Like Grandad and not allowing himself to ask Flora out even though it's obvious to everyone that they would make a lovely couple. She's only going on holiday. She's not completely relocating!'

Erin nodded in agreement, although part of her wondered was there something a bit more to Harry's reluctance. It must be quite daunting to put yourself out there like that with someone you've been friends with for decades.

Lorcan continued, 'So I'd decided I was just going to go for it because I didn't want to wait any longer to ask her to marry me. We both want to start a family and I know that Jo would love us to be married first. But then with you and Aaron breaking up... I didn't want to appear cruel or insensitive. Us celebrating our love while, you know... you're heartbroken.'

He spoke with such sincerity that Erin couldn't help but feel a rush of affection towards him. 'Lorcan,' she said, 'you don't have a cruel bone in your body. Everyone knows that. And you are absolutely one hundred per cent right about waiting for the right moment. There will always be something to get in the way of big decisions if you let it. We all use it to justify not taking chances or pushing ourselves out of our comfort zones. Don't let marrying the woman you love be something you put on the long finger while you wait for some imaginary perfect time. When something is working, grab on to it and realise that it's already perfect.'

'You're so right,' Lorcan said, 'and so kind.'

She shrugged, unable to speak. All those unspoken words swirled around in her head. She was not kind enough to have Aaron continue to love her, apparently.

Sensing her emotional state, Lorcan took her hand and pulled her into a hug, which she welcomed, allowing herself to be comforted by him. He was a friend who was there for her when she needed it and she hadn't even realised how much she had needed a hug until that moment.

'You're stronger than you think,' Lorcan said. 'I admire you so much for going after what you want with the bakery. The fact that you are not letting this break-up wear you down is admirable. But it's okay to let your feelings out sometimes too,' he added as he squeezed her a little tighter. 'No one is going to judge you for being upset about Aaron leaving. Most of us have at least one bad break-up in our past – we know what it's like. You don't have to pretend with us. You matter to us.'

Dear God, what was it with the menfolk of Ivy Lane coming over all emotionally mature and empathetic today? While she certainly admired whatever it was Libby and Jo were doing to have two men so comfortable expressing their feelings, she couldn't help but wonder where she had gone wrong with Aaron that he seemed to have the emotional maturity of a sock.

19

Erin's legs were heavy by the time she heaved herself up the two flights of stairs to her flat. It had been a long and draining day and all she wanted was a quick shower, some fresh PJs and her bed. She had never been so glad to see her own front door and to slide the key into the lock. Pushing it open, she noticed a white envelope on the floor, which must have been slipped under it at some stage during the day.

She knew straight away it wasn't regular post because the postman did not venture as far the flats, instead using the individual post boxes in the entrance hall. It was probably from Aaron, but why he hadn't contacted her via phone or just called at the pub? She'd made it quite clear that he wasn't welcome in the flat, and he had at least obliged and returned his key when he came to pick up the manky food and tatty towels. Perhaps he wasn't feeling quite so obliging after she'd told him – or Connor, to be more precise – exactly what she thought of his request to be added back to her Netflix account.

Her body ached as she bent to pick the envelope up. And her heart ached when she saw the familiar handwriting on the front of it. Her mother's. Her mother who had only ever visited this flat once before – and that had been a duty visit when she and Aaron had moved in together. Unsurprisingly, Helen Donohue had turned her nose up at almost every aspect of her daughter's new home, including Erin's more eclectic interior design preferences. Helen Donohue was all about whatever minimalist trend was currently featuring in the pages of the *Ulster Tatler Interiors* magazine.

After that particular visit, all subsequent meet-ups were conducted either at whatever restaurant her parents were currently bestowing their patronage on or back at the family home. All it took was the rumour that her daughter's relationship was on the skids and that her mother might not get the big day out she had been pining for all along and Helen Donohue had deigned to grace the Lane with her presence.

Her adrenaline spiked in that way only her mother could make it spike, Erin slumped onto her sofa and opened the letter, wondering how her mother had managed to get into the building in the first place. She'd have to pin yet another note to the notice-board in the hall about not letting strangers in.

She opened the letter and saw a curt note in her mother's trademark cursive writing – and, of course, it was written with a fountain pen because her mother was the very definition of 'notions'.

Erin,

As you have not had the manners to reply to my text message, I thought this would be an appropriate way to get in touch. Your father and I would like to know what on earth is going on with you. We have it on good authority that you and Aaron are no longer cohabiting.

Please get in touch at your earliest convenience,

Mum x

Erin could hear her mother's judgy words in her voice as she read and the faux posh accent she liked to adopt. Maybe on another day, she would've felt really sad that her mother hadn't even bothered to ask how she was, but instead she felt angry. In fact, she felt so completely rage-filled that she wanted to go over to her parents' house and knock on their door and order them out of their beds just so she could tell them that she was worth more than her relationship.

The only problem with that was that it would most likely just fall on deaf ears, as so many of the things she told her parents about her life did. So, instead she decided to channel her rage – now so immense that despite her exhaustion she knew there was no chance she would sleep – into something productive.

Erin knew her kitchen like the back of her hand. She knew at any time what ingredients she had. She kept her cupboards well-stocked with many cooking and baking basics. She had the tools and equipment she needed to bake the lightest sponge or make the richest caramel. She had her beloved KitchenAid mixer, piping bags, rolling pins and measuring cups and spoons – although she was often able to measure simply by sight. When Erin baked, it felt like she was following a choreographed routine. It wasn't just about the ingredients, it was about how she moved around them – how effortless it felt to mix and measure, to whisk and simmer. It was about getting the shapes and flavours just right. She would accept nothing less than perfect. Maybe that's what she took from her parents – their impossibly high standards. Yet this was okay, because this she knew she was good at. This was just a part of her.

She mixed flour and sugar and eggs. She melted butter and added chocolate and watched it transform into a silky ganache.

She made a sugar syrup before adding espresso and more than a little cognac and mixed it into a rich buttercream. She baked. She cut her cake into perfectly even-sized rectangles. She assembled layer upon layer. She piped the words The Ivy Inn in a delicate chocolate script on the top of them and stood back to admire the finished opera cakes – one of the first delicacies she had made when she was in Paris. The anger had left her by then. It was three in the morning and tiredness took its place, but at least when she went to bed, she knew she would sleep.

* * *

When morning came, Erin met Jo in the beer garden at The Ivy Inn for coffee – her self-baked cakes with her to share around.

'These are not good for my diet,' Jo said as she took a large bite of her second cake. 'I've heard that there's a condition called writer's arse, and the more books I write, the more arse I'll gain because it seems I can't stop eating.'

'Maybe I should stop baking for you then,' Erin laughed, 'and ban you from the pâtisserie before I even know if it's ever going to open.'

'Don't you dare!' Jo warned. 'But you do have to tell me why you baked these last night when you were dead on your feet leaving my house. And don't try to bluff your way out of this. I know for a fact these are not some "packet mix, add an egg and throw them in the oven for ten minutes" efforts. These took time. And you'd only do that if you were angry about something. This is a rage bake if ever I saw one.'

'If you don't want them, I can take them away again,' Erin said, feeling a little embarrassed that she was so transparent to her friend.

'I have already warned you that if you do that, I will not be responsible for my actions and you will end up in a book. It's up to you to decide if you'll be the villain or the hero,' Jo said but Erin could see the concern on her face and she knew that Jo was acting from a place of love.

'My mother,' Erin started, before she stopped, took a deep breath to settle herself and continued. 'She came to my flat yesterday, at some stage, and left a handwritten note expressing her concern at rumours of the demise of my relationship. She has ordered that I get in touch at my "earliest convenience" or some such nonsense.' Erin was doing her best to make light of it because she was determined not to cry. Her head was still sore from yesterday's sob fest with Noah, coupled with the wine after work and the exceptionally late night.

'Oh,' Jo said and grimaced, because Jo knew enough of Helen Donohue to know that this message would not have been out of concern for her daughter.

'Exactly,' Erin said, as she felt her chest tighten with the threat of another emotional outburst. 'But I will not cry,' she insisted. 'I will not let her do this to me.'

'Crying isn't a bad thing,' Jo said. 'A good cry is like a good fart. Better out than in.'

'It's words as beautiful as those which make you such a great writer,' Erin laughed, so very grateful to have a friend as wonderful as Jo on her side. 'I mean, how have you not won every literary award going yet? It's beyond me!'

'Clearly all the other writers in the world are intimidated by the exquisite nature of my prose,' Jo said, as she eyed a third opera cake before she shook her head in disgust at herself. 'These really are epic. And I love the icing. Noah will love them. We'll have to get them on menu once you're up and running in the shop.'

'*If* I get up and running,' Erin said. She didn't want to presume things would go in her favour.

'We're manifesting this,' Jo said. 'So it will happen. But, tell me, what are you going to do about your mother?'

That was a good question. As good as any Erin had been asked. She supposed if her mother had already resorted to visiting her home and leaving a note, then chances were, she wasn't going to be satisfied until she had seen Erin in person, and for the sake of her own sanity, Erin knew that really would have to be at her earliest convenience. But first, she had to get her work out of the way.

'I'll have to face the music, I suppose,' she told Jo.

'But you don't have to dance to it,' Jo replied. 'Don't let her get under your skin.'

'Might be a bit too late for that,' Erin said, glumly. 'But I'll do my best to remain calm when I see her.'

'Good woman,' Jo said, and reached across to give her friend's hand a reassuring squeeze.

'Can I ask a favour though?' Erin said. 'Could you put her in your next book? She'd definitely be the villain... or maybe the victim.'

Jo laughed, in the delightfully unselfconscious way Jo always laughed – loud, throaty and exuding nothing but joy. 'Oh, absolutely. With pleasure,' she said.

Erin felt a surge of gratitude for her best friend – who never judged and never made her feel bad about anything, apart from that time they had the war of attrition over the loo rolls. She had to resist the urge to get up from her seat and pull Jo into a giant hug and tell her how much she was truly loved, before calling first dibs on being her bridesmaid. She didn't care if Clara already had her name all over that role – she wouldn't be above going hand to hand with an eight-year-old for the title of chief bridesmaid and the chance to wear a pretty frock.

Having left Jo and made her way to the kitchen, Erin was

delighted to see Paul had everything under control, and the kitchen staff were already hard at work.

'Hi, boss,' Paul said, with a grin. 'Nice to see you.'

'Always lovely to be here,' Erin called as she went to the staffroom to change into her chef's whites. She could hear the chatter of her staff and the way in which Paul was able to issue instructions without sounding like a pompous bully – she may have trained with some chefs with big egos, but she didn't believe in taking that approach in her work. She'd rather have the respect of her staff than have them fear her. Thankfully, Paul, who had joined her team four years before, believed in taking much the same approach. The result was a hardworking team, who, most of the time, all rubbed along nicely and were able to banter with each other. It would be a big wrench for Erin to leave them if she got the pâtisserie, but she knew she would be just a few doors away. She would still be able to oversee the menu, although the kitchen would no longer be her domain. That, she realised, would be tough – but she couldn't deny that it would also be really exciting.

For now, though, she was going to focus on her work and enjoy how smoothly this particular ship sailed. She knew she wasn't going to hear from Mr Mole today – she doubted even the most diligent estate agents tried to confirm deals on a Sunday – so she could just concentrate on doing what she did best, and whenever she wasn't busy, she could plan exactly what kind of cake she was going to make for Lorcan and Jo's wedding. Something non-traditional, she figured. No stodgy fruit cake, unless Jo really wanted a tier of it. Maybe a light vanilla sponge. It was hard to beat the classics. Depending on the time of year, she could even persuade Jo to opt for a naked cake – no fondant or buttercream icing. A crumb coating maybe, decorated with fresh berries and edible flowers. It would be exquisite.

20

The following few hours passed quickly. There was no time for Erin to think about Aaron, or her mother, or Lorcan's forthcoming proposal to Jo. There wasn't even any time to think about how tired she was after her few hours' sleep.

Still, she was grateful to get a short break and to be able to escape the heat and noise of the kitchen for fifteen minutes. She grabbed a bottle of water and took herself outside to sit on the small wall at the front of The Ivy Inn. She turned her face up towards the sun. If she wasn't mistaken, it was a little cooler than it had been the day before, and the clear blue skies that they had been treated to over the course of the previous week were now decorated with wisps of white and even grey. A gentle breeze blew through the branches of the nearby trees.

From where she sat, Erin could see the bakery, closed of course. Its buttery vanilla-coloured exterior gleaming in the morning sun. The red of the for sale sign attached to the wall seemed at odds with the peaceful vibe to the Lane, but she hoped it would be taken down soon – preferably when she herself was handed the keys.

'It will be sad to see it close,' she heard a voice from behind her. It was a voice she recognised only too well, and her heart sank. Of all the quaint little lanes in all the world, he had to walk into hers.

'Aaron,' she said, as she turned to see her ex standing across the street staring up at Flora's. What on earth was he doing? Why was he here? Her heart lurched, and her stomach. In fact, it was fair to say she experienced a shitstorm of feelings all piling in on top of each other at the same time. Her brain was so used to identifying him as friend and not foe that it jarred to swivel straight to anger, confusion and sadness. This was not on her terms, and she had wanted whenever they met again to be on her terms – after all, he had taken full control of their last goodbye. Not that he'd afforded her the chance to say goodbye. She'd obviously wanted to look amazing, to be in control and to show him he'd, in the words of Julia Roberts in *Pretty Woman*, made a 'big mistake'. 'Huge,' in fact.

Instead, her face was beetroot red, her curls had turned to frizz, she was exhausted and she was wearing her food-splatted chef whites. Try as she might to form the appropriate thing to say to him, she just couldn't speak. He had completely caught her off guard, which was brutally unfair of him.

'I hope whoever buys it doesn't turn it into some bougie little hipster spot,' Aaron said, eyes still on the bakery. 'Gentrification is never cool.'

She took in his appearance. He was wearing clothes she didn't recognise. Clothes that still had the brand-new-still-starched-from-the-shop look about them. Clothes that made him look like he'd been a victim of a dodgy makeover TV show. He was dressed in khaki cargo trousers, with a crisp, blindingly white T-shirt and a black utility waistcoat, like those worn by photographers, or people on safari. The pièce de resistance was a pair of slip-on canvas mules, worn without socks so they showcased his also blindingly white ankles. None of this was anywhere near his usual look. On any given Sunday, he'd be more likely to be found in jeans or joggers and a comfy T-shirt. She didn't think she'd ever seen him wear a waistcoat before – let alone a utility jacket. It had enough zips, buttons and Velcro on it to look like one of those toys you get to teach toddlers to dress themselves.

These clothes won't have come in cheaply, she thought, and yet the same man had been begging food from her because he had paid for the last big shop. There he stood, there talking about gentrification as if he wasn't looking like a born-again hipster. All that was missing was a quirky moustache, waxed into a point on either side.

What a gobshite.

Erin blinked, willed her mouth to work and say something. 'I'm sure whoever gets it will do something that fits well with the Lane,' she managed, as she bit back the urge to tell him about her hopes and dreams for it. He was no longer someone who was entitled access to her wishes and wants. 'I'd better get on,' she told him. 'Sunday lunch waits for no one.'

He shuffled from one foot to the other and looked down before raising his head and looking her directly in the eyes. There was something about the whole move that gave her cheesy boyband vibes. Who was this man who was stood in front of her, with Aaron's voice but dressed and behaving in a very un-Aaron like way? She could feel her heartbeat quicken as the urge to get away from him battled with her curiosity about why the hell he had showed up outside The Ivy Inn.

'But I thought you wanted to talk?' he said. 'Connor told me you wanted to meet to chat? I've been trying to get hold of you all day yesterday and this morning. But it just keeps going straight to voicemail. Do you have me blocked?'

She blinked hard at him, dumbfounded at his gall. '*You* blocked me,' she said. '*You* walked out. *You* left, and *You* gave me nothing to go on.' Mentally, she jabbed him hard in the chest with her index finger at every emphasised word, somehow having found the strength not to actually jab him in the chest. Or punch him in the face. 'But now you want to talk? Here? Now? After you left without so much as finding the time in your schedule to talk to your girlfriend of three years or tell her you were leaving her with not so much as an explanation?'

'I did what I could,' Aaron said. 'I paid up the rent for a bit so you wouldn't be left high and dry.'

'Well, that's okay then. All is forgiven. You paid your share of the rent. How dare I have expected more?' To her surprise, Erin found her voice wasn't shaky and she wasn't worried that she would burst into tears at any second. She didn't even sound angry. She sounded incredulous more than anything – which, she realised, was her primary emotion at that moment.

'Of course not,' he said. 'But I came here because you wanted to talk, so can we please talk? Properly?'

'You came here on a Sunday lunchtime, mid-service – when you know the kitchen is busiest and you just expect me to leave them to it and suddenly make time for you because it suits you now?'

'You have a good team, Erin. Paul can run the kitchen any other time when you are off. I'm sure he can keep things going while you talk with me about our relationship,' Aaron said, a bitter tone having crept into his voice.

'This is my work, and it is important,' she said, aware that her break was up and she needed to be back in the kitchen.

'And that,' he said, throwing his hands in the air, 'sums it all up in one sentence. This is your work, and it is important. It is the most important thing in your life and it always was. It came before me and it came before us. If you want to know why I left, that is the reason. I can't compete with your work obsession.'

She felt as if he had slapped her in the face. Was he right? Had she put work first? 'If you felt that way, why didn't you talk to me about it?' she asked, the wind taken out of her sails.

'When?' he said, and this time she heard hurt in his words. 'You were always either at work, or so exhausted from work you didn't have the energy to talk. I tried talking to you; I tried making time for us, but I just wasn't your priority. Surely you felt it too. I was spending every evening home alone thinking this is not what a relationship is supposed to look like, or feel like. I was so lonely, Erin, and I don't think you even realised. I didn't think you'd care if I left. I doubted you'd even notice,' he bit with a sting of bitterness.

Erin shook her head. Was that how it was? Was she neglectful? Was this all her fault? 'I love my job,' she said, feeling chastened by his words, 'I'm not going to pretend I don't, or apologise for it. But I love... loved you too. I put everything of myself into us. And maybe we'd become complacent, but I didn't shut you out, Aaron. That's not fair.' She scanned her memory for times he had asked to speak but she'd been too tired or too distracted to engage. Was he right to be angry and accuse of her caring about the Inn more than their relationship? Did he really want her to claim responsibility for everything that had gone wrong between them? Should she?

'If it's easier for you to believe that you didn't shut me out,' he said, with a sad shrug of his shoulders, 'then you go ahead and believe that.' It was the dramatic sigh after that did it. It brought Erin out of a spiral towards self-blame back into a reality she wasn't going to let him get away with.

'You're not being fair, Aaron,' she said. 'You want to come here and put every ounce of blame at my doorstep? There were plenty of chances for us to talk – but you seemed to like to choose late night, after a long shift. Or five minutes before I was due to go out the door. Why did you never suggest chatting in the mornings, or on the nights you played football with the lads? Or when we were having a night out?'

He opened his mouth to speak but closed it again. He must've realised, Erin thought, that she was right.

'And none of it – not one tiny bit – is an excuse for just packing up and moving out,' she continued. 'You never gave me the chance to fix it. You never gave *us* the chance to fix it – and didn't we deserve that at least? If it wasn't working, didn't we deserve the chance to work that out together, instead of you pulling the rug out from under my feet and leaving me humiliated in front of our friends?'

'Our friends?' Aaron snorted. 'There's no such thing as "our friends". They're your friends – the Ivy Lane crew. It's not like you enjoyed hanging out with Connor and the lads.'

'Connor and the lads?' she said. 'You really wanted me to come along on one of your booze cruises or pissed-up football days? Or play Dungeons and Dragons with you? You'd have had a conniption at the very thought.'

'No, I wouldn't,' Aaron replied, but it was clear from the blush on his face he knew she had called him out.

'I have to go back to work,' she said, as she stood up. 'It seems clear to me that there isn't anything left to say. Just leave me alone. Don't pretend you were doing me a favour by paying the rent – because I don't need favours from you.'

She turned to leave and hoped with every ounce of her heart that he had turned to walk away in the opposite direction, leaving her alone. Her calmness was giving way to anger now. And shame too, maybe. Shame and fear that he had been telling the truth and she had let them down so badly he felt he had no choice but to leave?

Goddamn it, she could feel her stupidly emotional body threatening to let her down once again.

By the time she was back in the kitchen and was trying to talk to her staff, her voice had taken on a thick and syrupy quality as she struggled to hold back tears.

'Everything okay, boss?' Paul asked her, his eyes wide with concern.

She could not bear to meet his gaze, so she shook her head and raised her hand in the universal sign language for 'Please don't talk to me or expect a response any time soon because I am too emotionally fragile right now'.

'Okay,' he said, thankfully completely fluent in all of her moods. 'Everything is on schedule. Desserts need your attention but I can look after that if...'

'I'll sort it out,' she said, her back to him so that he could not see her shame written large all over her face. 'Thank you, Paul,' she added. 'You're a great asset here.'

'Yes, chef,' he replied, 'And if you need to talk about it, or scream into the void, I'm here for you,' But Erin didn't think she had the strength to talk or scream about it. All she wanted to do was hide under her duvet and hibernate until she felt stronger.

But that simply wasn't an option with a pub full of hungry customers to feed. If people were going to spend their hard-earned cash on going out to eat, she was going to make sure they got the best that she could offer. If the desserts needed attention, then she would focus on that.

It was a process she always lost herself in – where she could enjoy bringing the raw ingredients together to make something beautiful and delicious. Where she could feel a sense of accomplishment each time she created the perfect pastry, or the lightest meringue – and when the orders started to come in, she felt a dopamine hit each time just from knowing that people were enjoying the food she had prepared.

The time passed quickly as her team worked efficiently around her, each of them so familiar with their roles and her standards that these busy services often ran like clockwork. It was just the distraction she needed from her confrontation with Aaron – except for his comments about gentrification.

Is that what she was trying to do? Was she trying to change the very fibre of the Lane? She didn't think so. What she wanted to do was add something beautiful to a street which had become a home for her. A big part of the appeal of wanting to buy Flora's shop was that she would be buying into this community – a community that was interwoven with multiple generations of residents. It wasn't a street that had forgotten its roots, it was a street that had grown and evolved but kept the sense of belonging and family at its very heart.

That was not a sign of gentrification. It was not some – how was it Aaron had put it? – some 'hipster bougie' nonsense. It was where she belonged. It was where she felt she mattered – more so than the house she had grown up in, where silence was more common than loving words and laughter. More so than in her flat with Aaron while they had slowly drifted apart and existed side by side but never together for longer than she could remember.

As she served the final dessert of the day after a long and busy service, she embraced the feeling that this was home and the reality that Aaron, with all his angry words, was not. She wanted this. She needed this. She needed the shop to be hers. She needed the new business. And a new home. A fresh start. She had no plan B, and she wasn't sure where to start on finding one. She had to believe that everything would come good.

Twenty minutes later, she was standing at the fire door

guzzling a glass of iced water to cool herself down when she spotted Noah walk into the kitchen and glance around until he spotted her.

'Erin, the very woman I need,' he said.

'I've been here the whole time,' she said. 'What's up?' It struck her that maybe something had been wrong with lunch. Had someone complained? If so, there was little she would be able to do about it now that service was done. She couldn't think of anything that could've been off – she was nothing if not meticulous and thankfully her team were just as focused as she was.

'Nothing's up,' Noah said. 'Well done on another successful service! I was just popping by to tell you that you have a visitor in the bar looking to talk to you.'

Erin's stomach tightened. 'It's not Aaron, is it?' she asked. 'Only he was here earlier and I don't want to talk to him again.'

'Has he been giving you trouble?' Noah asked, his face flooded with concern. 'I mean outside of him being an absolute shite-hawk and walking out?'

Erin shook her head. 'No. Not really. He said since I wanted to talk, he was there to talk – knowing full well what a typical Sunday looks like for me here. And then he started harping on about gentrification or some other such shite. I didn't tell him about my hopes for the bakery, so please, if you do see him, keep it to yourself?'

'I'd be hard pushed to be civil to him, so you've nothing to worry about when it comes to me spilling the beans to him. The beans will be staying in the tin,' Noah said.

Erin couldn't help but smile. 'I appreciate that,' she replied, and felt it in her very core. She felt deep gratitude that Noah, and Lorcan too for that matter, hadn't even questioned which side of the big break-up divide they should land on. They had her back.

'Hang in there, kid,' Noah smiled back. 'Which brings me

back to my original point. There's someone in the bar waiting to see you. They said they've been trying to get you on your phone, but it's been going to straight to voicemail.'

'I haven't had a moment to look at it all day. It's been too busy. Who is it?' Erin asked as she placed the glass of iced water against her forehead, closed her eyes and savoured the cooling sensation of the condensation on her skin.

'Flora,' he said. 'It's Flora.'

21

'Flora?' Erin asked, her eyes having sprung open.

'Is there an echo in this room?' she heard Paul's voice from across the kitchen and looked in his direction just in time to see him grinning to himself, clearly delighted with his own joke.

'Very funny!' she called, before directing her attention back to Noah. 'And how does she look? Does she look sad? Does she look like she's about to pish on my chips?'

'For a chef, you have such a beautiful turn of phrase when it comes to food images,' Noah said, sarcastically.

Erin ignored him and kept on talking. 'Well, does she? Does it look like she's about to break my heart?'

From the other side of the kitchen, Paul could be heard singing 'Achy Breaky Heart' as he walked into the pantry to stock-check and Erin swore she was about two seconds from bashing him over the head with a copper-bottomed pot.

'Does he know you're hoping to buy the bakery?' Noah whispered, and nodded in Paul's direction.

'No. I think he just has end-of-Sunday-service giddiness. But it doesn't matter. I just need you to tell me the craic. What does she want? It can't be about the bakery? Wasn't Mr Mole supposed to call us? He hasn't called. So why would she want to talk to me? Unless she's beset by guilt at letting me down and... Oh God...'

Erin felt Noah's hand, warm and reassuring on her arm. 'Just breathe, Erin,' he said. 'And trust that what's for you won't pass you.'

'We shouldn't keep her waiting then,' Erin said with faux bravado.

'You really shouldn't,' Noah said with distinct emphasis on the 'you', but Erin was smart enough to know it was always wise to bring backup, especially when feeling emotionally fragile.

'Hey, business partner, we're in this together. If this is about the bakery, you signed up to help me with that. I'm not walking into this alone.'

'C'mon then,' Noah said. 'I'll be your wingman on this one. And I'll walk away if it doesn't concern me.'

'Cheers, boss,' Erin said, taking a deep breath to steady herself before following Noah back into the bar. He led her to one of the booths close to the front of the bar, where she was surprised to see Flora deep in conversation with Harry. She watched them for a while, and took in the quiet, easy way they were with each other. If she wasn't mistaken, there was a cheeky little glint in Flora's eyes and her smile was warm and bright. And, of course, what she saw in Harry's eyes as he spoke was boyish and roguish and she got an inkling of the very handsome man he must've been all those years ago in his young adulthood. She could see a trace of Lorcan in him too. But mostly she just saw a man who was totally entranced by the woman opposite him, and a woman who looked positively illuminated as she talked back to him. She could've stood and watched them all day.

'Flora!' Noah said, a little bit too loudly perhaps. 'I tracked Erin down for you.'

There was the briefest of moments when Erin could sense the effort it took for Harry and Flora to break their gaze from each other before Flora looked up at her and grinned.

'There you are now!' she said. 'I've been trying to get hold of you. I thought maybe I had the wrong number, but Noah here tells me I didn't.'

'The kitchen has been so busy, I've not had a chance to look at my phone all afternoon,' Erin said.

'Ah, well that explains it,' Flora replied. 'I didn't leave a voice message because my granddaughter told me that you young ones never listen to messages anyway.'

'All that technology and they don't make use of the half of it,' Harry interjected. 'Imagine that! They were all crying out for mobile phones when they first came out. Didn't want anything to do with having a house phone any more. Wanted to be able to talk to anyone no matter where they were. And now? You'd be hard pushed to get a young one to answer the phone in the first place. It's all texts and the like. Don't even get me started on the language they use – it's like no one ever heard of a vowel or it would be too much effort to type a full word out. I don't know...'

Erin was grateful when Flora reached her hand across the table and rested it gently on Harry's. The touch was enough to stop him in his tracks before he launched into the twenty-minute full-length version of why technology was a cursed thing and how people had been much happier back in his day. As if he wasn't still living and breathing in the world now and didn't have his very own mobile phone which he insisted on wearing in a holder on his belt.

'I'm rambling on again, aren't I?' Harry said with just a touch of a smile.

'Just a bit, Harry,' Flora said and the smile that had been on Harry's face morphed into a grin.

'Good thing I've you to keep me right,' he said and Erin almost hoped that Flora wouldn't return to telling her what she had been trying to get in touch about. She'd be happy to sit and watch the pair, with their gentle teasing and innocent flirtation. It was so wholesome and lovely.

'Someone needs to!' Flora teased. 'But here, Erin, sit down, pet. So we can have a wee chat.'

'I'll leave you to it,' Harry said, groaning a little as he stood up to leave the booth. 'My knee is giving me gyp. A wee medicinal whiskey might just help with that,' he smiled.

'Mine's a gin and slim,' Flora said with a smile,

'Erin, what would you like to drink?' Harry asked. 'And Noah?'

'I'm fine, thank you,' Erin said. 'I've to finish cleaning up in the kitchen yet.'

'And I always have more work to do,' Noah said.

'No rest for the wicked, eh?' Harry said with a cheeky wink. It really was very heart-warming to see him so at ease.

'Even less for the good, Harry,' Noah rejoined. 'But how about I skip you to the front of the queue to save your gypy hip?'

'That would be much appreciated,' Harry said, before he doffed an imaginary cap at both ladies and headed to the bar, leaving Erin to slip into the still warm seat opposite Flora. There was something deeply unsettling about sitting in someone else's bum-generated warmth, but Erin pushed through uncomfortable thoughts about Harry's rear end and tried to focus on the task at hand.

She had to use every ounce of her strength of character to look Flora in the eye and keep her voice steady as she said, 'And so, what can I help you with today, Flora?'

Flora tilted her head to one side and looked at Erin, a soft smile crinkling the wrinkles which framed her eyes and mouth so perfectly. There was a life well lived in her appearance and the feeling that every line told a story of its own.

'Here's the thing, pet,' Flora began. 'I got your offer. And I wanted to talk to you about it myself, you know. It didn't seem right putting everything through the estate agents, not for you. It's different for the people I don't know, but I know you and I care about you.'

As lovely as it was to hear that Flora did indeed care about her, Erin couldn't help but wish she would just cut to the chase. She nodded. 'Thanks, Flora. I appreciate you taking the time to talk to me.'

'I'm going to be honest,' Flora said, 'your offer is just a little short of what my Rachel thinks I should be holding out for.'

Erin's heart sank. She knew that she had stretched her budget as far as she could and she didn't want to ask the others to up their investment either. She didn't know yet what it would take to pull together the refurbishment of the flat, or the fitting out work in the shop, or to market her new business for that matter. She knew enough from watching back-to-back episodes of *Homes Under the Hammer* that contingency funds generally got blown out of the water when unforeseen extras were needed and she didn't want to start her new business already in fear for her financial future. At the same time she completely understood Flora's position – and she would never want to short-change the older woman. Not in a million years.

'And there is other interest. More than I thought there would be, to be honest. Even a couple of chains – a coffee place and a chemists, you know.'

Erin knew only too well. What chance would she have against the buying power of the corporate world?

'It's not easy,' Flora continued. 'You know? To make decisions as big as these. I don't think I ever really thought the day would come when I would be selling up at all. I always said I'd work 'til I couldn't any more, and my children would tease me that there was nothing that would stop me from going into that bakery. Even when they were new-born, I'd just enough time off to get back on my feet and no more. And when my Johnny died, I was back in the day after his funeral, because the thing is, Erin, I have loved it. And I have loved that it has always been there to keep me going, even at times when I didn't think I wanted to keep going at all.'

Flora blinked back tears and Erin feared she'd join her in giving in to her emotions – the biggest feeling in her heart right then being disappointment at the news she was sure was headed her way.

Flora continued. 'It kept me going – that place. But it's more than that. People might say, sure, it's only a bun for your morning cup of tea, but it's not, you know. It's somewhere for people to meet and have a chat, even if only in the queue. The people I see come through those doors. There's people out there who first came in the bakery in their mammy's bellies, and then in their prams, and now they're pushing the prams of their own grandchildren. So even though I needed the place to keep me going, I like to think it kept other people going too. Whether it be thinking about who they'd meet or what they'd treat themselves to. I never wanted to let those people down, you know. Because you shouldn't ever do that if you can help it. You shouldn't let your own down.' Flora sniffed, but it was Erin who noticed that her own face was wet too. She didn't dare speak. 'So, anyway, after talking it through with my Rachel, and the rest of my children, and with Harry just now, I've decided I don't want to let the community of Ivy Lane down. Certainly not for the sake of a few pounds.'

Erin felt her breath catch in her throat. Did Flora mean what Erin thought she meant?

'But... sure you need that money for your retirement. And your travels! You should absolutely get the best price for the place.'

'And that's what I'm intending on doing,' Flora said, leaving Erin once again confused. Her feelings must have been obvious on her face because Flora tilted her head and gave her a smile. 'I'm talking in riddles, aren't I? It's spending too much time with that Harry one! Sure, you'd never know what nonsense you'd be coming out with. And there's no such thing as a long story short with him, so let me get to the point.'

Please God, Erin thought but managed not to say.

'Sometimes getting the best price involves more than just money. I want that sense of community to continue. I want the Lane to be well looked after and not over-run by big chain operations who aren't part of the fabric of the place. I know your business idea isn't to keep the shop running as it is, and things are going to change. I'm not a naive oul' doll with no wit about me. But the thought that it's someone who knows and loves this place and who wants to make it better is worth more than a sack of money to me. You young ones bring so much to this place. And God above knows you have helped keep us old farts going.' At that, Flora's voice cracked and she glanced over to the bar, where Harry was making a show of rubbing his sore leg before taking a grand big sip of his whiskey. If Erin wasn't mistaken, there was more than a little fondness to her tone, and to the expression on her face. 'I don't think he'd still be going if it wasn't for you lot. Grumpy old devil that he is, you all kept him going when he wanted to give up, and now look – Lorcan is back here and working with him. You never know, Lorcan might even marry young Jo and they might have a baby like Libby and Noah, and there could be children running around this place again sooner than you think.'

Not for me, Erin thought with a sigh before she chided herself for not focusing on the big picture. Maybe she was scared too. Because everything was about to get real, really quick, and she didn't know if she should cry, or laugh, or scream, or all three.

'Are you saying that you're going to accept my offer?' Erin asked, hoping with all her heart.

'I am, pet,' Flora replied and gave her hand a squeeze. 'And I'm delighted to do so. Just knowing the place will be in good hands gives me such a sense of peace. It will make it easier to walk away. I know people say it's only bricks and mortar, but it's so much more than that. It's been my whole life.'

Erin couldn't speak for the tears that openly coursed down her face. All she could do was put her free hand on top of Flora's and squeeze back.

'My goodness, ladies, who died?' Harry's voice boomed as he appeared beside the table with a gin and slim for Flora and a whiskey for himself. The pair shared a smile that said more than words could ever say. 'Hang on!' he added. 'We haven't forgotten you, young Erin!' Harry stepped to the side, revealing Noah carrying a tray replete with a bottle of champagne and several glasses. 'I believe congratulations are in order,' Harry said with a wink.

If Erin wasn't mistaken, there was a hint of emotion in his voice too.

22

It was sometime around eight in the evening when Harry, having consumed more than enough medicinal whiskeys to treat a dose of the bubonic plague, decided to lead the way into a bit of a singsong.

Erin was feeling just the nice side of tipsy as she sipped a cooling vodka and cranberry juice after moving on from the champagne. The bubbles from the former had gone straight to her head and she'd found herself cleaning the kitchen while several sheets to the wind, grateful that there was no food service on a Sunday night to deal with.

Paul had looked at her, one eyebrow raised, as she had bopped around the kitchen after Flora's big announcement.

'Why are you looking at me like that?' she'd asked him, a wave of self-consciousness washing over her.

'You look happy,' he'd said.

'It has been known that I can in fact be happy some of the time,' she'd replied, with a lopsided smile.

'I'm not saying you can't,' Paul had said, 'but I'm sure I didn't pick up wrong that you looked upset earlier?'

The gentle way in which he asked the question had made Erin realise he was asking out of concern for her and not nosiness. It was, she realised, probably exactly the right time to give him a potted highlights rundown of the last week. So, she had told him that she had split with Aaron, and then opened up about all her hopes for the bakery, stopping just shy of filling him in that she had him in mind for the head chef position in The Ivy Inn, deciding to hold that nugget of information until she had signed contracts and discussed the promotion with Noah and Jo.

He had listened intently and expressed sympathy and excitement in the right places. 'I had a feeling something was off with Aaron,' he'd said. 'If you don't mind me saying so.'

'I don't mind at all,' she'd said. 'But can I ask what gave you that idea?'

Paul had shrugged. 'It's nothing much, really. But you didn't seem to talk about him very much any more. There was no "Aaron and I watched *Bake Off*", or "Aaron and I are going away for the weekend".'

He wasn't wrong, Erin thought.

'And there were a few times I wondered if you were hanging on a little later than usual or coming in early just to be away from home,' Paul had said, but couldn't quite meet her eye. Clearly, he didn't want to offend her, but while his words did sting a little, there was nothing untruthful in them. That's exactly how it had been, she realised. When Erin really thought about it, she knew there had been times when she came to work early on the pretence of catching up with Noah or Jo, or to do a stock-check, when, really, she had just found the increasing silence between her and Aaron too much.

'Was it that obvious?' she'd asked.

Paul had shaken his head. 'No. I don't think so. Unless someone was paying attention.'

She'd paused. Did this mean he was paying attention? To her movements or to the status of her relationship? For a moment, she didn't know what to say next. She certainly didn't feel ready to pull at that particular thread.

'Okay,' she had muttered before opting to change the subject entirely, which was sometimes the best course of action when embarrassment threatens to floor you. 'Well, I suppose it's no bad thing since I'll be so very busy with my new business – if I can get my mortgage approved.'

'It will happen,' Paul had said. 'When you want things to happen, you tend to chase after them until they do. Think of all the changes you've implemented here, Erin. I think you will be incredible... I mean... *it* will be incredible.'

For the shortest of moments, Erin had wondered if she should read anything into his slip of the tongue. He'd said *she* would be incredible. He had definitely said that first, but he'd corrected himself so quickly.

Whatever, Paul did not give her the chance to think about it any more as he launched in with all the right questions. The kind of questions that could only be asked by someone who shared a love of food prep and baking and the unique satisfaction that came with preparing a mouth-watering meal. She realised how refreshing it was not to have someone's eyes glaze over when she spoke about her proposed menu, or what she had learned in Paris. In fact, she could see her excitement reflected back at her in his expression. Unlike Aaron, he didn't steer the conversation back round to himself, or pick up his phone halfway through to check the football scores.

'I hope it all happens for you, boss,' Paul had said as he'd grabbed his bag at the end of his shift. 'I've always had a feeling you were going to go further than this place.'

Those words, along with the company of her friends in the

bar, gave Erin a warm fuzzy feeling in the pit of her stomach. It was the opposite of how she'd felt when Aaron had come to see her earlier in the day, and it was a much nicer headspace to reside in.

This side of tipsy was a nice place to be and imbued her with a sense that all was right in the world, but not enough that she decided to dance on the tables, or anything equally embarrassing.

Harry, it turned out, was quite the singer, even if his choice of songs wouldn't have been Erin's first choice. She was more of an Ed Sheeran/Lewis Capaldi kind of a girl and Harry preferred singing the songs of John Denver and, perhaps more fittingly for the location, a rather impassioned rendition of 'The Town I Loved So Well' – the old Phil Coulter song about Derry at the height of the Troubles.

Erin allowed the deep sound of his voice to wash over her as she sat beside Flora, holding her hand, and closed her eyes. She was well aware she was too young to really feel the true meaning of the lyrics, but she felt a lump rise in her throat anyway. Maybe it was how Harry's own voice showed signs of emotion as he sang of the music that was always in the Derry air and of the hope for peace that the community had carried in their hearts.

The Inn, she noticed, had all but fallen silent as Harry sang. Even Paddy seemed to be enjoying the performance, having laid himself on the floor at Harry's feet so he could stare up at him and wag his tail at the high notes.

By that stage, they had been joined by Jo and Lorcan, and also by Libby and Noah, who sat hand in hand, Libby resting her head on Noah's shoulder. The pair looked as if they just fitted together, like two pieces of a jigsaw puzzle. When Erin saw Noah kiss the top of his wife's head tenderly, she felt a spark of excitement for the journey they were on. They were going to be parents. There was going to be a little baby as part of the fabric of Ivy Lane and at the centre of their friendship group. It would change things, of course, but she had a feeling it would be in a good way. Just as she was sure Lorcan and Jo would have the perfect wedding and enjoy their own happy ever after.

As good days went, it had been the best. Even with the run-in with Aaron earlier. To be fair, since Flora had revealed she was going to accept Erin's offer, she had barely given Aaron and his claims a thought. Her mind had been filled with a sense of positivity for what was to come and love for the people who were going to help her get there. That and, as she realised once the applause died down for Harry, the need to pee. There was nothing as true as the curse of the first fatal pee when drinking. Just like opening a can of Pringles – once you pop, you can't stop.

Having let go of Flora's hand, Erin sidled out of the booth and away from her friends towards the Ladies'. It was only now that she felt the slightly disorientating effects of her last two drinks and she realised she had to concentrate a little more on walking across the bar.

Relieved to find there wasn't a queue for the facilities, she sat down to wee and allowed herself a moment to think about just how quickly a life could change. Surely this last week would rival any plot twist Jo could come up with in her books. Erin would never have said she was a fan of change, but she had to concede not all change was bad.

She was still enjoying her little moment of self-reflection when she heard the door to the Ladies' open and two women, clearly also enjoying a little Sunday libation, walked in.

'Did you see her with that oul' fella singing?' said the first and Erin bristled, annoyed at the description of Harry simply as an 'oul' fella'. Maybe it was the alcohol in her bloodstream, but she wanted to protest that he was more than just an old man. He was the very cornerstone of Ivy Lane.

'I did and all,' the second woman replied. 'It's no shocker why he left her, is it? That hair looks like she stuck her fingers in the electric socket and you'd think she could put on a bit of make-up.'

Erin's hands moved to her head, where she tried to flatten her mass of red curls, now frizzy from the heat of the kitchen and with extra kinks thanks to having been tied up during service. She had known, of course, that the women were talking about her. Neither Libby nor Jo were single, and the only other woman in the company of the 'oul' fella' apart from her was Flora. As far as she knew, Flora had not just been unceremoniously dumped and whereas Erin's face was indeed bare of make-up, Flora wore an elegant dusting of powder and a soft pink lipstick. That, and the knowledge that people very rarely bad-mouth a woman in her seventies who supplies the entire street with buns day in and day out.

Erin froze where she sat – and wished that the women would both shut up but also that they would keep talking until she could identify their treacherous voices.

'She's no threat to you,' she heard the first woman say.

'I don't think she ever was,' the second replied. 'Coming home every night reeking of chip fat.'

There was a loud, mawkish laugh and that was what tipped Erin over the edge. She flushed the toilet and walked out of the cubicle with her head held high to see two women she didn't know gawping in the mirror as they caught sight of her reflection. Erin enjoyed watching the colour drain from their faces. She didn't know which one of these 'ladies' was Aaron's current bit of stuff – not that it really mattered. They were almost carbon copies of each other. Tall, slim, blonde, fake-tanned and fake lips. Probably fake boobs too, not that she wanted to stare in that direction.

'Okay girls?' She said, as she pasted the biggest smile she could manage on her face. 'You're absolutely right – I am no threat to whichever one of you is with Aaron just now. But here's the secret, I am actually one hundred per cent okay with that. I hope you're very happy. But maybe, just maybe, you should stock up your kitchen a bit. The poor pet had to come begging for food this week. From my cupboards.'

'That's only because you've made him pay for that flat even though he's moved out and everything,' the slightly taller of the two girls said, the colour having returned with gusto to her cheeks.

'That's what he told you?' Erin rejoined. 'Take my advice and work on your communication.' Erin looked at herself in the mirror and pulled a loose curl behind her ear. Yes, she looked tired and overheated, but there was also a glint in her eye that outshone her make-upless, frizzy-haired state. 'But here, before I go. Do either of you have a spray of perfume I could borrow – just to cover the chip fat smell?'

When the girls just looked at her open-mouthed as they tried to think of a fitting comeback, Erin tilted her head to one side.

'No? Ah well, never mind. I'm sure I'll survive.'

She felt a little shaky walking back to the table with the new knowledge of Aaron's betrayal racing around her head. But the scene before her was as happy as when she had left it, and she was reluctant to put any form of dampener on proceedings by bringing Aaron's infidelity into the equation. So she decided to hold the knowledge close to her chest for now, slipping back into her seat and resuming her relaxed pose listening to Harry launch into another song.

She did her best to remain as chatty and smiley as she had been and to keep bad thoughts from rushing into her mind and taking over. However, she should have known she'd never be able to get anything past Jo, who could read her as well as she could any of her own crime novels.

Her first indication that Jo had cottoned on that all was not as it seemed, was feeling a less than gentle kick to her shins, which caused her to swear loudly and almost put Harry off his stride. There was he ready for the high note in 'Danny Boy' when she took the Lord's name in vain. He blinked but, admirably, kept on singing.

Erin looked across the table to where Jo was rolling her eyes in an exaggerated manner and bobbing her head ever so slightly in the direction of the door to the beer garden in a very clear 'outside, now!' movement.

Reluctantly, Erin slid off her seat again and followed Jo to the far side of the garden, where they perched on the low stone wall and sat for a moment in silence.

'Are you going to tell me what's up or am I going to have to beat it out of you?' Jo said eventually.

'What makes you think anything is wrong?' Erin asked, but she knew she sounded less than convincing.

'Because since you came back from the toilets you've had a face on you that would sour milk,' Jo said. 'And you'd been so happy before. Oh my God, you didn't take a pregnancy test in there and find out you're up the duff, did you?'

That was enough to make Erin laugh out loud. 'Wise up!' she said. 'I know you're a writer, but jumping to a conclusion I must be pregnant is a bit far-fetched. You know I've no plans for babies any time soon, if ever. And did you not just order me another drink and watch me drink half of it?'

'Stranger things have happened!' Jo said defensively. 'So, if you're not pregnant, are you going to tell me what it is that is eating at you?'

Erin shrugged. She didn't really want to get into it. She needed time to process it all and decide just how she felt about it. Then again, maybe this was a situation where – like ripping off a plaster

– it was best to get it all over and done with in one go. Then she could take her time to concentrate on the positive things in her life.

'Aaron was cheating,' she said, her voice low. 'I just overheard two women talking about it when I was in the toilet.'

'Oh shit, that absolute bastard!' Jo exclaimed. 'I'm so sorry, dote. I'd no idea. That can't be easy to hear. How do you feel about it?'

'You're right, it wasn't easy to hear. I've heard a few things today that haven't been easy to hear actually and I've been putting them all in a little box because I want to concentrate on the things that make me happy. So I don't know how I feel really,' Erin told her, as she closed her eyes and looked up to the sky. She needed a moment to think. 'Part of me wants to track him down and kick him square in the testicles.'

'I'll help!' Jo said. 'I'll even borrow Lorcan's steel-capped boots to do it! One swift boot to the balls and...'

Erin placed her hand on her friend's, grateful for the solidarity but also wanting to finish talking herself. 'I love you for that,' she said. 'But the thing is, while part of me wants to cause him actual physical pain, another part of me just feels relieved.'

'Relieved?' Jo asked, incredulity written large across her face.

'That I dodged a bullet,' she said, and the realisation that this was true landed with a thud. 'He's clearly not the man I thought he was. And to be honest, yes, I'm a bit shaky, and I'm sick at the thought of him cheating, but it could've been worse. He wanted to push to get married, to buy a house, to settle down. I could've been stuck with him – a liar and a cheat – and it would have been ten times as hard to escape that years down the line than it is now.'

Jo nodded. 'I love you, Erin,' she said. 'And I know I've had a few drinks, but I'd say it to you sober. You're class and you're going to smash this out of the park, and someday down the line Aaron will get his comeuppance. Karma is a bitch.'

'So are those two hallions over there,' Erin said, nodding to a table to her left where the two creatures from the Ladies' were sat drinking their Prosecco as they tapped their overlong false nails on their phones.

'Was it them you overheard? So one of them is seeing Aaron and also had the brass neck to come to this pub where you work and bad-mouth you?' Jo asked and Erin could already feel her friend start to get up. She tried to grab her hand and urge her to sit back down, but it was pointless. Jo Campbell may have been small, but she was mighty, and there was no one in this world more loyal than her.

Erin watched with a mixture of pride and fear as Jo stomped to the table and politely told the two ladies that they had to leave and that they were, from this point on, barred from The Ivy Inn.

'You can't do that!' one of them – the one Erin suspected was the other woman – said.

'I think you'll find I can, and I have,' Jo said, by now attracting the attention of their fellow drinkers.

'But we're still finishing our drinks,' the woman responded.

'So you are,' Jo said, lifting the two Prosecco glasses from the table. 'So, I'll do you a favour. You can take these with you. I won't even trouble you to bring the glasses back. Consider them on the house.'

'I want to talk to the manager!' the second of the women said.

'I am the manager,' Jo replied. 'And one of the owners. The other owner, I can assure you, would tell you exactly the same as I am telling you. Now, do as you're told and be on your way before I tell everyone listening in just what kind of people you really are.'

Erin watched, her heart full of love and admiration for her best friend, as the two women gingerly took the glasses from Jo, gathered their things and left in silence, their heads down. They didn't so much as glance in Jo's direction. The fact that they had left restored a sense of equilibrium to Erin, and the smile she gave Jo as she walked back to her was a genuine one.

It would take more than two bitchy women to put her off her stride. It would, she realised, also take more than the news that Aaron was seeing someone else to break her. She'd done her crying already. She'd channel the energy from any residual feelings – positive and negative – into showing Aaron, and herself, just how much she could achieve and how she absolutely did not have to rely on any man to bring her happiness.

23

On Monday morning, Erin sent a text message to her mother to ask if it was okay for her to call round that morning before she went to work. She had long learned that it was not good manners to simply show up at the family home unannounced.

Of all the things in the history of time that ever made a Monday morning suck, visiting Helen and Gerry Donohue was at the top of the list, but Erin knew that it would be better for her just to get it over and done with. The alternative would be Helen escalating a campaign of passive aggressiveness so intense that Erin's head would spin.

Erin was therefore both delighted and horrified when her mother replied to say a visit would suit and that she looked forward to catching up with her daughter to find out 'what on earth' was going on in her life. There was no escaping it then.

She showered and dressed in a maxi dress her mother would approve of. She styled her hair – which felt like a lot of effort given that a couple of hours in the kitchen would reduce it to its usual frizzy state – and did her make-up. She even stopped at M&S on the way and bought a bouquet of flowers. Erin didn't actively hate her mother – she just found her incredibly hard work – but she had never been able to lose the desire to please her.

Erin's family home was everything that Erin herself was not – formal, curated, neat and organised. As an exercise in beautiful interior design, it was a winner, but what it offered in terms of Carrara marble floors and high-end kitchen appliances, it lacked in comfort, colour and warmth. Even as a child, Erin had been afraid to spill anything or colour outside the lines, for fear she would mark something of her mother's. Maybe that was part of the reason she rebelled against minimalism in her life and her work.

Helen Donohue would never contemplate a coloured glass chandelier in a pâtisserie, or using pastel-coloured wax paper, possibly with a gold trim, to wrap her produce in. She would never embrace the original features of the bakery, or countenance spending the day getting flour in her hair and dough under her fingernails. Had it not been for their matching heads of red hair, Erin might have wondered if she and her mother were related at all.

It was Gerry who answered the door when Erin arrived. He worked in a successful solicitors' practice managing the conveyancing side of the business. He was not a short man, but there was something about his demeanour when Helen was around that made him look smaller than he was.

'Erin! It's lovely to see you,' he said. 'Your mum is just finishing up on a Zoom meeting, but she will be through shortly.' He nodded towards the downstairs office that was her mother's domain. 'Shall we go and put the kettle on?'

'That would be lovely,' Erin said and dutifully followed her father through to the kitchen, where she took a seat at the island and watched him fill the kettle.

'Your mother is very concerned about you,' he said. Gerry Donohue was the kind of man who would never tell his daughter directly how he felt, always voicing his feelings on behalf of her mother.

'There's no need to be concerned about me,' Erin replied. 'I'm fine. Look, why don't you sit down and I'll make the tea?'

'There's no need for that. Sure, you'll be spending enough time on your feet when you go to that job of yours.'

'I'm well used to that, Dad,' she said. 'Making a cup of tea isn't going to hurt me.'

He didn't answer but carried on taking cups out of the cupboard and dropping teabags into them. Eventually, once the kettle had quietened, he spoke. 'So, your mother tells me you and Aaron have decided to split up?'

Erin took a deep breath. She wasn't sure that she and Aaron had decided to split up. Aaron had made that decision all on his own. That said, after the revelations of the day before and her confrontation with him outside the bar, she was very much happy that they were no longer an item.

'We have split up, yes,' she said. 'But it's okay. It was the right thing to do.'

'Was it though, Erin?' her mother asked, as she arrived silently into the room. 'I mean, you had been together a long time and you're in your thirties now. It's time to settle down and behave like a grown-up – get married, have babies. You'll have to start all over again. At your age.'

'Being together for a long time isn't a great reason to stay together if things have gone wrong,' Erin said, as her father handed over her cup of tea, along with an apologetic half-smile.

'But did you even try to fix them?' her mother asked, taking a seat beside her daughter and instructing Gerry to put some biscuits on a plate. Erin didn't know why her mother insisted on doing this. It wasn't as if she was going to eat any; Erin wasn't sure she'd seen Helen Donohue eat a biscuit in her life.

'That's the problem with young people these days,' her father said. 'They don't know how to stick with things when they get tough. They just want the world to offer them an easy ride and at the first sign of trouble they scarper.'

Erin felt herself tense.

'I'm sure if you and Aaron just sat down and talked it through there would be a way to make everything okay again. I hope you know it doesn't hurt to say sorry when you've messed up,' her mother added. Her father nodded in agreement before he sipped his tea from a china cup.

Being in the company of her parents was, Erin thought, probably akin to being put into a giant vacuum-sealed storage bag – the kind you put your winter blankets in – and having all the life sucked out of you.

'Now, Helen, who's to say Erin messed anything up? It might not have been her fault,' her father offered in a move that Erin thought was either remarkably brave or remarkably stupid. Whatever it was, it caught Erin off-guard. Was he actually sticking up for her?

She didn't have time to contemplate it any further before her mother's snort of derision filled her ears. 'Do you know our daughter at all? She seems to have encountered a lot of little blips along the road. Too many to point the blame at other people.'

'What blips?' Erin asked, unable to hide her confusion and her hurt. She may not have lived the life her parents had dreamed for her but she hadn't stumbled through her existence leaving a trail of destruction in her wake. Actually, she was quite successful if her parents could bring themselves to open their eyes and see it.

'Oh, not going to study law, then wasting all that time, money and effort you spent training at that fancy culinary school to come back here and work in a pub. I mean, come on, darling. Do you realise how foolish we've looked telling our friends about our Cordon Bleu-trained child, who perfected her art in the finest kitchens in Paris, only to have you serving up chips and chicken goujons down the local.'

Gobsmacked, Erin tried to find a polite way to tell her mother what she thought of her. She tried to find a way to say no, she didn't serve chips and chicken goujons, but even if she did, there was no shame in feeding people for a living. She tried to find a way to tell them about her plans for the pâtisserie, and her new executive chef title. But she realised it didn't matter. It wouldn't make a difference how or what she told her mother, and her father for that matter, who had gone silent after his moment of solidarity. They would always, always, find fault in her decisions. She had come home to work 'down the local' because her mother had been unwell and she had needed to be there to help her through chemo appointments and to recover from surgery. But that was long forgotten now. Now her return was just a source of shame.

Erin thought of Flora and Harry and their effusive praise for the young people on Ivy Lane and how much life and vitality they had brought to the place. She thought of Jo and Noah's parents and how they beamed with pride every time they came to The Ivy Inn, and of Libby's dad who was one of the gentlest, warmest souls she had ever met and who had already offered to do his share of the work on the flat renovation at a very generously discounted mates' rate.

Then she looked at her parents, the consternation and judgement on their faces. The uneaten biscuits on the plate on the sterile marble kitchen island where not so much as a crumb was out of place. She loved her parents, but she did not like them, and she was not prepared to sit and listen to them tear her life to pieces without even taking the time to listen to her. They didn't deserve to share in her hopes and dreams.

'Mum, Dad, it's been lovely to see you, but actually, I think I need to be on my way. Those potatoes aren't going to chip themselves,' she said.

'Oh, don't be like that, darling,' her mother cooed. 'You've only just arrived, and we haven't talked about Aaron at all yet. Please, sit down and finish your tea.'

Her father pleaded with her eyes for her to stay, but if he didn't have the balls to ask her out loud, then she didn't have the obligation to fulfil his wishes.

'I am finished with my tea, thank you,' she said. 'And there is nothing else to discuss about Aaron. We are not together, and we will not be getting back together. That's all you need to know. I'm sorry that me and my "blips" have been such a colossal disappointment to you both, but I'm not sorry for living my life on my own terms. I love you both, but I'm choosing not to spend any more time in your company today.'

With that, Erin got up and walked out of the door without so much as a backward glance.

She expected that tears would follow, but they didn't. Instead, she felt empowered at her decision to walk away. Just as she had walked away from Aaron's nonsense the previous day. Certain things were to be left in the past, and her future, one her parents did not have the right to know about yet, was waiting for her.

* * *

The next few weeks blurred into each other. There were times when Erin felt so exhausted she found it hard to track what day of the week it was. Without Jo and Libby's help in compiling the mother of all to-do lists, there was a good chance she'd have made some monumental mistake and bought the wrong shop, or forgot about a wedding reception in the Inn, or forgot to put a crucial order through for some of the equipment she needed for the bakery.

It was overwhelming, but in the best way, she thought. Yes, it was stressful and, yes, she was acutely aware she was investing every penny of her savings, as well as a considerable chunk of money from her best friends, but it was also very, very exciting. Once she had got over the hurdle of getting accepted for a commercial mortgage, she felt she could embrace the chaotic stress of it all.

Having Noah and Jo among her business partners meant they were fully briefed on what she was doing and were happy to cut her some slack at the Inn so that she could take what time she needed for appointments and meetings and to sign her life away.

Paul was only too happy to take ownership of the kitchen when Erin couldn't be there and though it tested her control-freak tendencies to entrust him with keeping things running smoothly, she couldn't deny he did a good job, which boded well for his eventual promotion.

Buying the bakery from Flora, with her blessing, meant Erin had access to the building to make plans and to get a sense of the place that would not only be her business premises but her home. The renovations to the upstairs rooms would be fairly basic given her limited budget. Thankfully, Libby's dad was pulling as many strings as he could to get her fixtures and fittings at a reduced cost, and Noah had promised to hire a van to do a run to Ikea to get whatever furniture Erin needed. Of course, she had some furniture of her own, which she would bring with her from the flat so she wasn't starting entirely from scratch.

The little savings here and there would be just about enough to allow her to get the pâtisserie just as she wanted it – complete with the multicoloured glass chandelier: her one big indulgence.

Flora loved hearing her plans, and told her on multiple occasions how thrilled she was that the ovens would still be switched on and the scent of fresh baking would still fill the air.

'I think this old building would miss it if all of a sudden the cooking stopped. I know it sounds a bit airy-fairy,' Flora said several weeks into the project as they drank tea in the kitchen after closing. 'But I think buildings absorb the atmosphere of a place. This place has been a bakery for longer than I can remember. It would seem an awful shame for that to stop completely now.'

'It would,' Erin agreed. 'I like that there will be a continuation of sorts of your legacy.'

At this, Flora blinked back tears and raised one shaking hand to her chest.

'Are you okay?' Erin asked, panicked. My God, but the last thing she needed was for poor Flora to cark it right there and then in the kitchen.

Flora sniffed loudly and laughed. 'Oh sweetheart, I'm fine. Well, fine to a point. It's all starting to feel a bit real now, you know.'

Erin knew only too well. She had handed in her notice at the flat and while she was looking forward to a fresh start, there was something about packing your life up into boxes that made you feel just a little bit nervous. She was so invested now, she couldn't help but worry she was tempting fate by daring to believe it was actually happening.

She couldn't imagine how unsettled Flora felt. No matter what the older woman might have said about being ready to retire and enjoy the rest of her life, the reality of seeing that day start to hurtle towards her must've been daunting.

Erin took a packet of tissues from her bag and handed one to Flora, who took it gratefully and dabbed at her eyes.

'I don't think I ever really believed the day would come when this place wouldn't be here in the same way again. I've loved it and I've hated it – sometimes both in the same day – but it's always been there for me. And yes, there are times when I'd rather have done anything else but set to work on another cake, or another batch of scones, but once I was there mixing the ingredients and bringing it all together, I never regretted it.'

Erin nodded.

'I know this sounds silly, or maybe not – you're a chef, you understand. But no matter how many times I made something, I was always just a wee bit surprised when it all turned out so well. Like there was a bit of magic in the making. And before you think I'm away with the fairies, I know it's science and not mumbo-jumbo, but sometimes it really did feel like a thousand mini-miracles. I'll miss the feeling of the flour in my hands, and the sound of the mixer beating the butter and sugar. It made up the sound-track to my life more than anything else,' Flora smiled.

'Did you never get bored with it? Ever? That's what I worry about sometimes. That I'll wake up one day and just think – nope, that's me done,' Erin said, and it was true it was something that did concern her. More so now she was investing every last penny she had into making baking and food the sole focus of her life.

'There were days I was bored. There were days I didn't want to come to work. I'll let you in on a little secret – the menopause years were a nightmare. Hot flushes and hot ovens were a combination from hell. And there were times when I was expecting, or when the wains were wee, that it was hard going. I know it wasn't a million years ago, but expectations were different, even then. A lot of women stopped working when they started their families – and it wasn't some lifestyle choice. There were barely enough jobs for the fellas, and there was no one else to watch the wains if you were out all day. We were all just trying to get on with things, you know. I'm sure my children would tell you there were days they hated this place too, but I'll let you in on another wee secret. See the days when they would come and sit by that workbench over there?' Flora pointed to a free-standing bench by the back wall of the kitchen, that had definitely seen better days. 'Those days, they were the happiest of my life. They'd come here after school, get a glass of milk and some fresh buttered scones and they'd sit there doing their homework until it was time to go home. They weren't angels, mind, but they were good. And most of the time, I didn't have any bother with them. Knowing they were here, with me, was just lovely.

'Sure, everyone who came in knew them and would spoil them rotten. The number of coins that were slipped into their hands behind my back was nothing normal. There were days I'd tell them that they made more than me and I was only exaggerating a wee bit. I dared not tell the neighbours to keep the money to themselves though – they'd have been offended, even though some of them had barely a penny between them, and others existed on tick.

'When the weather was good, they'd be out in the street kicking a ball about with Harry and Mary's boys. And the other kids from the street too. There weren't many cars in those days. No fear, and sure, I could watch them out the front of the shop and give the window a good rattle if they were getting too rowdy.' Flora's eyes had misted over again and Erin could tell she was lost in her recollections of tough times, but simpler times in so many ways.

'You're really going to miss it, aren't you?' Erin asked, as she wondered what her story would be here. Would there be times she would be overheated and over-stressed? Probably. She was,

after all, known for her fiery temper. Would there ever be children
of her own sitting at a table doing their homework? She doubted
health and safety would be quite so lax with that in this day and
age, but maybe, just maybe, there would be a time when there
might be one or two children of her own upstairs. And a partner
too, hopefully? Not that she was interested in anything romantic
these days. Aside from Lorcan's forthcoming proposal. With how
she felt about Aaron and his betrayal, Erin wasn't sure she ever
wanted to put her trust in another man again. If she decided she
did want to be a mother she might just have to throw caution to
the wind and take matters into her own hands.

'I *am* going to miss it,' Flora replied, 'but I have to be realistic.
I'm not getting any younger and if I want to see anything of the
world, I'd be best to do it now before I start to lose my marbles –
although there are many out there who would tell you I've lost my
marbles already anyway.' Flora gave a small laugh. 'It's going to be
strange not seeing all your faces day in and day out, though – you
have all become as much of a family to me as my own lot. There
are people here who are incredibly special to me.'

Flora had not yet admitted her feelings for Harry, nor he his
feelings for her, but Erin couldn't help but notice the way her
head subconsciously bobbed just a little to the right in the direction of his shop when she spoke about people who were incredibly special to her. She wondered whether she should just ask
Flora outright. The two women had become closer over the last
few weeks and as they had talked about the sale and purchase of
the bakery, they had discussed so many other things too. Funny
things initially and, increasingly, heavier topics. Topics infused
with feelings. The kind of chatting normally reserved for best
friends. The kind of no-holds-barred chatter where nothing was
off limits.

Erin had confided in Flora about the rude blondes in the

toilets who had bad-mouthed her within earshot, and how she had discovered one of them was currently warming Aaron's bed. Flora had replied with a facial expression that would curdle milk and the brutal honesty of a Derry born-and-raised granny – vowing that should she see that Aaron fella again she would give him 'a good boot up the arse'. Erin had almost choked at Flora's turn of phrase before she had given in to kinks of laughter instead.

She'd even told Flora about her parents. That time, Flora had just given her a tight hug and told her that some people struggle to express their emotions, but she was sure that Erin's parents loved her all the same. 'It would be impossible not to,' she'd said.

'I do love you, Flora,' Erin had replied, and she'd meant it.

Sitting here with her now, Erin was starting to realise that Flora retiring would also leave a Flora-sized hole in her life.

'I will miss you so much when you go. If nothing else, who is going to make my bread for me?'

Flora rolled her eyes to heaven. 'The girl who can create all those fancy French pastries that look like works of art but who can't made a good bread roll! I'm sure you won't have much use for them in your fancy bakery, but I'll make it my mission anyway to teach you my tricks before I leave.'

'Many have tried, and many have failed,' Erin said, as she remembered all the times she hadn't proved her bread long enough, or she had over-baked it, or it hadn't risen and ended up dense and inedible. Even the few successful attempts she had made weren't a patch of Flora's light and delicious breads. At best, they were passable, while Flora's were heavenly.

'The many who have tried are not me,' Flora said with a knowing wink. 'There's a knack to these things and it's all about timing it just right and being patient!'

'Isn't that true about everything in this world?' Erin said.

Opportunities had presented themselves to her before, but the timing had just never been quite right. Or she had been so focused on other plans, she hadn't recognised them for just what they were until it was much too late. There were so many times she had looked back and wept over missed chances or kicked herself over choosing the wrong path, believing she had messed up without believing that other chances – better chances – would come in the future.

'That's true,' Flora answered. 'But it's not *just* timing. Do you know what else it takes to be a success?'

Erin shrugged. 'Money? The alignment of the stars? Sacrificing a small animal?'

The look on Flora's face at the mention of the sacrifice of a small animal told Erin that her friend's sense of humour probably didn't run quite as darkly as hers did.

'I *am* joking,' she said quickly. 'No animals were hurt in the making of any of these plans.'

'I'm glad to hear it,' Flora replied. 'Blood sacrifices can be very messy.' She winked and Erin could not hold in the bubble of laughter that burst from her. 'Anyway,' Flora said, her face giving away just the hint of a smile, 'it's not about any of that. It's about courage. Now, excuse my language here, but it takes balls to do what you're doing. Just as it did for Libby to open the bookshop and Jo to start writing her novels. You young ones are blazing a trail.'

'You did your own share of trailblazing,' Erin replied. 'For you to take over the running of this place when you were just a young thing and shops were getting bombed out left, right and centre – now that was courage.'

Flora just shrugged. 'That was how it was, though. We just got on with things, because we had no choice.'

'I don't buy that. It was more than that. Maybe take a moment to think about how much courage getting on with things in such uncertain times took and give yourself some credit! Plus what you are doing now? Selling up, going travelling? It's a brave move too. You're an inspiration, Flora.'

Flora shook her head and turned away, making herself busy with wiping down one of the surfaces she had already cleaned. 'Maybe,' she said, with a little wobble in her voice and her back still turned towards Erin. 'Maybe I could do with a little more bravery though? Because I am scared, you know. I don't know who I am without this place and all the people in it.'

Erin noticed her shoulders were hunched and shaking just ever so slightly. She reached out and placed one hand very gently on Flora's shoulder. 'You'll still be the same wonderful you, just off having wonderful new adventures. Of course it's scary. But think of going to Australia and spending time with your son and his children. All that lovely sunshine too. You'll have the best time.'

Flora sniffed and turned back to Erin, just as she hastily wiped tears from her face. 'Can I tell you a secret?' she asked as she dabbed her eyes again. 'I hate flying and I hate the sunshine even more.'

24

A conversation like this required a pot of tea and a comfortable seat. Erin and Flora made the decision to cross the road to Once Upon a Book, where they could get both in the small coffee bar area Libby had set up. It was quiet in the shop – a few customers milled around leafing through books as they tried to decide what their next purchase would be. Two of the writers' spaces were in use by people frantically scribbling away, brows furrowed in concentration. Erin wondered what they were working on. A book? Some truly awful poetry? A history essay? Or were they just doom-scrolling Twitter or arranging their Tesco delivery?

She pulled her attention away from them and led Flora to the two comfy high-backed armchairs which sat facing each other in the cosy coffee nook. This was perhaps Erin's favourite part of the bookshop. The exposed brick walls, copper lights and shelves loaded with potted plants gave the space a New York loft living vibe, while the framed prints on the walls of the covers of local authors' books reminded Erin that she came from a place of great storytelling history. The print of the cover of Jo's first novel never failed to make her smile. She hoped Flora would find this as relaxing and inspiring a place as she did.

'Now, a wee pot of tea?' she asked.

'Actually, pet, could I get a latte with oat milk and an extra shot?' Flora replied, and Erin's eyes widened. That would teach her to be so presumptuous. 'You young ones aren't the only coffee addicts in the world,' Flora laughed. 'Or the only ones with mild lactose intolerances either. I'll spare you the details!'

'You're a gem,' Erin smiled, trying to banish the unbidden image of Flora's IBS from her head. 'One oat milk latte on the way.'

'With an extra shot,' Flora reminded her with a smile that was still a little uneven, as if hiding a wealth of unshed emotions.

'With an extra shot!' Erin repeated and nodded before she turned to go and order at the counter behind which Libby was seated, with a book open in front of her. It was clear, however, that she was deep in thought and not actually reading the words on the page.

Erin coughed lightly to get Libby's attention, and although the cough was quiet and genteel, it still managed to startle Libby, who gave a little jump before she blinked twice in rapid succession, pulling herself back into reality.

'Erin! Lovely to see you, and Flora too, of course. What can I get you?'

Erin recited her order, choosing a plain old cup of tea for herself.

'If you don't mind me saying so,' Libby whispered, and glanced once again at where Flora was staring into space, 'Flora doesn't quite look herself. Is everything okay?'

'A touch of cold feet, I think,' Erin said, as she remembered the older woman's expression as she'd admitted how much she hated flying and how she hated the sun even more. It unsettled her on a number of levels – most selfishly perhaps that it made her worry Flora could change her mind about her imminent retirement and revert to her earlier plan of working in the bakery until she dropped dead of old age over the treacle scones and was carried out.

Erin hoped for a suitably reassuring response to her worries from Libby – but Libby instead pulled a facial expression that directly mirrored the one Erin's internal fear demon was wearing. It screamed 'What if Flora backs out?'

The paperwork was well underway, but it hadn't been finalised yet. Nothing had been signed. No deposits paid. It didn't matter that a closing-down day for the bakery had been announced, or that plans were already underway for Flora's retirement party at The Ivy Inn. It didn't even matter that Erin had invested in building materials and had paid deposits to secure some handymen for the refurb of the flat. It was still possible it could all go tits up, even at this stage of proceedings.

'I'm sure everything will all work out and this is just a natural stage in the process. I mean, it's a big change for her,' Libby said, eventually, as she fumbled with Erin's change. 'And isn't it natural for everyone to have cold feet?' The uncertainly in her voice made Erin question whether or not it really was natural, but when Erin looked up and saw how pale Libby was, she wondered if Libby was a little off-kilter herself.

'Are *you* okay?' Erin asked. 'You seem a little off? Still feeling sick?' Though Libby hadn't been hitting her up for freshly buttered toast quite so often these days, she looked a little on the gaunt side and her skin and was pale.

'I'm not too bad with the sickness,' she said. 'The anti-emetics have been a lifesaver. I was just reading this book about birth, because forewarned is forearmed, but now I think I've made a terrible mistake in not waiting until they can beam the baby out of me, using some Star Trek-type technology. Do you know how big ten centimetres dilated actually is? Because it's big...'

'You poor thing!' Erin soothed, glad that it wasn't she who was facing the prospect of childbirth. 'Thousands of women do it every day, so it can't be that bad, can it? And there are drugs? Epidurals and whatnot?'

Libby nodded.

'And you get to meet your son or daughter at the end of it all. That will be amazing,' Erin said and was rewarded by a smile from Libby.

'It will be. I suppose I have to keep my eyes on the prize.'

'Attagirl!' Erin said. 'And if you have a girl, I have it on good authority that Erin is a lovely name!'

Libby laughed. 'I'll put it on the list, along with Paddy,' she said, as she set about preparing their drinks.

'Do you know when you'll be taking maternity leave? Do you have cover organised?' Erin asked.

'The baby is due in early January, so I'm hoping to get through the Christmas rush, but we'll see how it goes. No cover organised yet, but Jo has said she might be willing to take over for a bit. She knows the shop, and my picky ways, and she says she can write when it's quiet.'

'Sounds like it could work,' Erin said.

'It might. I don't think I'll be taking too much time off, but I'm lucky. Home is only up some stairs, so it should be relatively easy to combine a bit of work and mothering. Although I'm saying that as someone probably very naïve about what's involved in running a shop and parenting a newborn.'

'You should get a chat with Flora,' Erin suggested. 'She was just filling me in on how she managed working with raising her kids.'

'That's a great idea,' Libby said. 'She's some woman for one woman. So impressive!'

Erin looked over towards the chair where Flora was sat and she felt a prickle of fear run down her back. Please God she wouldn't let Flora, and Libby, Noah and Jo down by sinking the business.

'You are some woman for one woman too, you know. I absolutely believe that with every part of me,' Libby said, wincing just slightly – which sent a bolt of panic through Erin. Wincing couldn't be good, could it?

'Are you okay?' she asked.

Libby put her hand to her stomach and smiled warmly. 'I am. This little one was just letting me know that they believe in you too.'

Erin felt tears prick at her eyes, surprised at just how moved she felt at the thought of a foetus's made-up confidence in her. This baby was becoming more and more real, and while she had, of course, known Libby was expecting, it hadn't really seemed real until just then. 'You can feel the baby move?' she asked, eyes wide at the thought of a tiny little person wriggling around in her friend's tummy.

'Yes. I can. It's a bit too light just yet for anyone to feel from the outside. Noah is so eager to feel the baby kick and wiggle. I tell him that's only because he won't have to deal with being kicked square in the bladder,' Libby smiled, and the pallor of her face gave way to a light blush of contentment. 'For now, it's nice for me that I am the only one who can feel it. It's like our own wee secret bond,' Libby said. 'And it's reassuring to feel the baby move. It saves me from calling Jess every three seconds to beg her to call round to listen for the heartbeat.'

With Libby's oldest friend being a GP, Erin often felt sorry for poor Jess when she'd been brave enough to attend any get-together with the Ivy Lane gang. There was rarely a birthday party or barbecue that didn't turn into some sort of informal walk-in clinic for Jess, who would spend the duration of the proceedings looking at rashes, talking about knee pain or agreeing that you don't hear too much about gout these days. It always amazed Erin how a group of adults in their early thirties could suddenly morph into hypochondriac geriatrics at the mention of a doctor being in the building. It also amazed her how Jess didn't tell them all to stop annoying her. It takes a special kind of a person to have infinite patience with people showing her manky parts of their bodies. Nonetheless, Jess and Libby were as close as friends could be and Erin was sure Jess wouldn't mind supporting her friend for one moment.

'You're lucky to have Jess,' Erin said. 'I imagine it's quite terrifying trying to grow an entire new human being, even without being as sick as you have been, but as you said, nothing worthwhile is easy got.'

Libby placed Flora's coffee on the tray and smiled. 'It's true and I am lucky. Even when I am feeling truly rotten, I know that I'm lucky and pregnancy doesn't last forever. And this stress over buying the bakery won't last forever either – not for you, or Flora. I don't think there are a lot of people who find change easy. Especially big change and there's a lot of that about at the moment. Feels like we're all in a state of flux on the Lane right now, but I have faith it will all work out. Things have a habit of working out here.'

Erin smiled. There was no doubt that a chat with Libby always ended up being reassuring, and, of course, Libby was right. Things did have a way of working out on the Lane. It had been a lucky home for so many of its residents. Surely it was her time to have a bit of luck too? She just had to help that luck along its way and make Flora feel equally as reassured and happy that the big change she was about to make in her life was the right one.

'You must think I'm a silly old bat,' Flora said as she sipped from her coffee and sighed appreciatively.

'Hardly,' Erin said. 'That place has been yours most of your life. I'm emotionally invested in it and I don't even own it yet, so I can't imagine the strength of your bond to the place. It must feel like home.'

'It does that,' Flora said. 'I think maybe I took that for granted for the longest time. It's only now when it's all about to end that I realise just how much it means to me and the full impact it had on my life. I'll tell you something for nothing, there's nothing like the prospect of flying to the other side of the world to put things in perspective.'

'At least you'll see your Peter and his family? He must be so excited at the thought of you coming,' Erin said.

Flora smiled. 'He is. And those grandchildren of mine are excited too. Peter says they are all going to come home to visit while I'm there, so we can have a big get-together. They were still so young the last time I saw them. Apart from on that FaceTime thing.'

Erin couldn't help but notice how the smile on Flora's face grew wider when she spoke about her grandchildren, in much the same way it did when she spoke about the bakery.

'And when you're back, you'll always be welcome to come through my door and help out whenever you want,' Erin said with a smile. 'It will always be your home, you know, and I promise you I won't let you down when it comes to looking after it.'

'I know you won't,' Flora said, 'And if I haven't said it already, I'm really excited for you. I've every faith that you are going to do something remarkable.'

'Even though my bread rolls inevitably turn out like rocks and

I can't master a scone that doesn't taste stodgy?' Erin asked, one eyebrow raised.

'An afternoon in the kitchen with me and we'll have that sorted,' Flora said. 'Come over some day at closing time – that way we can work uninterrupted. Or come over in the mornings. I'm usually there for five. I'll tell you all my secrets.'

Erin was wowed once again. How did a woman of Flora's age keep on her feet for up to twelve hours at a time working in a busy kitchen and shop when Erin still had to haul herself out of bed every morning, drink a bucket of coffee, then stand under a cold shower to wake herself up? Even with those interventions, Erin still dreamed of a nap or maybe an early night most days and certainly on days when she didn't have to work that evening.

There'd be no such thing as days off when the pâtisserie opened, she thought. Certainly not at first. Erin knew initially she'd have to operate with a small staff until she was on a better financial footing, which would mean that her working day would extend well into the evenings too. She'd have to do the lion's share of the admin, and promotion at first – and although Libby and Noah had offered to help, and Lorcan had promised to build a website for her – she knew she was facing a very steep learning curve.

When she thought about that and still overseeing the kitchen at The Ivy Inn, she felt a mixture of excitement and sheer unadulterated terror. Thankfully, most of the time the excitement won, but sometimes the sheer unadulterated terror got the better of her.

She supposed that was what it must feel like for Flora when she thought of getting on a plane and flying to the other side of the world – hoping it all worked out.

'I'll come over one morning,' Erin told Flora. 'That way, you won't have to stay at work longer than you need to, and maybe I can even help you prepare for the day ahead.'

'First rule of business,' Flora said with a wink, 'Never ignore the offer of help! I'd be more than happy to have you as my glamorous assistant for the morning. The ladies who work with me are brilliant, but there is always room for more help.'

'It will be you that's helping me,' Erin reminded her. 'You're like my fairy godmother these days. If it wasn't for your generosity in accepting my offer, I wouldn't even be doing this.'

Flora shook her head. 'Nonsense,' she said. 'You'd have found a way. There's a determination in you, Erin. I recognise it from myself. I don't think you've let it out too much in recent years, but it's there now and it's that which is making this happen for you. Don't downplay your role in making this happen for yourself. Take that from an old lady who has seen a lot of things. We women are much too quick to put our success down to other people or play down our role in it. Men don't do that. Not as much. They claim it all. So don't feel bad about claiming your success for yourself. It's amazing what can happen for you if you just find a little inner bravery and let it out.'

Erin's chest constricted with unbridled affection for this incredible woman, who, in the space of just a few months, had treated her with more kindness and support than her own family ever had. It dawned on her that family was not always just the people who you were related to by birth, but it could be the people who chose to be in your life, and to show you love and support with no expectations. She had yet to hear from her own parents after walking out of their house when she'd had enough of their criticism. As far as she knew, they didn't even know about the bakery yet and she was happy for it to stay that way. She had people in her life who really did care about her.

'Jeez, Flora!' she said. 'You should be available on the NHS to boost people's morale and self-esteem.' It wasn't going to be easy for her to see this wonderful woman leave. And what if she decided to stay in Australia with her family? It would be great for Flora, of course – but there was no denying that Erin would miss her. That realisation hit hard. 'I'm going to miss you,' she blurted.

'Luckily for you, I'm not dying,' Flora said before she added, 'not that I know of anyway,' with a cheeky wink. 'You said I could call in any time to the bakery, and you know what, I might just take you up on that. You'll not have the chance to miss me!'

'I'm sure Harry will be just as happy as I am to hear that,' Erin said with a cheeky smile.

'Now you're just being silly,' Flora blushed.

'I am not!' Erin protested. 'There's a spark there, Flora. We've all seen it.'

Flora shook her head. 'Both of us are much too long in the tooth for that kind of nonsense. We care about each other, of course, but let's just stop any talk of sparks.'

Erin nodded in response but took note of the twinkle in Flora's eyes all the same and the seed of an idea started to grow in her mind.

25

―――――

'Harold,' Erin said as she walked into the shop and spotted Harry perched on his usual spot behind the counter. 'How are you today?'

'Well, young Erin, I'm still alive, so I'll take that as a positive thing,' Harry said with a smile, and of course a little grimace as he stood up. 'I creak a bit, though. Need to oil the old joints.'

'You need to stop living on sausage rolls and hot buttered toast,' a voice from the stockroom shouted before Lorcan walked into the shop with a stern expression. 'Some vegetables wouldn't do your joints any harm, Grandad. Nor your heart!'

'At the age of me, what do I need to be worrying about my heart for? I'll not be around for much longer anyway,' Harry said, his face a picture of misery.

'You off on your travels too, Harry?' Erin asked, familiar enough with Harry to know when he was playing the sympathy card.

'Aye,' Harry said. 'The ultimate trip. One-way ticket. Once you check in you can never leave.'

'The Hotel California doesn't want you, Grandad,' Lorcan said with a wry shake of the head.

'It's not the Hotel California I'm talking about, son,' Harry replied, his mouth turned downwards in an exaggerated manner which reminded Erin of when Clara was desperate to get her own way over something so would bring out the big guns. All Harry was missing was the puppy dog eyes. 'I mean the afterlife. Be it heaven or be it hell, I don't know where God will send me, but I won't be sat here on this chair any more and that's for sure.'

If Harry was hoping his words would engender sympathy and reassurance from Lorcan or Erin, he was very much mistaken.

'You'll outlive us all, Grandad,' Lorcan said. 'So I don't want any more of your nonsense.'

'Harry, you can't go anywhere,' Erin added. 'We need you here.'

'And I've already told you, I need you to be my best man when I get round to marrying Jo,' Lorcan said.

'Aye, you did tell me that,' Harry replied. 'And it would do an old man's heart good to stand beside you on your big day, but what I'm saying to you now, sunshine, is that you'd need to get the finger out and actually do the asking. It's time for you to settle down and start a family.'

'Well, you need to stick around then,' Lorcan said. 'I will do the asking, and I'll even start on the wedding plans, but it will be a while yet before there are babies in the picture, and if and when they do come along, I'd really like them to get to know you – and know you for as long a time as possible. Which brings me back to my first point. Less sausage rolls and buttery toast and more fruit and veg. It's not like we don't make you a dinner every night or invite you down to the bar to eat some of Erin's fine cooking.'

Harry nodded. 'Ach, I know. And I'm very grateful, but I don't like being a burden on you young ones.'

'But, Harry, you're not a burden on anyone!' Erin insisted. 'We love you.'

Harry beamed, his whole face illuminated by the brightest of smiles. 'See that, son,' he said to Lorcan. 'The ladies love me! Even this fine young woman here. Now, if only I was a bit younger...'

'A bit?' Lorcan snorted.

'Aye, well, more than a bit maybe,' Harry said, his smile still broad. 'Or if young Erin here was a bit older. She'd be the perfect woman for me. A beautiful Irish colleen!'

'Oh Harry, you romantic old devil,' Erin teased, as she enjoyed their playful banter. 'It's not often a man tells me I'm beautiful. I am delighted!'

'And so you should be!' Harry said with a smile. 'And you've a good heart too. You're right, I don't want to miss out on the big wedding, or any great-grand babies when they come. Not to put any pressure on you, Lorcan, but I'd like to meet them when I can still hold them and only one of the pair of us needs to wear a nappy.'

Lorcan laughed. 'Fair point, Grandad. Sure I'll talk to Jo. Just as soon as I'm done proposing to her.' He turned his head to look at Erin. 'Are you still okay to come ring-shopping with me tomorrow?'

'I'm looking forward to it,' Erin said. She enjoyed a good mooch around the jewellery shops, even if she wasn't buying something for herself. She would, after all, be helping the love of her best friend's life and that would be an incredible honour in itself. Jo loved Lorcan so deeply, and so deserved to have her own happy ever after that Erin was sure she could handle not being the recipient of any bling herself.

Lorcan smiled brightly. 'I'm nervous,' he said. 'But excited.'

'Why on earth are you going shopping for a ring?' Harry interrupted and neither Erin nor Lorcan could hide the look of confusion from their faces. Surely, Erin thought, Harry wasn't in the process of losing his marbles. She hadn't noticed any other signs that would cause her to worry Harry was heading into his dotage.

'So that I can propose to Jo...' Lorcan said, slowly. 'You know, like we've talked about a hundred times over the last couple of weeks?'

Harry rolled his eyes. 'I know that,' he said. 'I'm old, not senile! What I mean is, why are you shopping for a ring when I have a perfectly good ring here that you can use.'

Erin felt her breath leave her body as it started to dawn on her just what Harry was getting at.

Lorcan, it seemed, was not so quick on the uptake. 'Grandad, I love you and I'm very grateful that you would part with one of your rings. Your generosity is amazing, but I really want to get her something truly special.'

'This is truly special,' Harry replied, his brow furrowed. 'I wouldn't want anything less than that for you or Jo. Do you think this is one of those times where I'm pawning off something that's past its best just to get rid of it? I know you young ones laugh at me for doing that in the shop.'

'We don't laugh,' Erin said. 'We love it. It's one of our favourite quirks.'

'Except when you do it with in-date milk that smells a big strange,' Lorcan added.

'Nothing wrong with milk that's not fully gone – cook it into something and you won't even taste it,' Harry said, his poise defensive. 'But, look, I know that I can be a gruff old bugger at times and so I didn't know how to do this. And I'll try not to be offended if you say no, but I picked it up earlier today. I wanted to get it cleaned and polished up a bit first.'

Erin looked on, felt tears prick in her eyes and was instantly annoyed with herself for coming over all emotional once again.

'I know it might not be to the taste of young women these days, but if you want to use it, I'd be very honoured. As would your granny. This was the start of our happy ever after. She was my big love, and my best friend. I've a feeling that's how you see your Jo and I can see that's how she feels about you.'

Erin felt as if she was an intruder on what should have been a very private moment and yet she absolutely was not going to look away or leave Harry and Lorcan to have their touching moment alone. Her heart thudded in her chest as Harry opened a small blue velvet box and presented the most exquisite engagement ring she had ever laid eyes on to Lorcan for his approval.

She couldn't help but gasp. There it sat, a sparkling emerald-cut diamond, set between two slender matching marquise cut stones on a white gold band that had been buffed and polished to within an inch of its life.

'I had the gold dipped again,' Harry said, a trace of pride in his voice. 'So it looks like new, even though it isn't. I promise there is a lot of love in that little band.'

Transfixed by how the light caught the diamonds and reflected their glimmer back into the room, Erin had to fight the urge to shout that she'd take it. For that ring, she wouldn't care about the age gap between herself and Harry. It would be a straight 'yes, thank you, I will marry you' from her – at least until the diamond drunkenness wore off. What she did know for sure, though, was that Jo would adore it. She'd not only love the beauty of the ring itself because it was absolutely bloody gorgeous, but she'd be touched beyond words that this ring came from Harry, and his much beloved wife.

Erin's eyes flicked to Lorcan as she willed him to love it just as much as she did. It was obvious how much it would mean to Harry if Lorcan said yes, and yet Lorcan seemed frozen to the spot, his face caught in an expression Erin couldn't quite identify.

'Well?' Harry said. 'This is a nerve-shredder.'

'I'm sorry,' Lorcan said and Erin felt as if she might just throw up and die right there at the end of the biscuit aisle. Cardiac arrest amid the custard creams. She'd want that put on her gravestone.

'Well, I...' Harry started.

'I just needed a moment,' Lorcan interjected and his voice wobbled. 'It's beautiful, Grandad. And perfect. So perfect. Are you sure?' Lorcan reached out and took the box to examine the ring closer.

'Well, what good is it doing me just sitting in a drawer? Your granny loved that ring. It was the first piece of fancy jewellery she owned and she wore it every day of her life. I don't think she ever took it off. I would've buried it with her, but she promised me I would take it and give it someone truly in love who would appreciate it.'

Any attempt not to cry was abandoned as Erin felt hot, salty tears course down her face. She didn't feel too embarrassed though, as she couldn't help but notice that Harry and Lorcan were both crying too.

What Mrs Grant from down the road thought as she walked through the door to grab a carton of milk and saw the three of them openly weeping was anyone's guess.

26

Erin no longer missed Aaron, but she did miss the idea of him. The idea of having someone waiting for her at home who she could share her day with. She missed the different energy that came with knowing she wasn't alone in the flat. That day, she missed having someone to curl up beside and regale with the story of Harry and Lorcan and the most beautiful engagement ring in the world. She missed making dinner while drinking wine and chatting about her plans and about her conversation with Flora.

But, she realised, it was not Aaron that she missed. She just missed having someone. There was so much running through her head that she wanted to talk it all out with someone she trusted not to start yawning ten minutes in. She wanted someone who would share in her excitement and who would make suggestions with as much enthusiasm as she felt. She missed having someone who would make her a cup of tea and tell her she was loved.

But she did her best to hang on to Flora's words about her being brave and bold as she made her own dinner. And she tried to think about how beautiful Lorcan's proposal would be to Jo. And how cute Libby and Noah's baby would be. There were so many good things in the world which weren't reliant on her having a man by her side – especially not one like Aaron, who had clearly already moved on to his own bit on the side.

Erin poured a glass of perfectly chilled Pinot Grigio and asked Alexa to play her favourite song from her favourite singer. She let the soulful sound of Foy Vance's deep and melodic voice wash over her, as she sang along about finding her way in life with the help of her friends. A simple dish of *pasta aglio e olio* with a sprinkle of chilli flakes made for a very simple, yet tasty meal for one and instead of slipping into a painful reverie about her single status, she took out her notebook and started scribbling more ideas – ideas for the perfect engagement party for two of her very best friends.

For a start, she didn't even have a name for her new business and she would really need to get a move on with putting together the marketing and design package if she wanted everything to be in place by opening night. She wanted the shop to look as beautiful as the food she would sell in it would taste.

With about four weeks left until the sale completed, everything was starting to ramp up a gear. Once the shop had been signed over, the plan was to close for a month to facilitate the refit before opening again in mid-October.

So, it was time to stop faffing around, and to finally choose a name for the shop. Inspiration was thin on the ground, though, and she was starting to worry she'd end up calling it something deeply uninspiring like 'The Bakery' – which, while functional, didn't exactly exude the artisanal vibes she was hoping for. Maybe she should take Aaron's smug lead and call it The Gentrified Bread Shoppe of Old Ivy Lane, she thought with a wry grin. Or maybe not.

With the aid of Google, she scribbled down name ideas from the sublime (Baked to Perfection) to the ridiculous (Huge Baps) and every pun she could think of (Dough My Dear and Roll With It). She remembered her conversation with Flora earlier. There was no doubt in her mind that Flora was genuinely sad to be leaving the bakery behind, but Erin was determined she would stay true to her word and make sure the pâtisserie would always be a home for Flora.

That's when she recalled the idea she'd had earlier as they had chatted in the bookshop. She wrote down the name that had popped into her mind and looked at it. Grabbing her laptop, she typed it several times in different fonts and tried to imagine what it could look like on the signage outside of the shop. She imagined the exterior with a fresh coat of paint, window boxes and a sandwich board complete with details of special offers, or inspiring quotes about cakes. The name which had come to mind would be absolutely perfect.

With the name chosen, Erin was able to send it to Lorcan, who had a designer pal only too happy to come up with branding ideas. There was signage of course, but also pâtisserie boxes, aprons for her staff and promotional literature to be worked on. Erin knew she would have quite the task bringing it all in on budget, but she'd figured the best way to work it out would be to write down her 'dream' list and then edit it.

By the time she went to bed, there were five different lists in five different notebooks scattered on the living-room floor, along with a three-quarters empty bottle of wine and her dirty pasta dishes. She was too tired and too tipsy to care as she got up, stretched and wandered through to bed, not even bothering to change out of her clothes before face-planting on top of her duvet and falling asleep.

Whether it was the wine, or the full moon which shone

through her still open curtains, she didn't know, but her dreams that night were vivid and varied as her subconscious cycled through every possible disastrous outcome for her new venture – and a few hugely successful but highly implausible ones too.

When Erin woke just after six, she felt as tired as she had the night before and her head was thumping. But despite that, her overwhelming feeling was of excitement and hope for her future. It was a gift, she thought, to be able to secure her very own shop on the Lane and she vowed to follow the tradition laid down by her fellow business owners and planned to bring as much extra joy to their wee part of Derry city as she could.

As she stood under the shower and let the cool water wake her up, she launched into another refrain of Foy Vance's 'Closed Hand Full Of Friends' – one of her favourite songs. As she lathered and rinsed her hair, she thought of all the people on the Lane – the people she truly thought of as friends, and even family. On that August morning, under water so cold it bit at her skin and made her feel alive, she felt as if a perfect clarity ran through her. All the conversations she'd had, all the dreams she'd talked about, all the history of the street and the future of its residents bounced around in her head and an idea of how to celebrate all that was good in her world started to form.

Of course, if she was going to pull all this off, then she was going to need help. She'd need to push her luck and ask her friends for even more favours, but she was as sure as sure could be that once she explained what exactly she had in mind, none of them would object to helping.

Switching off the cold water before hypothermia set in, Erin jumped out of the shower and roughly towelled herself dry. She dressed, sleeked some serum through her hair to smooth her curls and grabbed her sunglasses. She felt an extra spring in her step as she, along with her five notebooks, made their way towards Ivy Lane.

Before she'd left her flat, she had sent a text to Lorcan, Jo, Libby and Noah with the request they all meet for a chat in the snug at the Inn that afternoon. It was time to start plotting...

27

'So,' Lorcan said as he looked Erin directly in the eye. 'You think we should set Flora and Grandad up. Romantically?'

'Yes,' Erin nodded. 'Isn't it obvious that they'd make a good pair?'

'Well, of course it is,' Lorcan said. 'But I'm not sure he's open to starting a new romance. I wish he was – because he deserves to be happy. Both of them are old, you know, and very stuck in their ways. I know we tease him about it, but at the end of the day, I think maybe romance is behind them.'

'Excuse me,' Libby chimed in. 'Don't you think old people can fall in love? I'd like to think that Noah and I will still be falling a little in love with each other every day in our seventies.'

Erin noticed how Libby glanced at her husband and he smiled back at her.

'Of course we will,' Noah said.

'Urrgh, get a room you two!' Jo teased.

'Don't be such a grump, Jo,' Noah laughed back. 'I'm sure you and Lorcan here have similar goals.'

Erin looked at Lorcan and watched him blush. Of course they

had similar goals. Lorcan was just trying to think of the perfect way to pop the question.

'Yes, if I don't scare him away with how much of a demon I become every time a book is due in,' Jo said and Erin noticed how frazzled she looked. It was less than a week until Jo's deadline and she had entered her wild-eyed and manic stage of writing.

'Not possible,' Lorcan said, reassuringly. 'It's a good thing I don't scare easy.'

Determined to pull the conversation back to the matter in hand, not least because the declarations of love in front of her were making her feel a little sad and a lot single, Erin cleared her throat. 'Lovely and all as this is,' she said, 'we're here to discuss how we can make Harry and Flora realise they have feelings for each other before Flora retires and we don't see her as much. The clock is ticking. We're less than four weeks from Wee Buns closing its doors, and Flora's retirement dinner.'

'And you're sure they do have feelings for one another?' Noah asked.

'Of course they do!' Libby said. 'Have you not noticed how Harry always seems to carry himself a little taller when Flora is around?'

'And how he adopts his best posh voice, just like the one he uses on the phone?' Jo added.

'He makes sure she gets all the best unsold flowers,' Lorcan said. 'A week ago, I noticed he brought her a bunch up and they were only fresh in from the supplier the day before. Not a wilted petal near them.'

'If that isn't proof he has feelings for her, then I don't know what is,' Erin said.

'And Flora?' Noah asked.

'Well, she hasn't said it outright,' Erin replied, 'but I feel it. I've spent a fair amount of time with her these past few weeks and there's no doubt there's a bigger smile on her face when she talks about him, and when she talks about leaving the Lane and missing the people here... well, she always nods in the direction of the shop. I don't even think she realises she does it.'

'The only problem is,' Libby said, as she stretched in her seat and stroked her burgeoning bump, 'Flora's going to Australia, so there's not much point in setting them up for some big romance when she's on the next plane out of here. We don't want to break poor Harry's heart.'

But Erin knew that Flora was only planning to go to Australia for a month. She'd declared herself to be a Derry woman through and through and said there was nowhere on earth she would rather live out her twilight years than on the banks of the River Foyle. 'Australia might have the Sydney Opera House and Uluru, but they don't have the Donegal hills or the Peace Bridge,' Flora had told her recently. And that was without taking into consideration the fact that Flora hated the sun, the heat and anything that resembled non typically Irish weather. 'Turkey on the beach on Christmas Day? Not a mission!' Flora had said, before she confessed she'd done the Christmas Day swim at Lisfannon one year and it had taken four shots of whiskey afterwards to warm her up. 'God knows what kind of dinner I served up that day. I was off my trolley while I was cooking. I think the wains abandoned the table halfway through the main course and thankfully, I was too giddy and delighted with myself to be annoyed about it,' Flora had laughed.

'She's not planning to stay there,' Erin told her friends. 'To be honest, she's not that keen on going in the first place. Poor woman is terrified of flying – and travelling all that way on her own has her weak with nerves. She told me she's going to ask her doctor for a few diazepam to calm her down.'

'Not that keen on going?' Lorcan asked. 'God, all Grandad

talks about these days is how he hasn't seen enough of the world. I think Flora's news has given him itchy feet. He says he'd love to go to Australia.'

Erin raised an eyebrow. It couldn't be that easy, could it? Would it be weird to suggest it? She noticed Lorcan was looking directly at her and she could tell by the expression on his face that he was on a similar wavelength.

'You don't think...' Lorcan began.

'Harry and Flora...' Erin continued.

'Together? To Australia? As travel companions?' Lorcan asked.

'It's worth suggesting, isn't it?' Erin said.

'But if Flora is going to stay with her son, would it not be awkward for Grandad to go along?' Lorcan said, his face falling.

He had a point. Erin didn't know Flora's son, Peter, and had no idea how he would feel if Harry landed on his doorstep too. There had to be a solution, though – especially since Flora had already said she was nervous about travelling on her own.

'Not if we book a hotel for Harry?' Libby said. 'And maybe some excursions? There's bound to be coach trips or sightseeing expeditions. We could suggest some options to Harry that would let Flora get the time with her family that she wants while Harry gets to see some of the big tourist attractions? They might even want to do some things together?'

Erin nodded. 'Absolutely. We don't want to hijack her big holiday – even if she has said she's terrified of travelling alone. And I really think it would be wise to have a little chat with her first, just to see what she thinks?'

'It could be risky,' Noah said. 'I don't mean to be a party pooper, but are we sure the two of them like each other enough – even as friends – to want to spend the better part of twenty-four hours sat together on a plane? That would test any friendship.'

'It is risky,' Erin agreed. 'But when has something being risky ever stopped any of us from giving it a go. Isn't that what we do on the Lane? We take risks and hope for the best. You've said it yourself that we all benefit from moving outside of our comfort zones. It could be the best thing we do for them.' She was impressed by her motivational speaker-like take on the issue. 'Obviously we get them on side. I'm not going to bundle Harry into a van and sneak him onto a plane or anything. But if we don't take this risk for them, then they will more than likely never take it themselves.'

'There's nothing to lose, in fairness,' Jo said with a shrug.

'Okay, so, if that's the case, we better get working on it then,' Erin said. 'Let's figure out how to make these two realise they have feelings for each other, and let's set Harry off on the holiday of a lifetime.'

'And then let's make sure we get them both home again,' Lorcan nodded.

'Well, that's the plan,' Erin agreed. 'No one gets left behind. So where do we start?'

'You've the closest relationship with Flora,' Noah said. 'So maybe you talk to her. Don't sell it as a dastardly scheme to get them to admit their feelings for one another, but just a way for her to have a travel companion by her side.'

'And I'll sow a few seeds with Grandad,' Lorcan said. 'I know he loves the shop, and the Lane, but I'd love it if he would at least once in his life leave Ireland. He's never been as far as England, never mind anywhere more exotic.'

'We'll have to see what we can do about that,' Erin said, and she added the grand plan to the list of things she would need to do over the coming weeks.

28

'Prey tell, boss, what has you in such high spirits today? More news to do with the pâtisserie?' Paul asked as they sat opposite each other discussing the menu plan for a private function the following week.

Erin felt positively giddy at the thought that Harry could keep Flora company on her trip, but she also felt positively terrified at the thought of discussing it with Flora. She didn't realise, however, that her feelings were displayed so obviously across her face.

'No, nothing pâtisserie related,' she said. 'Everything there is just progressing as it has been. This is much sneakier,' she smiled.

'I do enjoy a bit of subterfuge,' Paul said. 'Care to share your secret? I am very trustworthy, as it happens.'

'I'm sure you are,' Erin smiled. 'But are you a romantic at heart?' If she wasn't mistaken Paul blushed a little in response.

'There's a question,' Paul said. 'As it happens, I am.' Erin realised Paul never really spoke about his romantic life to her. As his boss, she never felt it appropriate to pry. Her staff could tell her whatever they felt comfortable with on their own terms. She supposed she'd always just assumed he had women on the go. The odd name was mentioned now and then for a few weeks and then he seemed to move on. It hadn't been any concern of hers.

'That's good to know,' she said. 'I can tell you of our secret plans to play matchmaker for two of the Lane's favourite people.' He smiled, put down his pen to signal a break in work and listened as Erin outlined her hopes for Harry and Flora.

She told him she hoped Flora wouldn't be annoyed at the suggestion that her neighbour from down the street could be her plus-one on her once-in-a-lifetime trip. Or that the hope was that their trip together would bring them both to the realisation that their friendship was not entirely platonic. Both deserved to be happy and if they could be happy together, that would be ideal.

'I think it's perfect,' he said. 'And I don't think she'll be annoyed at all. They're friends, it's not that unthinkable they would travel together. I love that it could possibly lead to a little romance too. Everyone deserves a happy ever after.'

'That's true,' Erin said. 'Not everyone gets one though. Some of them get Aaron instead. My happy never after.' She laughed but it was a little brittle. All she wanted was someone to look at her the way Harry looked at Flora. Someone to bring her slightly wilted flowers and who knew the best and worst of her.

'You can't possibly say that,' Paul said. 'You're what? In your late twenties?'

'Early thirties as it happens, but I'm happy to go with your estimate,' she smiled.

'And Flora is in her seventies. You've a lot of time to find love,' Paul said. 'It might even be right under your nose but you just haven't noticed yet?'

Erin raised an eyebrow. Was he hinting at something? No. Surely not.

'There's Harry and Flora – and by the sounds of it neither of them aware that they have someone in love with them all this time. So don't be writing yourself off as a spinster of the parish just yet,' Paul said with a smile before directing their conversation back to the function which still needed to be planned.

As she cleared up later that day, Erin came to the realisation that she had to have her big chat with Flora sooner rather than later. There needed to be enough time to plan the trip properly and, it turned out, to get Harry a passport. In all his seventy-seven years, he had never had the need for one, and they'd have to move quickly to make sure they had enough time for an application to be processed. And there would need to be shopping done for suitable clothes, time devoted to planning the excursions and making sure his travel insurance was up to scratch. Erin dreaded to think how much that would cost, but she had been assured that due to his frugal nature, Harry had more than enough in savings to cover a voyage into space with Elon Musk, never mind a trip to Australia. Although she was pretty sure Lorcan was exaggerating just a little.

She decided that she would chat with Flora about it when she went to Wee Buns for her first bread-making masterclass.

It was after five in the afternoon and the bakery was closed and all Flora's staff had gone home. Erin paused as she stood outside the front door and read the sign in the window.

All good things.

Dear Customers and Friends,

We are sad to announce that we will be closing the doors at Wee Buns for the last time on 14 September.

It is finally time for me to hang up my apron and retire.

Thank you for your loyalty, your custom and your laughter through all our years on Ivy Lane. We hope you will support our successor in due course!

Much love,
Flora & Staff

Erin felt a lump in her throat, and an enormous sense of responsibility to live up to Flora's legacy. The first step of that, of course, was to master the art of the bread roll – not that she anticipated the pâtisserie having much call for bread rolls. Still, it had always annoyed her that she could construct great works of delicious art but couldn't master this basic.

She was no sooner in the door than Flora had handed her an apron and told her the key to good bread was in the 'knocking back'. Of course, this could be done by machine, especially on big orders, but Flora said she always found it deeply satisfying to do it by hand. It was the perfect way to get rid of all her stress. 'We didn't need fancy boxing exercise classes in my day. We just did this for an hour in the morning and that kept the bingo wings at bay.'

Knocking back, of course, was the process of punching and pummelling proven dough to disperse air bubbles and create a smoother texture in the final bake. Flora slapped two mounds of wet dough on the workbench and showed Erin her technique for pounding and stretching the dough over and over on top of itself.

'Just a fine dusting of flour on your hands,' Flora said, as Erin hung on her every word.

Flora was right that it was very satisfying to punch the dough and think of the faces of your enemies. Erin had dislodged a particularly big air bubble while thinking of the blonde in the toilet who had mocked her appearance. She now knew that the blonde was called Marnie, and she worked alongside Aaron. He was such a cliché, it was almost laughable. But instead of laughing, she punched another dough ball until she felt better.

Having underestimated just how physical it was to knock back twenty loaves of bread, Erin sat and took a cool drink of water while her arms ached. That Flora, at more than twice Erin's age, did this and more every day – and never complained of aches and pains – was beyond impressive. The older woman must have guns of steel, Erin thought, and it was no wonder she was ready for retirement.

'The process of making bread isn't quick and nor should it be. The second prove is where the magic happens,' Flora said. 'But it happens overnight. You can come back in the morning when I'm baking them if you want?'

'I'd like that,' Erin agreed. 'It would be nice to see the whole process through. But since I'm here right now, would you mind if we had a quick chat?' She felt nervous about the conversation they were about to have, but she knew she wouldn't get many better moments than this.

'Of course I don't mind, pet. Sure, I always have time to chat to you. Are you okay? Is there something wrong with the sale? Or is it boy trouble? I don't judge, you know,' Flora said, as she sat on a stool beside Erin with her own glass of water.

'Look, please don't be cross...' Erin began, and her stomach clenched just a little. She hoped this would go well.

Flora pulled a face. 'I'm not sure anything good ever starts with don't be cross,' she said.

'It's not something bad,' Erin insisted. 'It's just an idea. And please don't feel under pressure or in any way obligated at all. But it's Harry, you see.'

'Harry?' Flora asked, her eyes immediately wide with concern. Her hand flew to her chest. 'Is he okay? God bless us, and save us, he's not ill, is he? You'd tell me. You'd not let me get on a plane to the other side of the world if he was ill!' The emotion which flooded Flora's voice and which was written all over her face proved to Erin that Flora was indeed very fond of Harry.

'Oh God, no. No. He's fine. I didn't mean to worry you!' Erin said.

Flora made a sign of the cross and looked skyward. 'Thank God for that. I know he's a narky old curmudgeon but... you know...'

'You care about him?' Erin asked.

Flora's face blushed pink. 'I do. Very much. I think him being here on the Lane was part of the reason I kept this place open so long. We have our own little routine and I don't expect you young ones to really understand, but we've been such a big part of each other's lives for a very long time,' she said and there was a shake to her voice. 'So, you're telling the truth when you tell me he is okay? Because it would be cruel to keep it from me if he was sick.'

'Honestly, Flora. He's fine. Actually, he's been talking to Lorcan about how he wishes he had seen more of the world, you know. How he admires you for taking off to Australia and it's somewhere he always dreamed of going. And look, I was just thinking, you told me you are terrified of travelling on your own and we – well, me and Noah and Libby and Jo and Lorcan – wondered if it would be worth suggesting to the pair of you that you go together? Now, Harry knows nothing about this, so there's no harm if you think that's a bad idea. And we thought we could book some excursions for Harry while he was there, and of course he would stay in a hotel, and we'd have that all arranged, but maybe you could be a bit of company for each other if you weren't totally tied up with all your family business.'

Flora didn't speak for what felt like forever, but which was probably no longer than about five seconds. Unable to read the expression on her face, Erin started to panic that she had made a dreadful mistake. Had she got this all wrong?

'I like it,' she said. 'I think that's a brilliant idea and not just because I won't have to travel on my own, but because I was actually a little worried my family would drive me insane if I spent too much time with them.' She let out a girlish giggle, and if Erin wasn't mistaken, that was a sign there was another reason Flora was a fan of the suggestion.

'And it's always nice to have someone to hold hands with in all the holiday snaps?' Erin said, with a little smile, as the tension started to leave her body. She had been right all along.

'It is,' said Flora, and she took a long drink from her water. 'I'm a little flustered,' she added and giggled again, whilst Erin basked in the warm and fuzzy feeling that was growing inside her.

* * *

'You seem to be in great form,' Paul remarked as Erin found herself humming 'Waltzing Matilda' as she cleaned up after service that night.

'That's because I *am* in great form,' she told him, realising that it was true. That realisation was enough to make her smile a little brighter.

'Anything in particular responsible for your sunny disposition?' Paul asked. 'Not that I'm knocking it. It's good to see you in a good mood, even if I could do without the singing.'

She threw a drying cloth at him. 'There's nothing wrong with my singing voice. I'll have you know I won a bronze medal in the Derry Feis when I was at primary school for my singing.' That there were only three people in the competition was neither here nor there, she thought and decided to keep that to herself.

'I didn't realise I was working with a full-on singing superstar,' Paul teased. 'She cooks, she sings, she does a really bad Australian accent. Is there no end to your talents?'

'Of course not,' she said. 'I just keep them hidden because I don't want you all to feel inferior!'

'That's very altruistic of you,' Paul laughed, and Erin realised she was going to miss the easy banter she had with him when she moved to the pâtisserie.

'It really is. You guys are going to miss me when I'm not here all the time watching over you,' she said.

'We will, you know,' he said, but his tone was not the playful teasing of just seconds before and there was something in the way he looked at her, his chocolate brown eyes staring intently in her direction, that made her feel a little funny. In a good way. In a 'how have I not noticed this man is really quite hot' kind of a way. Was it possible he was flirting with her? Or was this the way he'd always spoken to her, and always looked at her?

Determined to keep her focus, Erin pushed aside her inappropriate thoughts and settled herself. 'Well, it's a good thing I'm not leaving altogether. I'll still be lurking around and calling in when you least expect it. As head chef, you'll have to run any proposed menu changes or adaptions past me first.'

'Head chef?' he said. 'You want me to be head chef?'

Erin blinked. Had she not made her intention obvious? Clearly not.

'Unless you don't want the position? But I think you'd be the perfect person to step up, and Noah and Jo happen to agree.'

'Are you taking the piss?' Paul asked, rubbing the stubble on his chin. 'You want me to step up? Here?'

Erin couldn't deny she was somewhat taken aback by his response. It wasn't what she had been expecting. She didn't think he would fall to his knees in gratitude, but the 'are you taking the piss?' was a bit too much in the other direction.

'Why would I be taking the piss?' she asked, her stomach now in knots. 'I thought you liked it here. And you've said you wanted to move up some day. Is it because I would still have final veto on the menu? Because you will get a say in how things operate.'

There was a pause while she tried desperately to read his expression. 'If it's not what you want, if you want to stay as sous or move on somewhere else, I understand.' Even though the truth was that she did not understand.

Paul started to shake his head slowly. 'No. No,' he said and the knot in her stomach tightened further. Would she have to start recruiting someone else now on top of everything else?

'I, uhh, didn't mean "taking the piss" in a bad way,' Paul said, 'more in a that-would-be-absolutely-epic kind of a way. I just wasn't expecting that.' He grinned, and the rush of adrenaline that had flooded Erin's body over the course of the last few minutes left her feeling giddy with relief.

'So you want it?' she asked.

His smile narrowed, his dark eyes flashed with something a little darker that went straight to her core.

'Oh,' he said. 'I do want it.'

29

'Noooooooo!' Jo said, her eyes wide. If she had been wearing pearls, Erin had no doubt that she would have clutched them tightly to her chest in mock horror.

'Yes!' Erin replied. 'Well, I think so. I mean I have been out of the dating pool for a couple of years, but I'm pretty sure this look' – she did her best to adopt the same smouldering expression Paul had worn the night before – 'and 'Oh, I want it' indicated some sort of nefarious intent.'

'But he didn't actually make a move on you?' Jo asked. The pair were in Jo's kitchen, where Jo had just made them each a cup of coffee. Erin had sliced and buttered two fruit scones and was now tidying up – her nervous energy forcing her to keep moving.

With her back to Jo, Erin felt her face redden as she remembered the sense of confusion that had washed over her when Paul had looked at her with longing and when she had finally realised it wasn't the first time he had looked at her that way. She'd just been too tied up in her relationship with Aaron, and then with opening the new business, to really take notice of it.

But as she had stood in front of him, his eyes locked on hers, she felt as if she were seeing him properly for the first time. Her heart had started to thud and, to her surprise, her stomach had tightened in lustful anticipation – before she had pulled herself together and moved to get herself out of the kitchen as quickly as possible. Without any sneaky snogging – even though she had wanted to – really wanted to.

She shook her head and Jo groaned. 'And this was Paul? Our Paul? Who you've worked with for the best part of three years and never once expressed any sort of interest in at all?'

'The very one,' Erin said. 'I've honestly never had any interest in him before. Aaron and I were together all that time – I didn't look at any other man in that way. Except that Scottish actor in *Outlander*.'

'Hmmm, he could call me Sassanach any day of the week and even though I'm Irish, I'd let him,' Jo said with a grin.

'I called him first,' Erin laughed. 'But look, maybe I read it wrong with Paul. Maybe I was just in a romantic frame of mind thinking of Harry and Flora jetting off into the sunset. And Paul might have just been buzzing at his promotion and not actually giving me the sexy eyes. But his voice had a definite kind of Christian Grey tone to it. Anyway, I will never know because I pretty much bolted and left him to lock up,' Erin said, as she slouched onto her chair. 'And now I'm worried that work is going to be hella awkward today. All that weird tension.'

Jo sighed. 'Ah, the weird tension stage. I kind of miss that. I mean, obviously it is hell on earth, but also the possibilities are endless, and you get that constant buzzy feeling in the pit of your stomach and the overwhelming horn.'

Erin's eyes widened. It was her turn to look as though she might clutch some imaginary pearls.

Jo simply laughed. 'Don't try to deny it. It's intoxicating – that crazy lust-fuelled stage. C'mon! I love Lorcan with all of my heart and I still find him outrageously sexy...'

'Vom!' Erin interjected.

'Let me finish and less of that vom carry-on. Anyway, I still find him outrageously sexy, but I do miss that insane animal lust that comes at the start of a relationship. You know, when you can barely keep your hands off each other and you don't even mind keeping your legs shaved just in case because you want each other so bad?'

'We're not at that stage though,' Erin said. 'There is no relationship. There's just a possible lustful glance over the pots. And, actually, I don't know if I ever want to be at that stage, you know, in a relationship, at all. And it's Paul! I've never thought of him like that, before now.'

'Before now,' Jo said. 'Because by the way your face has turned scarlet, I'm pretty sure you've thought about him in that way since your special moment last night.'

Erin would have been lying if she had denied this and Jo could always, *always* tell when Erin was lying. 'I plead the fifth,' she told her friend and took a huge bite of her scone so that she was unable to say anything more. But yes, she had thought of him in that way. She'd been unable to get his look of longing out of her head and her mind kept wandering to the fullness of his lips.

'Look, it doesn't have to be that big of a deal,' Jo said, pulling her back to reality. 'You won't be working together as much any more so that will help if it's a road you don't want to go down. And if he was just buzzing about his promotion, then I'd imagine that will become fairly obvious when he carries on as normal in the kitchen. Don't let it get to you or overthink it too much,' Jo said.

Erin shrugged as she finished chewing on her bite of scone. 'You have met me, haven't you? Overthinking is what I do best. So if I suddenly and unexpectedly develop feelings of a romantic or sexual nature – don't you think this would absolutely be the worst time in my life to even think about the possibility of a new relationship? I'm just out of a relationship – one I didn't end by choice, as it happens. Aaron might be a complete dick, but he was my dick and I still have to properly process how all that ended.'

'But you don't regret that it's over,' Jo said. 'Or do you?'

Erin put her coffee down on the table. Did she regret that things between her and Aaron were over? It was a yes-and-no kind of situation. Did she regret that a relationship she'd invested three years of her life in had come to a sudden and unexpected end? Yes, of course. She had, at one stage, thought they'd be forever.

But did she miss Aaron? Did she miss how she was when she was with Aaron? The person she had become? She couldn't say that she did. She much preferred the person that had emerged over the last number of weeks. Still as chaotic as she had ever been, but not settling for a life made for someone else. She was no longer ploughing all her savings into planning for a wedding they'd never actually got round to agreeing to have. It was just an abstract idea in some unknown future. No engagement had taken place. No concrete plans had been made. It was all on the list of things to happen 'one day'. For the first time in years, she was able to think outside of her previously mundane expectations.

'No, I don't regret it. And not just because he turned out to be a deceiving little prick, but because that wasn't the life I was supposed to live. Maybe that was my *Sliding Doors* moment and there is an alternate me in another universe who is living that safe, boring life and who is planning a wedding right now,' Erin said as she shuddered at the thought.

'So this has allowed you to live your very best life and do things you hadn't fully considered before?' Jo asked.

Erin nodded.

'And what if, for example, engaging in a little intense romance with Paul is on the "new you" agenda too?'

'The new me has enough to be worrying about without having to factor in fledgling relationships and keeping my legs and lady bits shaved. I'm setting up a new business and playing matchmaker for two stubborn pensioners. That's enough to keep anyone busy.'

'Maybe,' Jo said, and she took a sip from her coffee cup. 'But maybe don't close the door to that possibility? It might not be Paul, but you deserve to fall in love – or at least enjoy some absolutely mind-blowing sex – some time in your life.'

Erin was annoyed to feel herself blush again. 'Can we not talk about my sex life, please?' she said. 'How about we focus on phase two of the Harry and Flora plan. Getting Harry to agree to go.'

'I have it on good authority that Lorcan is working on that right now,' Jo said. 'Poor man was almost sick with nerves this morning. He can't believe he's actually trying to set his grandad up with someone.'

Erin smiled. 'It's not just someone, though, it's Flora, and we're not pulling the idea out of thin air. They both like each other but are too stubborn to admit it. At least this way it's just the suggestion of a trip together – we're not forcing them to be romantic.'

Jo took a drink of her tea. 'Maybe we should, though? Well, not force, but more like give them both a gentle nudge in the right direction. Agreeing to the holiday is one thing – despite his nerves, I do think Lorcan can talk Harry into that, especially now he knows that Flora's on board with the idea.'

Erin listened, intrigued about where Jo was going with this.

'But I was also thinking. They're not young. I know they're not at death's door, and no one knows how long they might have, but what we do know is how much pride and stubbornness both of them possess. And yes, I know we're nudging them in the right direction with the trip – but maybe we need to go full-strength matchmaker here.'

'What do you have in mind?' Erin asked.

'I was thinking a sort of blind date, although obviously they both know each other,' Jo said.

'So you mean just a regular date then?' Erin asked, smiling.

'Okay, smart-arse, a regular date then, but I think we might have to resort to subterfuge to get them to agree to it. Disguise it as something else.'

'Lie to them?' Erin asked. She never felt very comfortable lying to people.

'Yes, I suppose,' Jo said. 'But for a good reason. It's just a little nudge in the right direction.'

'Isn't persuading them to fly halfway round the world not a big enough nudge for them?' But even as Erin asked the question, she realised she knew the answer already. The pair had worked side by side for more than fifty years, seen each other most days and clearly had feelings for each other but had never found the courage to admit it.

Jo shook her head. 'No, I don't think it is. I think we have to use all available weapons at our disposal.'

'So what do you suggest?' Erin asked.

'Occam's razor,' Jo said.

'What have razors to do with it and who's Occam when he's at home?' Erin asked, completely baffled. Her head was starting to hurt and she didn't have the mental energy to decipher riddles. There were so many other things she needed to do.

'Occam's razor is the theory that the simplest solution is usually the right one,' Jo explained. 'I don't think we need to reinvent the wheel. We just need to set the mood. It could be as simple as a romantic meal together.'

But this being Ivy Lane, nothing is ever simple, Erin thought. And if they were going to do this at all, they'd be best to do it right.

A romantic meal was a great idea, but they decided The Ivy Inn might be a little too noisy for them to whisper sweet nothings to each other, and it might make them both much too self-conscious to have the clientele of the pub all staring at them.

They both agreed that opting for a fancy restaurant wasn't a goer. Harry was a man of simple tastes and an unfamiliar menu might put him off his stride. Besides, Erin really wanted to help prepare something special.

'Okay, so if you cook, how about we find a suitable venue that means something to them both?' Jo suggested. 'Apologies for using corporate jargon, but we need to think outside the box.'

'Somewhere that means something to them,' Erin repeated and she tried to run possibilities through her mind. The shop was out – there wasn't enough room for a table and chairs set-up and no one wants to get romantic next to the tinned tuna and copies of *Take A Break* magazine. Not even a full bucket of near-dated flowers would be enough to create an intimate ambiance. A distinct lack of any kind of a kitchen also made it a very poor choice.

Her mind flashed to some of the ideas she had for the pâtisserie. Obviously she wasn't going to be able to sneak in a full makeover without Flora noticing, but there were some little touches she could put into action quite easily. And with a bit of decoration – if she plundered the stock of fairy lights, soft voile drapes and centre pieces that were stored upstairs in The Ivy Inn for their wedding functions – she was sure she could create something lovely. Jo had a real eye for creative detail, as did Libby. Both would only be too willing to help. If she then moved things around, set up a little table and chairs, the bakery could actually look quite appealing and it would, of course, have significant meaning for both Flora and Harry.

She shared the idea with Jo, who reacted with enough enthusiasm to let her know it was a good idea.

'I'll ask Flora for the keys, say I want to measure up upstairs. She's already told me she's fine with me doing that at any time, so let's just choose a day and time and get planning. We have to figure out how to get Flora to come back to the bakery after hours and we have get Harry there too,' Erin said, her mind flooded with thoughts and ideas.

'And we have to hope it doesn't all go wrong so they end up falling out,' Jo said, her brow creased with concern.

Erin had to admit this was something they just had to have faith in. They'd have to trust that the glimmers of real affection they saw between the pair were real. All this dinner would be doing would be giving them a helping hand over finish line into their own happy ever after.

Have courage, she thought. Nothing worth having was ever easily won.

30

The target completion date was only two weeks away and Erin had never found herself so busy. In fact, everyone on the Lane seemed to be caught up in a flurry of activity. Jo was at the very final stages of writing her book. Noah was helping Erin prepare for her big move and the renovation of her new flat. There was little that Noah Simpson liked more than driving a van to the big Ikea outside of Belfast and filling it to the gills. Libby had started nesting, something that Erin thought was really nice to see after all her sickness, but also mildly terrifying. She was determined to give their flat a facelift before the baby arrived and while Noah had told her time and time again that he would do the heavy painting work and furniture moving, Libby was not to be stopped.

Lorcan had pulled a blinder in persuading Harry to go on his big once-in-a-lifetime trip, but was now buried under a sea of paperwork and admin. Not only was he trying to make sure his grandad had everything he needed for his big trip, including his passport, he was also trying to make sure he himself had everything under control for the shop. On top of all that, he was still thinking of the perfect way to propose to Jo, which he hoped to do after her novel was handed in.

It was all very exciting but also quite exhausting too. Still, Erin was finding joy in picking paint colours for her flat, and choosing the final fonts and logo for the pâtisserie. She could finally see it all coming together. She managed to keep her cool and cope with the exhaustion as long as she focused on the good things and not the worries that niggled at her in the wee small hours of the morning. She hadn't, for example, spoken to her parents since the day she had visited them and they had expressed her disappointment in her once again. She was surprised to find herself longing to tell them all about her new venture – showing them she was making the most of her Cordon Bleu training. Surely her mother in particular would find something to boast to her cronies about in that. But then she would find herself worried the business would fall flat around her ears and scared that her parents would revel in their 'told you so's. Ultimately she decided she did not need their negativity in her life.

And there was Paul, who she couldn't look at quite the same since their frisson of sexual tension after hours. There were times when she caught herself staring at him for just a moment too long. And there were times she was sure she caught him looking at her too, but they both kept things professional when they spoke. Yes, there was still the occasional banter back and forth, and they'd started sending each other memes on WhatsApp and would message each other throughout *MasterChef* to discuss their competition favourites. It was as much as she could allow herself to do at that time – her mind too busy and her heart still too bruised to contemplate more.

Erin's ultimate lifesaver in these extra busy times was Flora. Erin had started to look forward to her early mornings baking bread and drinking tea with her new best friend and Flora was just so easy to talk to. Plus, it did Erin's heart good to hear Flora speak with excitement about her trip now that her fears of travelling alone had been laid to rest. In fact, Flora and Harry had already made quite a few plans and their itinerary was starting to fill up nicely. Harry, notoriously the most frugal man in Ireland, had surprised them when all when he had insisted they would fly to Australia in business class. According to Lorcan, he hadn't even baulked at the price.

Even though they were only going for a month, Erin had surprised herself with the realisation she was going to miss Flora very much – although all being well, she'd be too busy with the new business to be able to dwell on it for very long.

The Indian summer that so often arrived at the start of September had failed to materialise, and the temperature dipped quickly. There was no more walking to work in a sun dress and feeling the early-morning sun on her shoulders. Erin arrived at Wee Buns at dawn, wearing her warm fleecy jumper and her oversized denim jacket. It wasn't long before the kitchen heated up though as the ovens were fired up and Erin swapped her fleece for an apron and got to work.

'I know this sounds like I'm a silly old woman,' Flora said as she prepared that morning's bread for baking, 'but the real secret to the perfect bake? Never bake in a bad mood. Always infuse a bit of positivity in what you are doing. Think happy thoughts.'

Erin smiled, that was about the fifth different 'real secret of a perfect bake' Flora had revealed to her, but this one definitely rang true. Erin thought of the times she cooked when angry, or distracted, or tired, and how it never had the same result as when her mood was better. But it wasn't possible to be in a good mood all the time, was it? This wasn't a Disney movie, it was real life and real life was messy at times.

'What do you do on the tough days?' she asked.

'Oh, well that's easy,' Flora replied. 'I do one of two things. The first is that I do all the swearing I need to do in the quick breaks I allow myself. That staff bathroom has heard language that would make a sailor blush,' Flora smiled. 'Then I don't so much as fake it 'til I make it, but fake it 'til I bake it.' She laughed. 'And on the days when even faking it is impossible? Well, those are the days someone might just get a sub-par loaf. But I'll make sure they get a brilliant one the next day!'

'I'll keep that in mind,' Erin said as she dusted her hands, ready to shape a few loaves of soda bread.

'To be honest, Erin. It's probably me who should be asking you for advice. You know a lot more about what you're doing than I do. Anybody can bake bread, or a good scone. And I've a good team who come in and help with the fussier jobs – the cream horns and the turnovers and the like. The ladies tend to look after that. But you? You run a full kitchen, multiple dishes, making sure they're perfect and hot and on time and then, aside from that, you make the most amazing desserts. I've seen pictures of some of your creations on your Facebook page and I could only dream of creating stuff like that.'

An idea ignited in Erin's mind. This could be the way she could make this romantic date with Harry happen.

'Flora, you've been so good to me here. Can I return the favour? Let me borrow your kitchen over the weekend, and you can come in and we'll cook up a dessert of your choice. It can be whatever you want it to be. A tarte or a croquembouche? Mille-feuille, or maybe even some baklava. Honey and pistachio is so good. You'd love some with your oat lattes!' She internally crossed her fingers and hoped it would be enough to do the trick.

'Oh...' Flora said, 'I would like that very much indeed. I love baklava and it won't trigger my lactose intolerance! I'll never say no to learning something new, even at my age!'

'Brilliant!' Erin said, a little too loudly, but she couldn't help it. She was just so delighted at having a plan in place to get Flora into the bakery after hours. 'Why don't we do it on Sunday night? Since I'm coming here after work anyway to do some more prep upstairs? I'll get us all set up and maybe you could come over about seven?'

'That sounds absolutely perfect,' Flora grinned. 'You're a great girl, Erin. You're making this all a lot easier than it could've been, you know.' At that, the smile faded from Flora's face a little and Erin could see tears form in her eyes. With a shake of her head and a sniff, Flora smiled brightly again. 'Look at me being silly!'

'It's okay to feel a bit wobbly,' Erin soothed. 'And you don't have to worry about holding it in in front of me.'

'See! I told you you're a great girl,' Flora said, her voice quiet. 'It's just getting very real. People have already been telling me they don't know what they will do without their morning buns. I know that I'm not letting people down, but a part of me feels like I am.'

'You couldn't let people down in a million years,' Erin assured her, as the alarm dinged on the oven to indicate the first lot of batched loaves were done.

'You're kind to say so,' Flora said, rolling the shelf of bread out of the oven and onto a cooling rack.

'It smells good,' Erin said, allowing the warm, floury smell to fill her senses. Such a simple food but it evoked such feelings. It was like a core memory. Calling in to see her granny after school and there always being a loaf fresh out of the oven. Her granny would cut her a nice thick slice and slather it in butter and Erin swore that no matter how many restaurants she had visited in multiple countries, under multiple award-winning chefs, there was no food in the world that ever tasted as good as that bread. It was better than every light-as-air pastry layer she'd ever eaten. It tasted of home and of love. Maybe that's what Flora meant by always bringing love to your cooking? It was Erin's turn to feel a little misty-eyed as she watched Flora slice the heel of the loaf for her and spread butter thick on it.

'You can be my taste-tester,' Flora said, and Erin could almost see her grandmother in her small kitchen, pouring a cup of tea that you could stand a spoon up in before the pair of them enjoyed their daily treat together.

'It's only a bloody slice of bread,' she chided herself inwardly as thick tears rolled down her cheeks, but she knew it was more than that.

'Would you look at the state of us eejits, bawling over some bread,' Flora said, her own voice cracked.

Neither of them needed to say that this was about much more than bread. This was about true friendship. Flora had made sure that Erin got her happy ending and that just made Erin even more determined that Flora would also have hers.

31

SEPTEMBER

'Houston, we have a problem,' Jo said, as she bustled in through the doors of Wee Buns, weighed down by a large box containing fairy lights, muslin drapes and crystal candle holders.

'What?' Erin asked, panic flowing freely through her veins. She had been kept later than she had planned at the Inn after her usual busy Sunday lunch service ran over. While she had done a fair bit of prep in the few-and-far-between lulls the day had offered her, there was much still to be done in the kitchen. Paul had looked at her with confusion as she had peeled and chopped extra veg, tenderised steak and then started on making a chocolate tart.

'What are you making?' he'd asked her.

'I'm making a romantic meal for two,' she'd smiled. 'In theory anyway.'

'Oh? who's the lucky guy?' Paul had asked, after a beat which Erin couldn't fail to notice.

'It's Harry,' she'd told him. 'That's why I'm sticking with the traditional options. Steak with all the trimmings.'

Paul had looked at her if she had lost the run of her senses. 'I didn't have him pegged as your type,' he'd said, a little awkwardly.

Erin had paused. Surely he didn't think... No. He wouldn't think that she and Harry were an item. Would he?

She'd burst into peals of laughter. 'Oh God, no! I mean he's a very charming gentleman and he was very handsome in his youth, no doubt, but no. It's for Harry and Flora.'

Relief had washed over Paul's face, which again Erin had noted but tried to file in the back of her head because she had so much to do, she didn't need to get distracted by thoughts of romance or lust with her sous-chef.

'Well that definitely makes more sense. I didn't realise they were a couple. I knew they were going to Australia, but I thought it was purely platonic,' Paul had said.

'Here's the thing,' Erin had told him. 'They are platonic, at the moment. But both have sort of confessed to having feelings for each other in small ways recently, so we – that's me, Jo, Noah, Libby and Lorcan – are trying to play matchmaker.'

'You're a devious woman,' Paul had said, but he had smiled at her in a way that had threatened to turn her legs to jelly.

'Earth to Erin,' Jo said, pulling Erin back into the present moment. 'The problem? It seems that Flora is ridiculously excited about learning how to make baklava. It's all she can talk about. Lorcan said she was in the shop earlier and was practically vibrating at the thought.'

'So you think she might be annoyed that it's a romantic dinner with Harry instead?' Erin asked, her heart sinking. It would be disastrous if this 'date' started off with a great disappointment.

'Hmmmm, maybe. Or maybe I'm just spiralling.'

'You're spiralling,' Noah said, as he followed his sister through the door with a second box of décor. 'It will be fine. And sure, it's happening now and we've no reason to change the plan, so we'd better just roll with the punches.'

Erin, who had rolled with more than her fair share of punches lately, was starting to wonder if the pressure building in her chest was the sign of an actual impending heart attack or just panic. At that stage, she wasn't sure which outcome she would prefer it to be.

'Promise to teach her another day,' Jo said. 'Or tonight, if she wants to kick Harry out.'

'But what if she's so annoyed with me she stops the sale?'

'Erin, you are spiralling so fast you might take flight. Stop for a moment and take a breath,' Noah said, just as the door rattled and Libby arrived carrying a record player.

'If music be the food of love... play on!' Libby declared.

'You should absolutely not be carrying that!' Noah said, before he dropped his box of décor and rushed to his wife to relieve her of the record player.

'I'm fine!' Libby protested. 'Noah, you need to realise I'll not do anything I shouldn't be doing,'

If Erin wasn't mistaken, there was an extra glow about Libby and she seemed more energised than she had in weeks.

'You doing okay?' Erin asked her.

'As it happens, I am doing the very best,' Libby grinned. 'I haven't been sick today, not even once!' She grinned widely. 'And I wasn't sick yesterday either. I am, however, ravenous, so if there are any sneaky baked goods hanging around this place, I won't say no.'

'It's a no treat day today, I'm afraid,' Erin told her. 'But there's carved ham or roast chicken in the fridge at the Inn. Second shelf. Oh and there is home-baked bread there too – baked by own fair hands using Flora's top-secret technique.'

'Which reminds me, we are having a baklava crisis,' Jo said, before she explained Erin's fear over the lack of baklava leading to a crisis of such epic proportions that it would stop the sale of the bakery.

As Jo spoke, and Erin listened intently, and just before Libby gave her a look that screamed 'I think you've lost your tiny mind', Erin realised a time was going to come when she would have to accept that this was happening. That there were no other bumps in the road to be met. Everything was on schedule, just as it should be. She had even taken delivery of the first batch of flyers for the business and was getting set to reveal the name she'd chosen to everyone.

'Darling, Erin,' Libby said. 'Let's keep our eyes on the prize and concentrate on what we can. Jo and I will do the set-up here. You work on the food side of things. Noah, can you help you bring anything Erin needs over from the Inn. Along with a ham sandwich for the mother of your unborn child. Lorcan is going to walk up past the shop with Harry in just over an hour. So, we've no time to waste worrying about bloody baklava.'

Erin had to concede that Libby had made a very valid point. 'Okay,' she said as she felt the weight lift from her chest. 'Let's do this. It's time to help some people fall in love!'

After what was undoubtedly the fastest turnaround in the history of fast turnarounds, Wee Buns was ready. It didn't look so much like a bakery any more. Libby, Jo and Noah had done an incredible job of dressing the place to give it an air of something really special. The Mamas and Papas were imploring those listening to dream a little dream of them, as the record Lorcan had sneaked out of Harry's house played, despite the occasional scratch. The food was prepared, thanks to Erin, who was given a helping hand by Paul, and the wine was chilling.

All they had to do now was wait for their guests of honour to arrive. Erin, now officially existing on adrenaline and not much else, insisted that both Jo and Libby wait with her. There was no way she was doing this alone. Oh no, it had been a joint venture from the start and they could all be there to deal with the fallout – whatever that may be. It was enough to tempt Erin to reach for the wine herself, but no, she needed a clear head.

It had no sooner turned seven before the door creaked open and Erin felt the breath leave her body. It was showtime.

Flora's face was a picture of bemusement as she looked around the shop she knew so well and tried to make sense of it. 'Erin?' she asked, her eyes wide. 'What is going on here? This doesn't look like... I mean...'

Flora glanced from Erin to Libby and Jo, and then looked around the room again before she finally rested on the table for two, so beautifully set in the middle of the room.

'Have I come on the wrong night? Is there something else going on here?' Her tone was a mixture of confusion and brusqueness. Wee Buns, after all, was not yet Erin's, and while Flora didn't mind allowing access so that Erin could get a head start on clearing out the flat upstairs and measuring up, maybe she thought it was a step too far for Erin to transform it into some sort of fancy eatery for her friends.

'No, no,' Erin said. 'This is the right night, but we do have a confession to make.' Erin wondered if she might actually throw up as she spoke. Either throw up or cry, or maybe both. She didn't know. 'We wanted to do something special for you,' she continued, her voice breaking. 'And we wanted it happen somewhere that was truly special for you. This seemed perfect.'

'Don't worry,' Libby chipped in. 'It will all be taken down and tidied away before the evening is done. We're not giving you any extra work.'

'So we aren't making baklava?' Flora asked, still clearly confused.

'Not tonight, but we are still on for that lesson,' Erin said. 'Tonight we wanted to treat you to a special meal with a special friend. As a surprise for you both. To mark your impending retirement and to celebrate your forthcoming trip of a lifetime together.'

At that, the door to the shop opened again and in walked Harry, followed by Lorcan. Erin waited for Harry to express the same confusion that Flora had, but he didn't. Yes, he looked around the room and took in all that had been done, but his eyes didn't rest on the table that was set for them. They rested on Flora, who was, Erin noted, blushing a deeper shade of pink than she had ever seen before.

'Harry, I didn't know about this,' Flora said. 'They've surprised me too.'

Harry rocked back on his heels and nodded. 'Is that so?'

'It is,' Flora said. 'But maybe, we could still have dinner?'

Erin wanted to punch the air. She was proud of Flora for having the courage not to run out of the room. God only knows what Erin would have done if she had.

'Maybe we could,' Harry said, a faint blush visible above his shirt collar. It was only then Erin noticed he was indeed wearing a suit. Freshly pressed, with a crisp white shirt underneath it. If she wasn't mistaken, he had brushed his hair too and she was pretty sure he was wearing some cologne. Had Harry Gallagher made an effort? Sure, this was a surprise to him too. Wasn't it?

'And I know you knew nothing about it. I managed to get this eejit here to explain the whole sorry situation to me,' Harry said.

Erin's stomach was like lead. Lorcan had the decency to look shame-faced.

'I won't say he tortured it out of me, but you know what Grandad is like when he gets going,' he said weakly.

'I knew there were shenanigans afoot,' Harry continued, 'and then this boyo here tells me I was being set up. On a date. With a very beautiful woman.'

Erin held her breath, as her eyes darted between Flora and Harry and back again.

'And I know I always said I was happy as I was, but here's the thing, Flora, I was only happy as I was because I had this great woman in my life who made every day easier. I only realised just how true that was when I heard you were selling this place and then the thought of coming to this street every day and you not being here, and not being able to chat and laugh with you like we always have, made my heart sore. You have become such a natural part of me, and of this place, and I need you to know that,' Harry said as Flora blinked back tears.

Erin felt Libby and Jo, who were stood either side of her, take her hands in theirs and squeeze. She couldn't speak. She could barely breathe. She was too invested in what was happening in front of her eyes.

'I'm not finished yet,' Harry said. 'You should all know by now I never tell a short story when a long one will do.' He turned his gaze back to Flora, who reached her hand out towards his. Harry wasted no time in taking hold of her hand and giving it a gentle squeeze. 'There's no one else on this planet that I could ever imagine flying to the other side of the world with. I never considered actually doing it before because I was always happy here in my comfort zone.' His voice cracked and Erin had to hold in a sob by biting down on her lip. 'But here's the thing, I've realised that you are my comfort zone.'

Flora hadn't spoken. She just stared at Harry and held his hand. She didn't shift her gaze, not even for one moment, to anyone else.

'You are the second great love of my life. And when I say that, I know that you more than anyone understand what Mary was to me. To us both. And you have always allowed me to love her and keep her memory alive. You have the same goodness in your heart that she did. So, Flora, these young ones have cooked us a dinner in this beautiful venue and—'

'Harry,' Flora said, and cut him off.

Bar the sound of the Mamas and Papas now dreaming about California, the room was silent.

'You do like to talk, don't you?' Flora said, but her tone was soft and warm. 'But sometimes, Harry, it would do you good to let someone else get a word in now and again. Because I feel it too, Harry. I love you too.'

Erin finally exhaled just as Harry stepped towards Flora, who beamed up at him as he lowered his head towards her and kissed her ever so softly on the lips. The collective sigh from Erin, Jo and Libby didn't interrupt the giant embrace which followed between the two old friends, but it did make the younger women laugh amid their happy tears.

When Harry and Flora eventually pulled apart, Erin got to work helping them to have a night of romance, friendship and, of course, great food. She spent as much time as was possible in the kitchen, keen to give the couple privacy to talk through all that they needed to talk through. From her spot just inside the slightly open door, she could hear them chat, with occasional peals of laughter ringing out. Her heart was as light as it was possible to be and she smiled so broadly, her facial muscles were starting to ache.

'I think that might be the most romantic thing I have ever seen in my entire life,' Libby, who was resting on a stool nursing a mug of tea, said. 'I was afraid it might go horribly wrong, but look at them!'

'And Harry!' Erin replied. 'Who would've thought the old goat had all that romance inside of him! Just waiting to get out!'

'Well,' Jo said, 'I know how romantic his grandson can be, so it doesn't necessarily surprise me.' She smiled smugly, and earned a tea towel directly to her face for her efforts.

'Oi, stop rubbing it in,' Erin said. 'Some of us are lonely, love-less spinsters of the parish!' But as she spoke, she realised that her relationship status really didn't bother her at all. She had enough in her life to more than fulfil her, and if she was being honest with herself, she was quite happy to spend some time working on herself. It didn't mean she couldn't enjoy the hints of growing unresolved sexual tension between her and Paul. In fact, it meant quite the opposite. She could very much enjoy the gentle back and forth without spending half her life overanalysing it.

She was in no rush to find all the answers to all of life's questions. Hadn't Harry and Flora proven that love would come along when it was good and ready?

What's for you won't pass you, she thought – recalling the conversation she'd had with Flora just a few weeks ago. It had become a mantra to her.

32

It was just a little after ten when Erin and Jo had finished putting things back to how they should be in Wee Buns and had locked up.

Harry and Flora had left an hour before, both with broad smiles and full stomachs, walking hand in hand down Ivy Lane together. Between courses, Flora had come to see Erin in the back kitchen.

'You're a minx,' Flora had said, her cheeks now pink with the rosy glow from a glass of wine. 'You lot coming up with this big scheme! I thought you were all done when we agreed to go on holiday, but now I realise there was a lot more that needed to be said.'

'And we didn't want to leave it to chance,' Erin had said. 'I know you believe in luck and timing, but sometimes I think luck just needs an extra helping hand.'

'I suppose I've not choice but to forgive you this time,' Flora had smiled. 'But my forgiveness is conditional on that baklava lesson! You won't get away with it that easy!'

Erin had laughed. 'I promise, Flora. I'm going to make you a pastry whizz!'

It had been as perfect an evening as it could have been, even with Erin's near panic attack earlier. Outside the shop, Erin took a moment to look at its facade and let a little shiver of excitement wash over her. This was going to be hers soon – more than her work, but her home too. The thought made her deliriously happy.

'I'm really delighted for you, you know,' Jo said, as they hugged their goodbyes. 'And I know this sounds really soppy, but I'm really bloody proud of you too, Erin. You're amazing, and that's for sure.'

Erin grinned as she let the warmth of the compliment wash over her. 'Get you home now before we start to get all emotional!' she said. 'There've been enough happy tears shed tonight.'

Jo just shook her head. 'No such thing as too many happy tears. Not unless your mascara isn't waterproof, anyway.'

'Well, I rarely wear mascara, so I guess I'm grand then,' Erin laughed as she gave Jo an extra-tight squeeze. Her heart was so full that if this scene was in a movie, it would be a musical and she would be singing and dancing down the street, clicking her heels in the air and swinging around lamp posts. As it wasn't, however, she simply told Jo she would see her the following morning and thanked her for her help before turning to walk home in the opposite direction.

She was only a few feet past the Lane when she became aware of footsteps behind her. Assuming it was Jo coming to tell her she had forgotten something, she turned with a smile bright across her face. 'What have I ballsed up now?' Erin asked.

But it wasn't Jo who was behind her. It was Aaron.

'I need to talk to you,' he said, gruffly and her heart sank.

'I don't think I want to talk to you,' Erin told him as she turned to continue her walk home.

'Erin! Please!' Aaron said and there was a pleading in his voice that she couldn't ignore.

She turned and took him in properly. He looked much the same as he had a few weeks ago. She couldn't say that he looked as if he had been pining for her. Nor did he look like he was thriving either. He just looked the same – and that same did not give her butterflies in the very pit of her stomach. It didn't give her the sense of longing she used to get when she looked at him. To her surprise, it didn't even make her sad or angry. He was just a boy standing in front of a girl when all she wanted to do was go home and put her feet up after twelve hours on them.

'Okay,' she said, straightening her shoulders. 'What do you need to say?'

'Can we go back to the flat and talk?' he asked.

'No, I don't think so,' she said calmly. 'It's late and that's my space now.'

He seemed to deflate a little in front of her eyes, his shoulders hunched ever so slightly and his gaze was downwards.

'My feet are killing me though,' she added, as she looked around her and spotted a low wall. 'So we can sit here, but I'm going to be honest with you. It's been a long day and I just want to go home and relax.'

'Rumour has it, you're moving soon?' he said as he followed her to the wall and sat down. She shuffled over a little to be a comfortable distance from him.

'Rumour has it, you were seeing some blonde behind my back when we were still together. Marnie, isn't it?'

Even in the darkness, she could see him visibly pale.

'We didn't sleep together until after I left,' he stuttered.

'Do you think that makes you a hero or something? I'll presume you did other stuff? Was it her house you ran to when you walked out without so much as a warning or explanation?'

'Does that matter now?' Aaron asked. 'It's in the past.'

The familiar and unwelcome ball of tension was back in the pit of Erin's stomach. 'Of course it bloody matters!' she said. 'You walked out and left me thinking it was all down to me. That I had been so unlovable, or unlikeable even, that you felt you had no choice but to clear out without warning. You made me blame myself when you had been seeing someone else behind my back! Someone who had no problem bad-mouthing me in my own place of work! You humiliated me the first time when you left, and I had to tell our friends that you'd cleared out, and you humiliated me again by jumping into a relationship with someone new straight away!' Erin's voice was firm but calm. She was surprised that she sounded as if she was in control of her emotions because her heart was racing and her stomach was churning. Shame, hurt, humiliation, anger – they bubbled away inside her and she realised she needed to let him know exactly how he had made her feel.

'It didn't mean anything,' he said.

'Oh, is that supposed to make me feel better?' Erin asked, her entire body pulsing with all the things she needed to say. 'Do you expect me to say it's okay, then? It doesn't count because it didn't mean anything to you. You hurt me, and it didn't mean anything to you? Jesus, Aaron! Don't you see that just makes it worse? If it was love... at least there would've been a reason.'

Aaron dropped his head into his hands. 'I'm sorry,' he said, and Erin realised it was the first time he had apologised for what he had done. She also realised just how much she'd needed to hear that. They sat in silence, and Erin could feel her heart rate start to slow.

'Rumour also has it that it's you that has bought Wee Buns, and you're moving in there to an upstairs flat?' Aaron said eventually. He looked up at her, his blue eyes flashing in the dark. It was hard to read his expression, but at a guess she'd say he wasn't happy.

'The rumour is not wrong,' she said, and bit back her usual urge to feel she had to explain herself and her decisions to him. He had walked out of her life and that included walking out on knowing her big decisions.

'I suppose you used your savings to do that?'

Erin bristled. Now there was a spark of annoyance there. What did it matter to him?

'I'm not sure it's any of your business,' she said, her voice even.

'Those were savings you had put aside for our future,' he replied.

'But we don't have a future, Aaron. Remember? And that was your decision. Whatever I saved or didn't save was always mine and it's up to me, and no one else, how I spend it.'

They fell silent again.

'Is that all you needed to talk about because, as I said, I'm tired and I want to go home.'

'I... I didn't think you would move on so quickly,' he said and Erin let out a short, sharp 'Ha!' in response.

'You moved on while we were still together,' she reminded him and he flinched. 'But, yes, an opportunity arose and I decided to take it. In a way, I've you to thank for helping me to wake up and realise what I really want from life.'

'What if I told you I made a mistake?' he said, his gaze now firmly on her. 'That it was a mid-life crisis or something.'

'You don't get to have a midlife crisis at thirty-two, Aaron,' she said.

He shook his head sadly. 'Things had become stagnant across of all my life and I, very foolishly dealt with that by hurting you. I needed to change something, and I knew I couldn't change my job, so I made a bad decision. I made the wrong decision. And I know I have no right at all to ask you to forgive me or give me another chance, but I'm going to ask you anyway. You have such a good and pure heart. And I know I hurt you,' he said, his voice croaky, his eyes teary. 'But you know what they say, you always hurt the ones you love. We could take that money and do something amazing. I could pack in my job and find something that I really love and we could build a life together.'

Erin stared at him in disbelief. She thought of the words of love and affection Harry had shared with Flora just hours before and how vulnerable he had made himself. Yet here was Aaron basically telling her she'd been an easy target and trying to get her to equate his awful treatment of her with love. On top of that, he had the audacity to suggest she use her savings to help him leave the job he hated? Of all the gaslighting, pig-headed, misogynistic takes in the world, this had to be top of the list.

'You are absolutely right,' she told him and she saw his face brighten momentarily. 'We could do all those things. Travel the world together even. Did you know Flora and Harry are flying business class to Melbourne? At their age. It's amazing.'

Aaron smiled. He looked animated now. 'It wouldn't even have to be a big trip like that,' he said. 'A few weeks in Spain would be perfect. And then I can look for a new job... Do you think we can hang on to the flat? I wonder if the landlord has a new tenant in mind yet.'

'Woah there!' Erin said. 'I said we *could* do all those things. I didn't say we would. We could get back together, for instance. But we won't. Because you might think you've made a mistake – and, to be honest, you absolutely have – but you don't want me back because you love me. I don't think you really love anyone other than yourself and it has taken me all this time to see that. Love doesn't look like what we had. And that saying about only hurting the ones you love – well, that's just bullshit. And for the longest time I believed it because I never grew up knowing that love could exist without hurt. I was never good enough for my parents, and I was never good enough for you. I was just easily moulded.'

Aaron stared at her open-mouthed. She dared him to speak because she would shut him down in a heartbeat, but he remained silent.

'And now you want me back because you've realised not all the girls in the world are as straightforward as I am. The grass isn't greener after all, and now that you hear a whisper that I'm investing my savings into a new business you decide to make a last-minute attempt to con the money out of me so you can pack in your job? Are you for real?'

'That's... not...' Aaron began.

Erin raised her hand to silence him. 'Yes it is, Aaron. It is exactly what you wanted to do. But I'm not the same Erin I was at the start of the summer. I can see clearly now how things really were. And look, I'm willing to put my hands up and admit to my imperfections. We were never meant to be. I kept wondering what I had done wrong that we seemed to have hit the "going through the motions" stage of our relationship so quickly when I see Noah and Libby and Jo and Lorcan are still in the process of falling in love. I thought I must've been doing everything wrong, but I wasn't. You'd checked out a long time before you left. I see that now. And I had pulled back into myself to protect my heart. I learned that particular skill when I was a teenager.'

'I love you,' Aaron interrupted.

'Oh for God's sake, would you just stop?' Erin exclaimed, completely exasperated. 'You don't. What we had was not what love looks like. I've seen love in my friends, even tonight with Harry and Flora, and it so different to what we had. So do us both a favour and just let it go. We are never getting back together. You are never going to get your hands on any of my savings. You want to change your life, Aaron? Then change it. But change it the hell away from me. What were we going to do? Get married and when the priest asked if we took each other to be husband and wife tell him, "Aye, I suppose. Might as well." Because that's not the kind of love I want. I'd rather have none than have that.' She stood up.

'Please,' Aaron pleaded. 'I get that you're angry, but can we just talk this through?'

She looked at the pathetic sight in front of her. She couldn't even be angry. She was just grateful that he wasn't a part of her life any more and never would be again.

Erin shook her head. 'No, Aaron. We can't.'

33

It was just two days until the purchase of Wee Buns was due to complete and Erin had not yet revealed the name of her business to her friends. She had been waiting for something very special to arrive from her suppliers and it had now landed. The rest of the marketing material – branded pastry boxes, bags, business cards and wax paper – arrived in several large boxes, as did her new chefs whites, but it was the all-important aprons that she had been waiting for most of all.

Of the five ladies who currently worked for Flora, two would be staying on, while the other three looked forward to their retirement. Erin certainly hoped she would be able to expand her staff fairly quickly, but for now, this would do. And each of her staff members would wear their very own apron with the logo of the pâtisserie embroidered onto it.

Erin cried buckets in the kitchen of The Ivy Inn as Jo and Libby helped her open the boxes to check her order. It felt real. More real even than when she had handed her share of the deposit over to her solicitor to allow the final stages of the purchase to proceed.

One item made her cry more than the others. 'Do you think she'll like it?' Erin asked as she pulled one of the aprons – the one she planned to gift to Flora – out of the box and looked at it.

'How could she not?' Libby, who had reached the '*cries at the drop of a hat*' stage of her pregnancy, asked with a shaky voice. 'It's beautiful. And the name is perfect.'

'I think so, and I hope Flora does too,' Erin said as she looked at the swirls and loops of her logo, tempted to pinch herself just to make sure she wasn't dreaming. Although the ache of every muscle in her body from packing up the flat and working all the hours God sent at the Inn to make sure the place would continue to run like clockwork when she had shifted over to her new premises told her she wasn't. Her head was full. She was surviving largely on caffeine and chocolate, and the occasional healthy meal Paul forced her to eat. Whatever of the flat that wasn't in boxes or wrapped in bubble wrap was covered in lists, sample menus and legal paperwork. There were at least fifteen different tabs open at any time on her laptop as she jumped between social media marketing strategies and 'How to use TikTok' tutorials, and she was so tired, she was sure she could fall asleep standing up if she closed her eyes for more than two seconds. But she was also deliriously, ridiculously happy. She hoped that what she was about to do would give Flora a similar sense of contentment. Although, from how things had been going with Harry, she was pretty sure her friend was already in that happy zone.

There was a certain spring in Flora's step each day now that she was officially 'courting' Harry Gallagher, and Harry himself seemed to have a sneaky wee glint in his eye. Lorcan had confided in her that he was starting to find Harry's constant crooning of old love songs a bit jarring.

'When are you going to give it to her?' Libby asked.

'I don't see the point of putting it off,' Erin said, belying the fact she was almost sick with nerves just in case it didn't hit right with her new but already very dear friend. 'We're finally making the baklava tonight, so perhaps that would be the ideal time.'

'You're both loving these mutual baking lessons, aren't you?' Libby asked.

'More than I expected,' Erin admitted. They took it in turns; one session cooking a delicious French dessert and the next mastering the art of the perfect soda bread or scone.

'You really should think about offering lessons once you have the place up and running. I think it would be brilliant,' Libby said.

'It's on the list already,' Erin told her. 'One-to-one lessons, or gifted weekend experiences, but I have to get myself settled and the business established first. If I can just hold my nerve.'

From the island where he was prepping veg, Paul looked up. 'Of course you can hold your nerve,' he said. 'And you've totally got this when it comes to getting your business off the ground. It will be a piece of cake for you,' he said with a cheeky wink.

Erin laughed. 'Yes, very funny, Paul.'

'You might even say, it will be wee buns!' he added, clearly delighted at himself for managing to use the business's old name, and the Derryism for 'easy' in such a well-timed pun.

'Watch it,' Erin warned him with a smile, her heart light and relaxed in his company. She was lucky to have him in her kitchen and, she realised, also in her life.

'Sorry, boss!' he said, raising his hands in mock surrender.

'You will be,' she teased back before she noticed that Libby was watching the exchange with the expression on her face she always wore when planning something. Erin knew she'd have to cut that one off at the pass before Libby's innate desire to find everyone their happy ending clicked in properly. She'd have that conversation later. For now, she just wanted to look at the contents of her lovely parcel and look forward to the day everything finally came together.

* * *

Erin couldn't remember the last time she had been so nervous. She didn't even think she'd been this nervous when she was waiting to find out if her offer had been accepted, or if her mortgage had been approved. This was the seal of approval she wanted most of all.

Flora had started to wind things down at the bakery. Some of her staff had already, tearfully, left. The countertop was awash with cards and flowers from loyal customers wishing Flora and her team all the very best on their retirement. A photographer from the *Derry Journal* had even been round to take her picture and a reporter was due out to interview her about all her years in business. There was no doubt in Erin's mind that it was a time of mixed emotions for Flora. Whatever sadness she carried with her about Wee Buns closing was tempered by her growing excitement at her forthcoming trip to Australia, which seemed to have finally kicked in properly once it was decided Harry was going too.

The door rattled as Erin pushed it open, the familiar and comforting smell of home-baked goodness wrapping itself around her like a hug as she walked in. She imagined this was what her new home upstairs would smell like all the time. She'd have to be careful to avoid the temptation to eat all her wares!

'There she is!' Flora smiled when she saw Erin. 'I hope you're ready for tonight's edition of the Great Ivy Lane Bake Off.'

'I am,' Erin said, although at this stage she didn't really feel there was anything she could teach Flora. There probably never had been. She could've given Flora the recipes on day one and she'd have knocked something exquisite together, but Erin so enjoyed their time together, she was happy to keep doing it. And she certainly hoped they would keep doing it in the future.

'Before we get started,' Erin said, 'could we just have a little chat first?'

Flora's face fell. 'Is something wrong?' she asked as she pulled out a stool and sat on it, sighing with relief when she took the weight off her feet. Her lined face further creased with concern.

'No, no. Nothing is wrong. I just wanted to talk to you about something. And I have a little something for you,' Erin said, and she reached into her bag and pulled out the package she had wrapped earlier. Anyone who knew Erin knew that wrapping gifts ranked in the top five of her least favourite things to do.

Her heart thudded as Flora carefully opened the package and pulled out the two items from inside.

'Look at the big one first,' Erin said, her chest tight with anticipation.

Flora raised one eye brow. 'You have me intrigued, Erin. But you know you didn't have to get me anything.'

'I know,' Erin said as Flora started to unfold the apron and blinked as she took in the logo on the front. There was silence. And for the first time, Erin feared it would be a bad silence and she had read this all wrong.

Flora looked from the apron to Erin and back again and time seemed to slow to a stop. The silence was unbearable. It felt like minutes when it was probably only a matter of seconds.

'I... I don't understand,' Flora said, her voice cracking and her hands shaking.

'Well, I'd tried out every name for the pâtisserie that I could think of and none of them felt right, and then it came to me, and I couldn't think of anything more appropriate. So now I'm really hoping that you are okay with it because all my branded supplies are in and it's probably too late to change and I probably should've checked first...' Erin was falling over her words and suddenly questioning every little decision she had ever made in her life and panic was setting in.

'Okay with it?' Flora said, as she blinked back tears. 'I've no words. It's perfect. And I am honoured and grateful.' The older woman lay the apron out on the counter to take in the tasteful logo and the name Erin had settled on. There in swirling black and white it was. Flora's of Ivy Lane. 'But it should be your name above the door,' Flora said.

'It's there too,' Erin replied, and took her phone out of her pocket to show Flora the new signage that was waiting to be hung outside. Underneath Flora's of Ivy Lane, in small letters it also read 'Bakes of Perfection by Erin Donohue of The Ivy Inn'. 'So, we both get our name in,' she smiled, 'because this place is home for us both, isn't it?'

Flora didn't speak. She couldn't speak.

But Erin had to power on because there were a couple of other surprises up her flour-dusted sleeves and if she gave in to the swell of emotion that was threatening to knock her sideways, she would be lost.

She reached out and gave Flora's hand a squeeze. 'You still have the second wee thing to open,' she croaked.

The second item that had been hidden in the package was a padded envelope. Brown and functional it didn't look like anything special.

'I'm sorry for the wrapping on that,' Erin said. 'It was all Harry's Shop had and I wanted to make sure it was properly padded so it wouldn't break.'

'Erin, this is too much,' Flora said. 'After everything you've done for Harry and I, I don't deserve this.'

'You deserve it, and more,' Erin replied. 'You don't know how you've helped me this last while. How you've always helped people here on the Lane. You might not even realise it, but you picked me up when I was on the floor and you pointed me in the right direction. And the time we've spent together...' Erin's voice cracked, and she had to gulp back a sob, 'Well, it has meant so much to me. It has reminded me what family should be like and I do think of you as family.' As Flora opened the envelope, Erin kept talking, 'Change is good, but there's something to be said for the way things have been. That's a sample flier for one of the services I'm going to offer. At the start, it will just be pre-orders on a Saturday, but we'll see how it goes. We'll have some overstock in the shop for customers to come in and pick up a treat of their choosing.'

Flora removed a crisp white piece of paper and looked at the front of it. It was adorned with the shop's logo, but also with a beautiful line drawing of a plate of some of Flora's most popular buns. There was a turnover, a cream finger, a gravy ring and, of course, a cream horn. Below the image it read: 'Wee Buns Buffet'.

'What on earth?' Flora said as she turned the page over to see a menu of services and prices.

'It's an homage to the history of this place,' Erin explained. 'A takeaway buffet, packaged up and delivered along with a selections of teas and coffees. Perfect for Saturday brunch.'

Flora beamed. 'I love it! I love it so much!' she enthused.

'There should be another wee thing in that envelope,' Erin told her – and waited for her to take out the final object, as she dared to hope that this would go down as well as the other items had. As Flora pulled out a small gold pinned brooch, Erin spoke. 'It's your name badge. For the days you want to come here, and sit on your stool behind the counter, much like Harry does, and survey this kingdom. If you want to bake a little, I'm sure I can trust you with that too.'

'Oh...' Flora said, before she walked out from behind the counter.

'It can be as often, or as little as you want,' Erin said. 'I just need you to know that you are a part of this place always. I know it was going to be a huge wrench for you to leave – but there's a seat here always. And I'll make sure it has your name on it.'

Erin couldn't speak any more as Flora, who had a surprising amount of strength for a woman of her age, hauled her into a tight hug and told her that Erin's place in heaven was assured.

34

OCTOBER

The weeks between Wee Buns closing and Flora's of Ivy Lane opening took on a life of their own. It was more than Erin could ever have dreamed it would be, and she knew it would only get better as time passed. It was also the singularly most stressful thing she had ever done in her life.

The refit to the shop and kitchens had been done without too much hassle. Libby's father was a superb project manager and he had promised Erin at the very start he would only speak to her about something if he needed to. She could put her trust in him – and she was happy to do that. There had been just one a minor crisis over a crack in the wall that Erin had immediately convinced herself was obviously a sign the building was about to collapse along with her investment, but it turned out that some Polyfilla and a coat of paint was all that was needed to sort that particular problem out.

The flat upstairs was well on its way to feeling homely. The kitchen still felt a little too new for Erin to really feel at home in it, but it had definitely been fun to design it from scratch for herself.

The scent of fresh paint hung thick in the air and Erin was finding it hard to remember the shell of a place that had existed there before. She would never be able to thank Noah enough for all his help in moving her belongings in and putting together all her flat-pack furniture without a single complaint.

The yard to the rear of the shop was still stark and fairly unimpressive. There'd be no time, or budget, to transform it into the beautiful outdoor space she dreamt of, but given that it was October and cold, she didn't think there was too much of a rush to get that done.

Inside, her beautiful coloured glass chandelier threw hints of pink and green and blue around the room. The old black and white photos of current and former residents of the Lane smiled down from the walls close to what was now named 'Flora's Corner'.

Erin had worked around the clock, with the help of Paul and Flora, to make sure the selection of treats she had ready for the grand opening were as impressive as they were delicious.

But her most ambitious creation of the evening was a croquembouche, decorated with finely spun caramel strands and fresh berries. She knew engagement cakes weren't exactly in keeping with tradition, but who doesn't enjoy cake? Especially a fancy French one made from profiteroles.

Erin had been forced to take Lorcan in hand the week before and ask him what was delaying his big romantic moment.

'I don't want to get it wrong,' he'd said. 'It has to be perfect. You should've heard Jo talking about Harry and Flora's romantic evening here – if my proposal doesn't at least match that, then I'm not doing it. I want her to know how much she's loved because I love her with all my heart.'

'Then let me help you get this wedding train moving!' Erin had said.

The plan they had hatched between them was relatively simple. Erin had kept Jo busy all day helping with the opening of the shop and the preparation for what Erin had said would be a night attended by local press and influencers. It had been a risk telling Jo this fib. Jo knew that Erin had no time for 'influencers' or the local media. She was reluctantly learning about social media only because Jo had told her it would be vital to market her business – but Erin wanted this special opening night event to be about something different than pushing the marketing of the shop. So the reality was that only those who mattered most to her were in attendance.

This night was about saying thank you to her friends and neighbours. It was about celebrating Flora and wishing Erin well. It was about drinking so much Prosecco that it would take a full cooked breakfast the following morning just to feel vaguely human again. It was about fun, and good food and even better friends.

And it was also about love. In particular, it was about Lorcan and Jo. Erin was fairly sure Jo had no idea about what was about to happen. She was much too relaxed to be aware the love of her life was about to get down on one knee and, with the help of her little sister, ask her to make him the happiest man on earth. Jo was too focused on making sure everything went smoothly for Erin that she didn't even question the croquembouche, impressive as it was. Erin had told her it was simply a centrepiece to showcase her talents and that had been enough for her.

Everything had gone as perfectly as they could've hoped and Erin was positively buzzing with happiness. This was everything she ever wanted but never believed she would ever have. The icing on the cake would be to see her friend so happy.

She lifted her glass and tapped a knife against it to silence the room. Erin knew she had to get this right. 'Ladies and gentlemen, and dogs of course,' she said, nodding to Paddy, who was sat beside a now blooming Libby at the back of the shop away from all the fun things he would enjoy eating or destroying. He looked up at Noah every now and again in the hope of getting a little sliver of cake, which of course he got. No one could ever say no to those particular puppy dog eyes. Harry and Flora were seated side by side, holding hands and looking more youthful than Erin had ever noticed before. Love, it seemed, agreed with them.

Erin took a breath and looked at all the familiar faces in front of her. The people that mattered. The people that cared. She thought of her parents and for the first time questioned her decision not to tell them about her new business. She'd have loved to have had them among the smiling faces in front of her, but that's not the kind of people they were. They'd hurt her too many times and sometimes the only way forward is to let go of the past. Completely. It didn't make it easy, but it did make her decision to cut them off the right decision.

She saw Paul smile at her and mouth 'You've got this!' and she steadied herself. She did have this. This was the life that was meant for her, in all its messy, eclectic, laughter filled glory.

'Thank you all for coming out tonight to help mark the opening of Flora's of Ivy Lane – a business I hope brings something new to the Lane as well as celebrating the best of what has been. A lot of people have worked their rear ends off to make this happen – from my business partners to my friends, to the people who I've come to think of as family.' She nodded to Flora, raised her glass just a little, and a wave of applause followed. 'I wasn't born on these cobbles. I can't, like so many of you, say I spent my childhood running up and down this street, but even as a blow-in you have made me feel like I belong and that's all any of us really wants at the end of the day. I know there are people here who think there is a little bit of magic in this place – and I'm starting to agree. Good things happen here to good people and there is something good always waiting around the corner. Which brings me to the real reason for tonight's proceedings. Libby, lights please!'

Erin stepped backwards as Libby stood up and flicked a switch by the door. Only the lights from the display cabinets still twinkled and a hushed silence fell over the room. Erin didn't know whether she might cry or laugh, but at least she didn't look like she was going to throw up, which was the exact expression on Lorcan's face as he cleared his throat and stepped forward.

'Lorcan,' Jo whispered. 'What are you doing?'

Lorcan – tall, handsome Lorcan – just smiled. 'Lights and music please!' he said, as Libby pressed another switch and the room was illuminated with swirling stars on the ceiling while a quiet instrumental version of 'A Thousand Years' began to play in the background.

Erin looked at her best friend, saw her expression change from confused, to horrified, to nervous and back to confused again.

'Miss Clara,' Lorcan said, and Jo's little sister, the child who had stolen all of their hearts, let go of her mum's hand and stepped forward, her smile so bright that it was contagious.

'Shall we?' Clara said, in a very posh voice, which made Jo laugh.

'I think we shall,' Lorcan replied, mimicking her.

Erin's heart was so full, she feared it might actually explode.

They both turned to look directly at Jo and in unison they spoke. 'Miss Jo, could we have the honour of this dance?' It was clear from their rhythmic pronunciation, they had planned and rehearsed this to the last detail.

As they reached out their hands, Jo stepped towards them, but not before turning back to let Erin know she would pay for this later.

As Jo, Lorcan and Clara stepped into the middle of the room, they seemed to naturally form into a giant hug of love and hope and joy until Lorcan and Clara took one step back and started to speak.

It was Clara's turn first. 'Jo, you are the best big sister in the entire universe and I love you very much.'

'I love you too,' Jo smiled through tears.

'Good!' Clara said with an authoritative nod. 'But please let me say my lines before I forget them.'

Jo nodded as a ripple of laughter spread around the room. One glare from Clara reminded the room that they should not stop her saying her lines either.

'Jo, I love you very much. And Lorcan loves you very much too. He loves you as high as a mountain, and as deep as the sea. He loves you more than I love hot chocolate. And that is a lot.'

Erin's eyes flitted between Clara and Jo and Lorcan and she felt the overwhelming sense that everything was going to be just fine.

'So, Jo, Lorcan wants you to know that he wants to marry you. And he wants me to be bridesmaid and not Erin or Libby. Sorry.' Clara pulled an exaggerated sad face, which let everyone know just how scripted and rehearsed her speech was. 'Mr Lorcan,' Clara said, and turned to nod at a now very pale and also tearful Lorcan who had just knelt on one knee and was holding a ring box in front of a very shocked Jo.

'I do love you as high as a mountain and as deep as the sea,' he said. 'And more than Clara loves hot chocolate. Erin said this place makes her feel like she is home,' he said. 'But you, Jo Campbell, you are my home and I want you to be my home forever. Will you marry me?'

There was not a dry eye in the house as Jo nodded, Clara jumped and punched the air with joy declaring 'I'm gonna be a bridesmaid!' and Lorcan looked as if he truly felt like the luckiest man on earth.

And in that moment, with all its beauty and love, Erin couldn't help but feel pretty damn happy too.

35

TWO MONTHS LATER – 21 DECEMBER

The afternoon air is crisp, and the sun hangs low in the sky, as if it would require too much effort to keep shining on this shortest day of the year. It may be a cold December day, but Ivy Lane is just as beautiful as it is on a summer's day – perhaps it's even more so. It could be the pinch of red on the cheeks of the people outside, standing in their fancy coats as their breath curls in misty clouds towards the sky. It might be the sprays of red berries, of green leaves, of soft eucalyptus and mistletoe bound together – glittering with frost – tied with twine to the iron fencing around The Ivy Inn. It could be the candles flickering in lanterns hung from the trees, or the warm white fairy lights twinkling overhead, glowing brighter and brighter as the sun sinks, turning the sky first pink and orange, then a soft inky blue, before giving way to a blanket of stars.

The chatter among the guests fills the air, along with the clink of champagne flutes and the whooshing sound of the outdoor heaters keeping the worst of the chill at bay. The atmosphere is thick with expectation of what is to come.

There's a certain magic about the wedding that is about to

happen on Ivy Lane. It's the climax of a love story that could only ever have happened on this street, between these people. It's only fitting that the happy couple have decided the courtyard garden of The Ivy Inn is the perfect place to say their vows. With its wide wooden gates open, the assembled guests have a clear view of the bookshop across the street – and the flat above it.

The bride and groom have surprised just about everyone by forgoing tradition and getting ready together in the flat owned by their very dear friends, Libby and Noah – the last couple to get married on the Lane, who also happen to be the owners of Once Upon a Book and The Ivy Inn.

Wanting as little fuss as possible, and clearly not taking into consideration how fondly they are regarded, the bride and groom have decided to simply walk across the street together, hand in hand, to their ceremony.

Noah has arranged for the street to be closed and cleared of traffic for the evening, which has made it possible for it to be decorated so beautifully. He's even gone to the trouble of having a red carpet laid across the cobbles – it wouldn't do to have either the bride or the groom lose their footing should the evening turn icy.

'I hope they aren't too much longer,' Erin says and she shuffles from foot to foot on impossibly high heels that are very much not her usual footwear. 'These shoes are strictly car to bar and I really want to make sure everything is going okay in the kitchen.'

Paul smiles at her reassuringly. 'Everything will be fine in the kitchen. You left very precise instructions. And you checked just ten minutes ago. Before you put those shoes back on.'

'And I can't wait to take them off,' she says. 'They were a bad idea. You should've told me they'd be a bad idea.'

Paul raises his hands in mock surrender. 'It takes a braver man than me to tell the ever-powerful Erin Donohue her idea might be a bad one,' he smiles. 'But hang in there. They won't be long now.

Erin isn't the only guest to be getting a little restless now, waiting for the main event. The happy couple should've arrived ten minutes ago. No matter how pretty the sparkling lights and how fragrant the cinnamon-scented candles, there is only so long anyone is prepared to stand out in the cold for. The patio heaters can't work miracles on a midwinter night.

'Maybe she's getting cold feet?' Paul whispers into her ear.

'She wouldn't be the only one,' Erin says, looking mournfully at her feet. 'I'd give my big toes for a pair of thermal socks right now.'

'You wouldn't look half as fetching though,' he tells her. 'And don't forget, this is their big night. It's important to them both that they have their ceremony under the stars. But hopefully it won't take too long and we'll all be back inside in no time, and you can go and annoy the kitchen staff.'

'And I'm going to change into my Converse and stay in them,' Erin says. 'I'll be throwing some shapes on the dance floor in comfort.'

'You look good to me whether you're in heels or trainers,' he smiles, and she allows him to pull her even closer which adds nicely to the warm and fuzzy feeling she now has inside.

There's more laughter and chatter now before a hush descends over the crowd.

'I see someone coming,' a voice shouts and everyone's gaze turns to the bookshop opposite, and the green door to the side from which the husband-and-wife-to-be are set to emerge.

At the creaking of the door to the side of the shop, music starts to play and the sound of the stunning Irish ballad 'She Moved Through the Fair', sung by the angelic-voiced Cara Dillon, fills the air.

But instead of a blushing bride walking through the door with her beau on her arm, there is a very flushed bookseller, her hand clamped to her swollen stomach. Her recently curled hair is already looking a little messy, her make-up streaked with sweat, or tears, or both.

Holding her up is her husband, Noah, whose face is ashen as he supports Libby, and tries to carry both her hospital bag and a baby bag into the street.

'Shit!' he proclaims. 'Bloody, shitting shit.'

The music screeches to a halt before the enchanting tune has even had the chance to really get started.

There's a moment or two of silence as the assembled crowd process the scene in front of them, before the sound of Libby, moaning in pain, jolts everyone into action.

'Why in God's name did we think it was a good idea to close the street and have everyone park somewhere else?' Noah babbles.

'I was supposed to have another week at least,' Libby sobs as Erin rushes over to her and pulls her into a reassuring hug. 'Everyone said first babies never come on time, never mind early. I can't believe I'm going to ruin the wedding.'

'You're not, Libby,' Erin tells her. 'You're just going to make it even more special.' Slipping into organisation mode, she continues, 'Noah, go get the car. Right, you guys,' she says, pointing at the other guests, 'some of you clear the road of these lanterns, flowers and the traffic cones at the top of the street, so Noah can drive down. Libby, let's get you sitting down. This is going to be the best day of your life. You're going to be a mama!'

'But the wedding...' Libby sobs.

'The wedding can still happen,' Erin says. 'If that's what the happy couple want. And it will still be amazing. You've helped them plan the most perfect day, but now you've more important things to be doing.'

Libby sniffs, but she knows Erin is right. Erin is always right. The last six months have proven she's a one-woman tour de force who could run the entirety of Ivy Lane if she put her mind to it. Her pâtisserie has been a runaway success, with extra staff already recruited to keep up with demand. There have been days when customers are queueing out the door and down the Lane just to try her incredible food. There's talk of her being nominated for Irish and UK-wide awards, and she has already attracted media attention. Though she hasn't made a final decision yet, there is truth in the rumour she has been invited to appear as a guest judge on *Bake Off*, which has made her parents very proud. Of course, Erin's reaction to that was to tell her parents they should've been proud of her anyway. She's quite enjoying standing her ground with her parents these days and displaying how she is, as the Irish saying goes 'some woman for one woman' – feisty, a little bit bossy (but in a good way) and exceptionally determined. Libby knows she will be wasting her time to even think about arguing with her friend.

As another contraction tightens across Libby's stomach, she realises nothing is going to stop this baby from making an appearance and there's no point in worrying about anything else just now. Apart from, that is, how long it will take Noah to get back with the car and whisk her to Altnagelvin hospital on the other side of Derry so she can get some gas and air!

She should have paid attention to these pains when they had started that morning. Instead, she had convinced herself they must just be Braxton Hicks because the liars on the internet had told her the baby wouldn't come early. The duration and strength of this particular contraction leads Libby to believe the internet mummy bloggers also lied when they said first labours tend to be long and slow.

When she is able to open her eyes again, she looks around, hoping against hope, she will see Noah pulling up ready to whisk her away to get all the good pain-relieving drugs.

Erin crouches down beside Libby and takes her hand.

'Hey, Libby,' she says softly.

Libby turns to look at her and Erin knows in that moment that this is exactly what Father Karras saw in *The Exorcist* just before Regan began spewing pea soup everywhere. Libby's face is now beaded in sweat and her eyes are red-rimmed. A voice, equally as demonic as Regan's had been in the movie, comes from Libby's mouth. 'What?'

'We... um... we were just wondering if we could help?' Erin asks.

Libby looks as if she is going to say something before a shot of pain clearly rips through her body and she closes her eyes to fight through the contraction. When she opens them again, they are wide with fear. 'They're not supposed to be this close together. Not yet!'

Erin has no idea what to say to reassure Libby. She knows as much about childbirth as she does quantum physics.

'Muuuuum!' Libby shouts, just as her mother totters out from the back of the crowd.

'I'd just gone inside for a wee,' she says, before gasping at the sight of her daughter on the bench outside the bookshop. 'Oh love,' Libby's mother soothes, while Erin takes the moment's reprieve to instruct Paul to ask all the guests to go into the bar. She wants to spare Libby the indignity of labouring in front of her neighbours.

The sound of a car engine makes them all look up as Noah drives down the street. His face is sheet white.

He is shaking like a leaf as he gets out of the car to get Libby.

'Are you safe to drive?' Erin asks.

Noah just stares at her wide-eyed. The panic has clearly set in.

'Okay,' Erin says. 'Let me deal with this. Libby, we're going to help you into the car. Has anyone got a towel or a blanket or something?' she shouts to the few people still on the street.

'I'm warm enough,' Libby huffs as she tries to stand up.

'I, erm, wanted it for the back seat in case your waters go,' Erin says.

'Oh God,' Noah chimes. 'I feel a bit dizzy.'

Erin looks back to Libby, whose eyes are closed tight again as another contraction starts to tear through her body. 'Stuff this for a game of soldiers,' she says, reaching into her bag to take out her phone. She calls for an ambulance, guessing by the length of Libby's contraction that the birth can't be that far off and guessing by the way Noah is hyperventilating that he is no fit state to drive. She'd drive herself but she had two glasses of Prosecco on an empty stomach and is feeling the effects.

As soon as Libby is able to open her eyes again, she pants, 'I think the baby's coming. I need to push!'

In unison, Erin and Libby's mum both shout, 'Don't push!' but Libby simply closes her eyes and starts breathing very heavily and occasionally swearing.

'I don't think she has much choice,' Erin says. 'Let's try and get her upstairs, if at all possible.'

With considerable effort and frequent swearing, they both manage to get Libby back upstairs and into her bedroom just as the sound of an ambulance siren floods the street – where Noah is waiting anxiously to direct the paramedics into the flat.

Jo, who had gone into The Ivy Inn to practice reading the verse she'd written for the ceremony, is drawn outside by the commotion, and runs immediately to Noah. 'It'll be okay,' she tells him, 'Let's get you inside too. Try and stay calm for Libby.'

'I think calm went out the window about ten minutes ago,' Noah says with a watery smile. 'Oh shit, Jo. I'm going to be a daddy.'

'You are, and you better get in there and hold your beautiful wife's hand as it happens.'

The brother and sister leave the cold of the street and lead the paramedics upstairs to the flat, which is now feeling more than a little crowded. In the living room, the bride, the groom and the best man are looking a little shell shocked at the arrival of a clearly labouring Libby and an assortment of excited friends and family members, followed, thankfully, by two paramedics.

'Oh thank you, God, for that,' Erin says as she sees help arrive.

It's only when she leaves Libby in the expert hands of the paramedics and walks back into the living room that she realises she too is shaking like a leaf. She has to sit down for fear she might faint.

Feeling a hand take hers, Erin catches her breath. 'That's it, good girl. A nice big breath, in and out...' Flora says, and when Erin looks up, she sees a picture of serenity in front of her. How is it that Flora can be so calm? It's her wedding day and she and Harry should be saying their vows right now, but instead paramedics have flooded the flat, all the guests are drinking mulled wine in The Ivy Inn and a baby is about to be born. 'Women do this every day. She'll be fine,' Flora soothes.

'But your wedding...' Erin cries.

'It can wait a few minutes,' Flora shrugs with a smile. 'God knows we've waited long enough.'

'Erm, Flora, my love,' Harry interrupts. 'Do you mind if I cross over to the Inn, you know, leave you ladies to it?'

'And get a little medicinal whiskey before you tie yourself to me for life?' Flora asks.

'I don't need any Dutch courage to marry you, pet,' Harry says. 'But I would enjoy one all the same.'

'Come on, Grandad,' Lorcan says. 'I'll take you over. And, Flora, don't worry. I take my best man duties very seriously. I'll make sure it's just the one.'

'Good man,' Flora says with a smile. 'And I'm sure he'll mind you just as well when your big day comes.'

'I will and all,' Harry says. 'Not a bother to me.'

'On you go then,' Flora says. 'We'll be over as soon as Erin here gets a moment to catch her breath. You don't get away with not marrying me that easy!' She grins.

As the men leave, Erin keeps holding Flora's hand. She takes a moment to take in everything around her. The Christmas tree in the corner, its coloured lights twinkling and casting a soft glow on the room. The packages wrapped under the tree, most of them labelled 'For Baby'. The scent of a cinnamon candle fills the air, and even though there is a new life emerging into this world just feet away, all is calm. There is silence for a moment and Erin drinks it in as she reflects on how momentous this occasion truly is, and how momentous this entire year has been.

She squeezes Flora's hand. Her friend has never looked more beautiful. Dressed in a simple cream shift dress, her white hair is decorated with a delicate feathered fascinator which sparkles with silver frosted crystals. The best thing, however, is that she looks as happy as she does beautiful. Harry, the old devil, had popped the question on the flight home after what had been a truly magical holiday to Australia. He even managed to get a good deal on an engagement ring – because not paying over the odds was still important, you know – even after he declared business class as 'the bee's knees' and vowed to see even more of the world.

Funnily enough, now that she had Harry for company, Flora had caught the travelling bug herself and couldn't wait to experience new countries with her soon to be new husband. They have already planned an extended honeymoon to kick off their new life together.

The happy couple decided to waste no time in saying 'I do' and Flora's son, Peter, has even made the trip over from Australia to give the marriage his blessing.

Today had been set to be perfect, until Libby's waters gushed all over the floor just as the bride and groom were getting ready to walk across to the Inn for their ceremony.

'You look stunning,' Erin tells Flora, who blushes in response.

'You do, Flora,' Jo adds. 'I'll have a lot to try to live up to for my day.'

'Ach, for goodness' sake,' Flora laughs. 'You could wear a sack cloth and be the most beautiful girl in every room. Now, Erin, pet, you tell me when you feel calm enough, and we'll go over and join the others in the pub. Let this wee baby come into the world in his or her time.'

Silence falls for just a moment before Libby lets out one hell of a roar – one so loud that all three women wince and try not to think about the toll pushing a baby takes on a woman's body.

Erin has never admired Libby more, she thinks.

But at just that moment, the shrill cry of new life rings through the flat and all is good and right with the world, and a little bit of magic has just shown itself once again on Ivy Lane.

ACKNOWLEDGMENTS

It's been a while since I took my readers to Ivy Lane, thanks in most part to some real-life plot twists, so my first and biggest thank you goes to my editor Caroline Ridding, and all at Boldwood Books for your understanding and support. Special thanks to Jade Craddock for her impeccable copy-editing skills, and Debra Newhouse for her keen eye during the proofread.

It has been such a joy to return to Ivy Lane after a two-year hiatus and to be able to write about this wonderful cast of characters again. Thank you so much for giving me the opportunity to do so, and for your guidance through the writing and editing process.

Thanks to all my fellow Boldwood authors who have welcomed me so warmly back into the fold and who helped make this return to rom-com writing great fun.

Thanks also, and as always, to my agent Ger Nichol, who has steered my career, in all guises, over the last seventeen years. We have been through a lot, and I have been lucky to have you in my corner.

Thanks to my family – my husband, and two children – for giving me the space to write and for understanding that I, just like Jo in this story, can get a bit feral when a deadline is imminent. Thankfully I can also, like Jo, be tamed with baked goods and Maltesers – and I thank you for supplying them, and good humour, when I'm in the final throes of a book.

Thanks to my parents, my brother, my sisters, assorted in-laws and my nieces and nephews for being a constant source of inspiration on what makes up a slightly weird, but incredibly loving and supportive family. I am so lucky to come from a family who value and promote creativity and chasing your dreams – no matter how seemingly unattainable. I am just as lucky to come from a family where neurodiversity is seen as a strength and where we all pretty much agree that 'normal' is a bit boring anyway. Just like the characters on Ivy Lane, we believe everyone deserves to feel as if we fit in somewhere. Special thanks to my sister, Emma, to whom this book is dedicated, for daily walks with the little dogs, Bebe, Demon and Whompas (not their real names), which have become therapy sessions.

Thank you to the friends who listen. And to the writing friends who have encouraged and supported me most in the last few years when I've been learning a whole lot about myself. Thank you especially to my soul sister Fionnuala Kearney.

Thanks to the librarians, booksellers, bloggers and promoters of books. We would have no profile without you and I appreciate you greatly.

And finally, thanks to all my readers, across genres, and to those who have got in touch to share how much they have enjoyed these books. It's a tough world out there at the moment, folks – we all need shades of light. Thank you for picking up my book and giving it, and me, a chance.

ABOUT THE AUTHOR

Freya Kennedy lives in Derry, Northern Ireland, with her husband, two children, two cats and a mad dog called Izzy. She worked as a journalist for eighteen years before deciding to write full time. When not writing, she can be found reading, hanging out with her nieces and nephews, cleaning up after her children (a lot) and telling her dog that she loves her.

Sign up to Freya Kennedy's mailing list for news, competitions and updates on future books.

Visit Freya's website: http://www.claireallan.com/freya-kennedy

Follow Freya on social media here:

ALSO BY FREYA KENNEDY

The Hopes and Dreams of Libby Quinn

In Pursuit of Happiness

Don't Stop Believing

Boldwood

Boldwood Books is an award-winning fiction publishing company seeking out the best stories from around the world.

Find out more at www.boldwoodbooks.com

Join our reader community for brilliant books, competitions and offers!

Follow us

@BoldwoodBooks

@TheBoldBookClub

Sign up to our weekly deals newsletter

https://bit.ly/BoldwoodBNewsletter

Printed in Great Britain
by Amazon